LOVE CANAL

A NOVEL

BY

TIMA SMITH

amarok books

LOVE CANAL

amarok books
ISBN: 978-1-944932-12-1

CHAPTER ONE

All right. He admitted it was possible she'd helped ruin his life. No question she'd ruined his marriage, or at least his expectations of it. And maybe, when it came right down to it, she'd ruined *him*. Little by little, but steadily, and from the very first time he'd closed his eyes and willed her presence.

The Flying Fortress B-17E with its dorsal fin. The white-nosed P-51 Mustang. The missile-nosed Black Widow. All hanging from his ceiling on their nylon filaments and trembling in the air as she came to him. Stepping barefoot over the jeans and flannel shirt he'd thrown on the floor, tapping one bright red fingernail on the green Nichinan transistor radio sitting on the edge of his desk. That tap, the audible signal that made him swallow hard as she fingered her top button and started the glorious rise of his thirteen-year-old prick.

He'd never been able to let her go, though god knows he'd tried.

Rosaries, novenas, pleading to St. Anthony for a miracle. And every Saturday, the dread of pushing aside the purple velvet curtain into the confessional. The old deaf priest behind the screen, hacking into his handkerchief and handing out the same meager penance week after week. Exactly what, Nate wondered, did the old fart hear out of *I masturbate?* I was late … missed a date … fasted, then ate…?

A hundred hundred our fathers hail marys acts of contrition. And then Auntie Miriam always on the attack. *St. Bartholomew's, Nathaniel? A school full of nuns? Oh pul-eez. If your mother's a Jew, you're a Jew. Don't you know anything?*

And then there were the prayers to Jehovah, on the chance the Jew in him was stronger than the Gentile, on the chance the god of Abraham might cooperate a little to get him back. Though the old Jew, it turned out, was as deaf as the old priest. Mortification. Punishing himself in a hundred little ways. Anything to avoid burning in hell through eternity, since, after all, it *was* world without end amen.

But nothing worked. He couldn't dispatch her. Or she wouldn't be dispatched. And eventually he gave up the guilt, the hair shirts, the self-mutilation, gave it all up along with the Faith. She stayed and he was glad of it. Glad to be possessed. That way she had of setting his skin on fire, teasing every nerve to the point of explosion.

He eased off a little now, wanting it to last, wanting to draw it out.

There'd been a real girl once who'd compared. In college. A French Canadian hooker with a vacuum powered pussy and a mouth that was so wet, so warm, so insistent that just thinking about it used to make his knees give. *Good, no?*, she'd say, while he lay there gasping. *I do ze exercize. A seecret I dun't tell all ze boyez. I show you how I do, huh?*

And then, on the other side of the universe, there was Roberta. And nineteen years of cardboard sex. Nineteen *years* and *she'd* been the one to walk out.

He took a breath and started again.

It was his own fault. He'd done too good a job. Made her too perfect. Little select pieces of only the best … Bergman Bacall

Monroe Turner Bardot. The great American 50s wet dream. And he let it take him now the way it had been taking him for forty years. Angel. Nymphet. Siren. Tease. Glorious indecent succubus.

Then the ringing started, on and on, and he felt his excitement slip. Church bells tolling him toward heaven, away from sin, temptation, the fires of hell. Sister Mary Angelica ringing them in from recess, impaling him on those pale blue rabid eyes because he, Nathaniel, the little Jewish kid, was the one she'd decided to save.

He tried to concentrate on the succubus, but with every ring something faded away — a breast, a hand, lips, a thigh, until finally she was gone, Taking his hard-on with her.

He opened his eyes.

Through the window, dawn was staining the sky, and he pictured a pool of deep orange spreading across Harbor Point, Savin Hill, Fields Corner, Codman Square, Ashmont. Day breaking across all of Dorchester. Home of Rose Kennedy and Mr. Spock, an Irish Catholic and a Jew. And now home of Nate Madigan, ditto.

He'd almost taken a crummy little apartment in Lynn, cheap and crawling with roaches, though it wasn't the roaches that had changed his mind. It was that damn rhyme that kept running through his head every time he thought about the place. Lynn Lynn, city of sin, you never come out the way you went in.

Above him, Nixon stared down from the cracks and spots in the plaster. The nose impossibly long, but with just the right lift, the beady eyes, the jowls. He pictured the hunched shoulders, the arms thrust in the air, the fingers doing twin Vs.

The one thing he could never figure was Pat. How she'd stayed with him through it all. Because there was simply no explanation. Except maybe an exceptional capacity for compassion. True compassion, the kind you gave to people who absolutely didn't deserve it. Or was she simply incapable of breaking a vow?

He pictured her standing behind her husband during the farewell speech, the wet eyes, the tight jaw. Was it possible she actually loved him? Loved Tricky Dick?

He closed his eyes again. It was a line of thinking he wasn't crazy about following, because it made him start to wonder about his own capacity. For love or for anything that was permanent or fine.

The only person he knew for sure he'd always loved was Kimmy. But somehow fatherly devotion didn't seem enough when he thought of all the people he didn't or hadn't loved enough — Esther, the original Mother Dearest; Priscilla, though he had tenderness for Priscilla, a feeling of protectiveness that had been there as long as he could remember. And empathy, both of them caught in the same powerlessness, the same craziness.

And Roberta. Had he ever really loved Roberta? But how could you live with someone for almost two decades, have a child together, and never be sure you loved her. Which made him wonder if he was malformed. Genetically damaged.

He grabbed a pillow and jammed it over his head, but the phone worked its way through the stuffing, and he knew it wasn't going to stop ... sixteen, seventeen, eighteen, nineteen. No one would let it ring that long. No one except Esther Neuburger Madigan, mother of the year.

Goddamn Priscilla anyway. Had to go and buy Esther yet one more offering, and then had to program the damn thing so all Esther had to do was push a button. One button for him, another button for Priscilla. A button for her sister Dolores, who'd been dead since 1977. So now she had real buttons to push instead of merely theoretical ones.

Now I know what it's like, she could say to him any time of the day or night ... *now I know what it's like to be treated like a dog. And by my own children! After I denied myself, after I went without so you could have what I never did ... after I wore the same pair of shoes two whole years and ruined my feet — only God knows how I've suffered* with these feet — so Priscilla could have the hoop skirts and those ugly sack dresses and the custom prom gowns like all her friends were wearing. And then what did she do? Let them hang in the closet, that's what! Nobody wears them anymore, ma, she'd say. How can I wear it to the dance again, ma? I wore it to the last one! So they hung, and I wore the cheap shoes that ended up turning me into a cripple.

And as for you, my first-born, my only son. For you I wore that awful second-hand coat four winters in a row. That ugly piece of cloth Miriam handed me like she was doing a charity, my own sister. Like I should have to wear her hand-me-downs my whole life. But I wore it anyway, so you, Mr. Big Shot, could go off to that fancy school and never want to have anything to do with your mother again. Sniffle. Sniffle. Big sigh.

It didn't matter that his father had never earned less than thirty grand a year when thirty grand a year was something. It didn't matter that they'd cleaned a hundred pairs of shoes out of her closet when they moved her to the nursing home, thirty winter coats, two dozen hats, rings big enough to eat a sandwich off of. And no matter how many times he explained it, she refused to hear that you couldn't go home when you couldn't walk six feet without falling over. When you left burners going under empty pots, opened all the windows in January and nearly died of pneumonia, called the police nine times a day because the planes flying over the house made too much noise.

Reasons, all of them, everyone but Esther understood. The only solution left, because they couldn't pay anyone enough to stay in the same house with her for even five days and because her children didn't want her – not her forty-nine year old daughter who lived on vodka and anti-depressants; not her fifty-two year old son who had a hole in his life the size of Milwaukee. But even if he and Pris were leading lives as solid as Walter Cronkite and Queen Elizabeth, they still wouldn't be taking care of her. Because they couldn't fucking stand her.

He tossed the pillow off the bed, tried to see something else in the cracked ceiling, but the Nixon image was too powerful to let anything else take shape. And then the phone stopped ringing and for a second the silence pounded.

Yes, he was a rotten son. Rotten being his own personal paradigm. A rotten husband, a rotten engineer, a rotten Jew, an even rottener Catholic. And somehow he'd managed to be a rotten philanderer, too. Handing Roberta the Valentine card with Ellen's name on it, leaving Maryann to wait for him at the motel half the night until she finally called him at home just to get even, knowing, somehow, that the phone was on Roberta's side of the bed. It was a bleak trail he'd left. Not a trail of tears, because tears were shed for things that mattered. More like a trail of shrugs, a trail of headshakes, a trail of confusion.

And now he couldn't even get it up for the succubus without extra effort. Fifty-two. A hundred and fifty-two. The way he was feeling, there was little difference. He sighed. How, he wondered, had his life turned into such a fucking bowl of cherries?

He looked at the pictures of Kimmy on the wall. An okay father. That he'd been. At least up until a month ago.

And the longer he didn't tell her, no, didn't tell *them* ... because as much as he wanted to, he couldn't make Roberta disappear ... so the longer he didn't tell *them*, the harder it got, until he'd rather do almost anything else. Go to jail, lose his mind, find out he had six months to live — always a good fantasy to fall back on, that — the effect of imminent death reducing all the other major failures. His finest hour. His one triumph over life.

Except he wasn't dying. At least not with any great speed. He was a fifty-two year old man, somewhat recently divorced, very recently canned from the one company he'd worked for since he was twenty-three, except nobody knew that yet because he didn't have the balls to admit it. A fifty-two year old man on unemployment, living in one bedroom of someone else's house, driving a car with no personality, and fucking an imaginary whore.

A fifty-two year old man with a college tuition bill he couldn't pay sitting on the desk, with a daughter who thought she was going to Wellesley in September when she'd be lucky if he could swing the ivied halls subsidized by the Commonwealth. With a sister who'd tried to slash her wrists ten times in the last ten years. With a crazy, bitter, petulant, shallow, self-obsessed mother who refused to get it over with and simply die.

Outside there was the sound of an engine starting. Seven-twelve. Which meant that at seven-thirteen the dog would start.

It had bothered him only peripherally up until a couple of months ago. An annoying snooze alarm. Barking when he turned on the shower, still barking when he turned it off, barking while he shaved, while he fixed his tie, while he snapped the top down on his travel mug. Sometimes he'd watch it through the windshield while he sipped coffee and waited for the engine to stop skipping, a big dog, a black and tan collie, handsome if you didn't know there wasn't enough room in that narrow head for more than a teaspoon-sized brain, straining against the line that linked it to the fancy dog house. A shingled peaked roof, a window on the side for christ's sake.

But now he had to listen to it all fucking day. And it wasn't like he hadn't mentioned it.

"Bark?" the guy said. Mel was his name, or was it Phil. "*This* dog?" Mel or Phil looked incredulous, shocked, disbelieving. "Bark? *This* dog?"

He'd nodded. "Yeah. *This* dog. From the time you leave until the time you come home."

Mel or Phil had scratched his head. "Funny, you know? Cuz we've had this dog four years. And no one's ever said a thing about barking. 'Til you. And you been here, what ...?"

"Six months."

"Yeah ... well."

As if somehow that explained it.

So now Mel or Phil wasn't friendly anymore, didn't wave across the fence like he used to. And the dog barked. Bark bark bark.

He swung his legs onto the floor and sat up, put his head in his hands. For thirty years his eyes had opened every morning by seven-o-one, but now, if it wasn't for the dog that didn't bark, he had the feeling he might be able to sleep all day.

But not this day. Because for once he had something to do besides looking through the Help Wanteds or sending out another useless resume.

Priscilla had hired him. Her deck needed staining.

"Hundred and fifty bucks," he'd told her after he looked it over. "Stain included."

"A hundred and fifty? Are you out of your mind? I can get the kid down the street to do it for seventy-five."

"Go ahead then, Pris. Be my guest. But don't call me in two weeks complaining about the lousy job he did. How much stain he got all over the ivy, how he didn't get the edges, how he laid his girlfriend on your chaise lounge and left the used rubber on the patio."

"Oh, shut up, Nate," she'd said, "okay, a hundred and fifty."

The way she acted, you'd think she didn't have two nickels to rub together. But he and Stan still ran into each other at the barber's once in a while, and he was about the only person Stan could talk to who understood. After all, he'd lived with Priscilla even longer than Stan.

Poor Stan. But not so poor anymore. Because after fifteen years of hell, Stan had traded Priscilla for someone normal. Stan's second wife didn't pass out face down in her spinach quiche. Didn't throw knives or lock herself in the bathroom just before everyone arrived for Thanksgiving dinner. Didn't try to kill herself once a year.

Stan's ulcer was gone. Even his hair had grown back a little. And he was guilty as hell about it all. Scared that somehow the life he'd had was the life he was supposed to have. That this new life was just something the gods were only teasing him with.

To appease them, he gave Priscilla more than she needed, more than she wanted, more than she could ever need or want. So now, instead of being a schizoid, suicidal, alcoholic, she was a schizoid, suicidal, rich alcoholic.

He heard the metallic click, girded himself against the assault of the WHDH morning maniac ... *a 1950 blast from the past for all you early risers!!!* He shot his hand out and tapped the off button, but not before Patti Page managed a Tennessee waltz step around his bedroom. Patti Page. He could still picture her — pretty, blonde, wholesome. Or at least she had been forty years ago. Which meant she could have been crooning her waltz the very first time he willed the succubus. The circle of life. How fucking fitting.

He decided to save the shower for tonight and pulled on an old pair of pants, a sweatshirt that had a hole over his heart, the sneakers he used to run in before he stepped off the curb and tore his trapezius maximus. He washed his face and hands, brushed his teeth and looked at the tint of blood when he spit. That was new. Relatively new. For a while he'd expected it to go away. But it hadn't. It was there every time, an insult. As if his own gums had turned against him, waiting to go soft and puscular until just after he'd lost his dental coverage. He buried his face in a towel that smelled faintly of mildew.

One by one all the certainties of his life had deserted him. Santa. Love and sex. Happiness. Security.

He dropped his toothbrush into a yellow plastic cup and opened the front door on a day that couldn't seem to make up its mind. The sun broke through the clouds, disappeared, broke through again, but thinly. No threat of more April rain, at least that's what Dickie the weatherman said last night on channel five.

Down the road, a motorcycle started up, revved, went steady. Across the street a sprinkler carelessly set was leaving most of its spray on asphalt instead of grass. Mrs. Cready, his landlady, was standing over a peony tree that looked more dead than alive, a cigarette dangling from the side of her mouth. She was wearing the black and white striped house dress she lived in, and the dirty pink bunny slippers.

"Morning." He nodded.

"Half a bag 'a cow shit," she said, taking a drag and blowing the smoke out the side of her mouth, "and this thing still looks like crap."

"Maybe it takes a while," he said, "you know, for it to sink in and take effect. The fertilizer?"

She shrugged. She wasn't a bad landlady. She didn't talk a lot. She wasn't nosey. It wasn't her fault the walls were thin. She had a bald friend who came every Thursday at four o'clock in the afternoon and stayed until the next morning. They played the same five or six records over and over ... Guy Lombardo, Artie Shaw, Benny Goodman. Doris Day, Rosie Clooney, Bing Crosby. He'd heard them so many times, he'd memorized all the lyrics. And then sometime around ten-thirty Thursday night, the last record would end and the needle would run in the groove for an hour or more.

There'd be grunts and various other animal noises, and sometimes he tried to imagine them, her without her black and white housedress, her saggy breasts between the bald guy's arthritic fingers, her bulgy purplish legs up in the air, his hairless ass driving against her. But it wasn't something you liked to linger on too long.

"Hope it makes it," he said, opening the gate and clicking it shut behind him.

"Yeah, well..." She coughed. "I ain't gonna hold my breath."

He slid onto the cracked front seat of the old Volvo, pulled the seat belt around him, sat there with his foot on the gas for a minute waiting for the engine to smooth out, listening to the announcer talk about orange juice. The collie was jumping around, straining at the end of its line and he brought the rpm's up until the engine drowned out the noise and it was merely a dog miming.

He watched it strain and jerk. Maybe it was insane, an insanity induced by being tied up for four years. By hitting the end of that rope over and over and over.

"Christ," he said under his breath.

It ran in the family on both sides. Insanity. A great-grandmother, a cousin, an aunt. And, of course, Esther, the non-certified one. The great-grandmother and the cousin he'd only heard stories about. Auntie May, though, they'd visited once when she was 'away.' One Sunday after church, driving in the opposite direction from home, Esther, his father, Priscilla and himself.

His father was driving. Maybe his mother hadn't learned to drive yet, but even after she did, his father always drove. He was sitting behind his father, Pricilla next to him, behind his mother.

"Where are we going?" he'd asked. He remembered the moment of his asking and the almost immediate realization that he shouldn't have. Remembered the silence that made the question seem like the wrongest thing he could have done.

And as it turned out, the whole terrible day was *his* fault. For asking that one stupid question.

He remembered Auntie May, who seemed perfectly right and perfectly wrong at the same time. Her eyes darting from one to the other of them, chain-smoking, crying and then laughing. And her white slip showing all around beneath her skirt. He remembered the slip most of all, the white lace hanging inches down. A sign of carelessness, sloppy habits. A sign of detachment. Women worried about slips that showed. Is my slip showing? His mother said it all the time. And her other sisters. Is my slip showing? Are my seams straight? But Auntie May didn't seem to care. Didn't even seem to notice.

It could come over you, the way it came over her. Everybody said it. *It just comes over her. And she can't do a thing about it.* So he was always waiting for it to come over him, too. Even now, it sometimes seemed not far away. Little inklings here and there, now and then. A random thought that never took center stage but knocked quickly and disappeared. Say, when he was driving on the freeway. *This is seriously dangerous this thing you're doing*, the thought would whisper, *seriously fucking dangerous*. And it would vaguely occur to him that if he held onto that warning, if he let himself really *think* about it, he wouldn't be able to do it anymore. Wouldn't be able to hurtle along with hundreds of other cars that were hurtling along at speeds that could kill you in the time it took to complete a breath. Strangers all around you at sixty, seventy, eighty miles an hour. Strangers you wouldn't trust next to your bag at the airport. But on Route 128, going seventy-five miles an hour, *then* you trusted them.

And the funny urges that came out of the blue. Senseless, ridiculous urges. Sitting across a table from someone — friend, foe, peer, stranger — and this crazy, almost overwhelming urge to throw his ginger ale or his beer or his coffee right in their face. The urge to blow his horn at the old lady passing by his car just to see her jump. The urge to reach across the counter and touch the blond teller's nipple through her silk shirt. Then there were the road lines he counted, the numbers he repeated in his head, the silk blanket edge he rubbed against his nose in bed.

He always managed to stop himself. Didn't blow the horn, toss the drink, touch the nipple. He stopped the counting, the repeating, the rubbing. He drove the expressway. As if sanity was a decision, something you chose or didn't choose.

Lately though, it was *in*sanity that seemed the saner choice because for one thing, it would be a whole lot easier. You wouldn't be responsible then. Not for the fact your slip showed or your hand touched things it wasn't supposed to. It would just be ... something that came over you.

He let the engine idle down and the dog started making noise again. The announcer on the radio was in the middle of a tire commercial. Mrs. Cready gave the peony tree a kick with one dirty pink slipper and went inside.

CHAPTER TWO

The sun finally decided to come out just after he got to Pricilla's. It worked its way around the peak of the roof, hitting the side of the deck, and he went and stood in it, let the warmth touch his shoulders, turned his face up and tried to remember the technique the meditation lady had explained to him.

He'd settled for walking after his ankle went bad, around the block three or four times, and when that got boring started leaving out some of the ninety-degree turns. He took different routes, almost all of which ended up at the park, ten acres more or less, in the center of town. Over the course of seventeen years, he'd probably driven by that park half a million times and never once been inside it. But now he knew it the way he'd known the neighborhood he grew up in.

The meditation lady was there every morning. She had her spot exactly half way between the pond and the larch grove. She was older than he was, but better preserved. She'd been a dancer, which she said gave her an edge. "Walking is good," she told him. "Everyone should do it two hours every day." She'd looked at him when he told her a lot of people didn't have two hours a day, her regard for him slipping a little. "Well," she said, "we all pick our priorities, don't we."

She practiced yoga positions for an hour, then she meditated for half an hour. Sometime she was finished by the time he came along, sitting watching the ducks on the pond or walking along the edge throwing cracker crumbs.

"I don't see how you do it," he told her, "the meditation. I mean, if I close my eyes for more than five minutes, I'm asleep."

So she showed him.

It turned out his breath had a shape and a sound. He hadn't fallen asleep. But things kept rushing into his mind, getting in between him and his concentration. "Maybe I'm afraid to see what's in there," he'd told her, "you know, that great empty void I am."

He closed his eyes now, standing in the sun, but that just made the noises he usually wasn't aware of get very loud. An airplane, insects, birds, someone slamming a car door down the street, the hum of the highway — which surprised him, that you could hear it this far away.

He swept, opened the first can of stain, stirred, breathed in the strong toxic smell of it as he started painting where the deck met the house. He didn't tape the edge. He knew how to be careful. After a while he fell into a rhythm, working slowly, liking the pace and the way the stain soaked into the grain. He liked wood, liked working with it. He'd set up a shop in the basement a few years ago, with the intention of making a few fine pieces — a sideboard for the dining room, a bookcase for the den. Maybe even a roll-top desk eventually, a small one. He'd managed a birdfeeder, and a cutting board Roberta never used because she said it gave her splinters.

He'd stained about four feet of the deck when he glanced up and caught Priscilla moving quickly away from a window. It startled him. Because for a second he didn't see Priscilla, he saw their mother. Poor Pris, who did everything she could to be different, but couldn't stop the genes that made Esther's face look back at her from every piece of glass. Poor poor Pris.

Ever since he could remember, his mother had hated her. And ever since he could remember, Pris had been wooing her. With rose-covered Mother mugs, bouquets of violets, jewelry and scarves she saved all her allowance for, straight-A report cards, a four-year scholarship to Yale. Now she did it with programmable phones, expensive gourmet cakes, silk bed jackets. And it was all received with the same indifference. A tougher Priscilla, a more realistic Priscilla would have thrown Esther over by the age of thirteen and spent her teenage years being merciless. The way he had. But instead of taking their mother out on their mother, Priscilla had taken her out on herself. Been merciless on the victim instead of on the victimizer.

"Look," he'd told her when she'd soaked herself in enough liquor to end up in ER for the forty-second time, "you gotta tell her to her face what she's done to you, Pris, tell her what she is. If nothing else, tell her to leave you the fuck alone. Tell her, for christ's sake. She's tough as nails. You can't hurt her. Nothing penetrates. But at least it might let you concentrate on unfucking yourself for a change. Jesus Christ, Pris, you're gonna be fifty years old. Isn't it time you finally pulled her goddamn claws out of your hide?"

But it was like talking to someone already in a coffin.

The way she'd been when he found her in the attic.

He dipped the brush into the stain.

She'd been sick all week that time, the Asian flu. Nineteen fifty-five, fifty-six. She'd been the only one to get it in the family, and he could still remember how sick she'd been. How he'd wake up in the middle of the night and hear her yelling — she'd always hallucinated when she had a fever — that her bed was on fire or there was someone with a knife in the closet or spiders were crawling all over her. But she was better by the time Esther went into tantrum mode. Just weak and cranky and bored. Fair game. And his mother had had it. Everybody had known that for a couple of days. You could feel Esther going brittle, cracking all around her edges. The attention had been on Pris too long. Esther needed to bring it back where it belonged. After a week with no coffeeklatches, no shopping; after a week of chicken soup and back rubs and nightmares, she needed to reconfigure the order of things.

He'd sensed it as he walked up the driveway after school. As if the black fallout of Esther's explosion had sifted through to the exterior of the house, put a smell in the air, dimmed the windows, dulled the paint.

He wiped his feet on the mat and slipped his shoes off, opened the kitchen door and went inside. Maybe nothing had happened. Maybe there'd be the smell of kugel and Esther would be brushing Pris's hair and they'd both be laughing. It was a game they were all good at. Pretend.

The kitchen was silent. No radio. No TV from the living room. He put his books on the counter and swallowed, went through the dining room, into the living room, then down the hall. He saw the aluminum TV tray first, the one his mother had been using to carry Pris's meals into her bedroom. It was leaning, broken, against the wall beside the bathroom door, the white wallpaper stained orange and red, the smell of Scotch Broth and tomato juice hanging in the air. He glanced into Pris's bedroom, saw the empty bed and sidestepped the broken pottery lying on the rug. His heart was beating now, his mouth dry. If he'd thought it was allowable, he'd have bolted back through the living room and the dining room, through the kitchen and out the door. Run until he found some other house where people smiled at you on a more or less consistent basis, where your world didn't hinge on the unpredictability of Esther's moods. But he was only ten years old. He didn't know then that running away was a viable option.

His mother's bedroom door was open, and she was lying there, staring at the ceiling. She hadn't heard him, but she must have sensed him because she suddenly sat up and looked at him. Her face crumpled. "Is this what my life has come to?" she wailed, "a prisoner in my own house? A nursemaid to that ... that devil!"

He stared at her and she lay back on the bed, sobbing. He checked his room, the guest room, then he noticed the door to the attic was open a crack. He flipped the light switch, but the bulb still hadn't been replaced, and he went up the dark stairs, his socks slipping on the painted steps. "Pris?" he whispered.

"That's right," Esther yelled down the hallway, "don't give any comfort to your mother. I'm only the maid around here, the slave. The person everybody steps over like a dog on the floor. You think *she* deserves your attention, your comfort, your love?!" Her voice cracked on the word love. "What about *me*?" And her bedroom door slammed hard enough to make the attic stairs shudder.

"Pris?" he whispered again.

He was so full of terror by then, her name stuck to his lips. Scared shitless by the pitch-black attic, which had terrified him for as long as he could remember, by his mother and the hell she was going to put them all through for the next few days, but most of all, right now, by the silence.

Where was Pris? And where was God? Where was *He* every time this happened?

It took several minutes for his eyes to adjust, for the tiny slits of light coming through the shuttered peak window to give shape to the rafters and the boxes and the unused furniture stored all around him.

"Pris?" he whispered, "Pris?"

She was lying in a crate of old clothes, a wooden crate they called 'the coffin,' and when he saw her, his skin crawled.

Her eyes were closed.

"Pris, c'mon, Pris, cut it out."

She didn't move.

"Pris. C'mon, get out of there."

Still she didn't move, and he was suddenly filled with a rage bigger than terror, bigger than anything he'd ever felt. He thought back to it sometime, could still feel the immensity of it, even after all this time, and he figured that at that moment he'd been capable of doing significant damage. That it could have been one of those revolting news stories they splash across the front page. *Boy, ten, massacres mother and sister. Father walks into blood-soaked house and finds son mumbling unintelligible sounds.*

For some reason, he didn't kill. Instead he reached inside the box, picked Pris up by the shoulders and shook her until she started flailing at him with her fists.

"Why didn't you answer me?" he hissed.

"Leave me alone," she wailed, "I want to die. I just want to be dead."

"Is that what you're going to be. Just like her?"

That had stopped her, and they'd stared at each other in the dark before he helped her climb out of the box. They'd waited up there until they heard their father come home.

Esther ranted and raved all night. Their father made them scrambled eggs while she stood in the kitchen and accused him of loving his children more than his own wife. "Who takes care of *me?*" she kept sobbing. "Who ever takes care of *me.*"

"I'm making enough eggs for all of us," his father said.

And she'd rushed out of the kitchen, back to the bedroom, but this time she'd left the door open so they could listen to her sobs the whole time they choked down the runny eggs and the burnt toast.

Pris had gone to school the next day. Their mother didn't speak to them for a long time, maybe four or five days. That was how she punished. She did nothing for them. She prepared food for herself and her husband. She didn't wash their clothes or pack their lunches. She didn't say good morning or good night or ask them about their day. She stopped talking if they came into the room. She didn't look at them.

Whenever she was like that, he used to watch the classroom clock all afternoon, wishing three o'clock would never come, and then he and Pris would walk home as slow as they could, hardly talking, go straight to their rooms and stay there until their father got home from work and they could breathe a little. And until then, the house would be silent. No TV, no radio, nothing that could be remotely construed as enjoyment.

Because as long as Esther was miserable, everyone had to be miserable.

Then on the fifth or sixth day, they'd walked into the kitchen and there were two gifts sitting on the kitchen table. One for him. One for Pris. It was over. Esther's way of saying they were forgiven. There were four plates of fried chicken and gravy for dinner, four plates of apple pie for dessert. Things were going to be okay again. At least for a while.

Somehow they survived. Somehow there were albums with pictures of what looked like normal children and normal parents. Somehow Esther believed she'd been a good mother and a good wife, better than any of them deserved. Aggrieved, that's how she saw herself. Overwhelmingly aggrieved.

At ten-thirty, he smelled coffee and set the top back onto the can of stain. He slid his brush into a plastic bag, snapped a rubber band around the handle, went to the basement door and let himself in, washed his hands at the utility sink next to the washer. Then he went upstairs. Pris was leaning against the kitchen counter, the ever-present cigarette between her fingers. Along with two mugs of coffee steaming on the table, there was a plate with two lemon Danish and two pecan sticky buns.

"Hi," he said. "You look at it yet? Make sure the color's right?"

She brought the cigarette up to her lips. "I don't care about the color."

"That's good. Because it's a lot darker than the old stain."

She shrugged. She'd been a pretty girl. Delicate, fine-boned. She was still good-looking, but the way she treated herself was starting to show. Her skin was coarse, slightly veiny. And there were downward lines around her eyes and mouth that hadn't been there just a couple of years ago. Still, she had the kind of looks men of a certain age responded to. She could find someone to spend time with if she gave it half a try.

He sat down and pulled a mug toward him. He looked up at her. "You sign up for any of the courses I told you about?"

She shook her head.

"It's not too late. We could take a ride over there this afternoon. You've probably only missed one class, maybe two. But that's not so important. I mean, it's non-credit."

She shook her head again. "I don't think so."

"How come? You used to like ceramics, sculpting."

"I don't have time."

He picked up his mug, set it down again. "Time? You don't have *time*?"

She took a deep drag. "Yeah. I don't have time, okay? I have this big house I have to keep up. And I have Esther. She's a full-time job all by herself."

They looked at each other.

"*Someone* has to do it, Nate."

"Whatever you say, Pris." She could try all she wanted, but the guilt thing wasn't going to work.

He took a sip. It was very fine coffee, the best Stan's money could buy. He took one of the sticky buns. "Aren't you having anything?"

"I guess." She came over and sat down across from him. "How's Kimberly?"

"Good. I saw her Wednesday night. We had pizza."

"Did you tell her yet?"

He took a bite of the bun and shook his head no.

"Are you going to wait until she shows up at Wellesley? Let *them* tell her she's been unenrolled?"

He set the bun onto the edge of the plate she pushed across the table to him. "Tonight." He looked at her. "It's not the easiest thing I've ever had to tell her, you know."

She shrugged. "I should think she'd be getting used to you telling her hard things by now."

She was referring to him and Roberta. Ever since Stan had left she was mad at every man in the world. Especially every man who wasn't still married to his first wife.

"I didn't leave Roberta, Pris. She left me, remember? She was the one who had something hard to tell Kim, not me."

"Well if that's the way you look at it, then she had a good reason for leaving you."

He decided to let it go. "Take a wild guess at who I ran into last week."

She narrowed her eyes, blew a puff of smoke toward the ceiling. She shrugged. "Gorbachov?"

"Close." He sipped more coffee. "Ray Gallerani."

Her eyes unnarrowed. "Ray?"

He nodded. In high school, Pris and Ray had been voted the couple most likely to get married. It had been such a sure thing, someone had given her monogrammed towels when she graduated with P.A.G. for Priscilla Ann Gallerani in fancy red initials. And then Ray went away to college. Not to Yale, like they'd planned together, but to Stanford, three thousand miles away. And by the time he came back for a visit nine months later, he had a different way of talking, a different sense of humor, and a different girlfriend.

"What's he here for," she asked, "doing a little slumming?"

"It turns out his bowl of cherries soured right along with everyone else's."

She didn't say anything, but he could sense she was holding her breath, waiting for whatever he was going to say.

"Three divorces, a bunch of kids he never sees, and a bad hair implant."

"He went *bald*?"

He nodded. "Aside from the plugs."

She smiled a little.

"Anyway he's back here for a while. He asked about you."

"And I suppose you told him."

"I said you were divorced, too, but you still had all your hair. He said he'd like to see you."

She shook her head. "Ray Gallerani."

"Maybe you should extend an invitation for lunch."

She was playing with her spoon. She looked up. "To him?" She sat back. "And talk about what? How it felt to be deserted at eighteen by the only person I'd ever felt I could trust?"

He didn't say anything. He picked up his mug.

"Besides you," she said, "but you I couldn't marry."

A dog started howling somewhere in the neighborhood. Then it barked. Then it went silent.

"Maybe it was the water," she said after a while, "maybe that's why we all turned out to be such losers."

"We're not losers," he said, "we just weren't as invincible as we thought."

She sighed, emptied her mug, and he could tell the way she licked her lips it wasn't just coffee in there.

She caught his look. "I have to go to the nursing home this afternoon. You'd need a little reinforcement, too. If you ever went."

"I go."

She laughed. "Twice a year? You call that *going*?" She shook her head. "You could help a little, you know Nate? Take some of her weight off my shoulders."

He put both hands up, palms toward her. "Don't go making it sound like I've got some role in this, Pris, in this masochistic thing you two have going. No one's bending your elbow behind your back, you're doing that all by yourself."

"Have you any idea what it's like sitting there with her for two hours every fucking day?"

He nodded. "Yeah, as a matter of fact, I do."

"No, you don't. You don't have a clue."

If words had sharp edges, he'd have been cut to ribbons by the way she said it. Maybe it was whatever she'd put in her coffee, or maybe deep down she hated him, too.

"You've always had this nice protective mantle around you, Nate. You were born male. Me..." she shrugged, "I'm nobody. A pair of ears for her to talk into, a set of wheels to take her shopping, a pain in her ass when things aren't exactly the way she wants them. But I'm nothing she takes seriously. Nothing she acknowledges." She sighed. "At least you get that, Nate, acknowledgement. It's *some*thing, you know? Gives you a place to start from."

She picked up her mug again, licked the last drop from the edge. "If you went once in a while, I wouldn't be the only one listening to how she's suffered and how not one thing she's ever done has been for herself and if she had to do it all over again, this time..." she held up one finger, "...this time she'd be different. She'd be selfish!" She leaned toward him. "And you know what? Sometimes I actually wonder if it really was that way, *her* way. If maybe *I'm* the one who's crazy."

He looked at her, remembering the way she used to imitate Olive Oyl —*hmmm, Popeye, hmmmm, yes.* She'd had a sense of humor once, but somewhere along the way she'd forgotten how to laugh. He set his mug down. "Give me three more hours to work, and I'll go with you."

She frowned at him. "You're serious?"

"Of course I'm serious. Why would I say it if I wasn't?"

She looked over at the clock. "We'll go at three-thirty. That'll give you time to clean up."

He pushed his chair back. "Three-thirty." He went down the basement steps and out the bulkhead. He couldn't believe he'd agreed to go. As if there wasn't enough bad stuff already built into this day. He wound the elastic off the brush, slid the plastic bag off, took the lid off the can and dipped the brush in the stain. There must have been something in *his* coffee, too. It was the only explanation.

CHAPTER THREE

Somehow, the nursing home was under the highway. It was at the end of a dead-end street, a one-story H-shaped wooden building painted white, with gray shutters flanking each window, and window boxes full of fake flowers that faded but never died. It was surrounded by grass and trees and six concrete pillars that soared seventy feet to support a section of the overpass. Down below there was the constant hum of the traffic, and probably a decade's worth of lead in the soil, but the old people didn't seem to notice the noise, and he'd never seen any of them outside growing tomatoes in the yard, so the poisoned soil probably didn't matter.

It had been the only nursing home they'd visited where the smell didn't take your breath away as soon as you stepped into the foyer. The only one where they'd been offered references without getting the feeling they were asking for one of the director's kidneys. There was a dog, an aging golden retriever who made the rounds of the rooms twice a day, not that Esther was impressed. She wasn't the type. There was bingo every night, movies on the weekends, daily priests bearing hosts and weekly rabbis bearing nothing, and in the dining room plastic flowers at every table.

Esther hated it. They hadn't expected anything else. She had never shown a knack for making bad situations better, only a knack for making any situation worse.

On the way over, they'd stopped and bought flowers, carnations. He'd intended to pick up roses, but Pris had said they wouldn't last more than a couple of days in the over-heated room, where carnations would still look good after a couple of weeks.

At the front entrance there was a semi-circle of wheelchairs on either side of the front door, seven or eight old women, and he set a smile on his face, nodded at them the way you would if you were going into someone's house and their relatives were all lined up on the porch, but no one smiled back. All they did was stare, like kids, with no self-consciousness. Except it didn't work here because there wasn't anything cute about this bunch. Not one damn thing.

Inside, there was another wooden semi-circle.

"They just sit there," he whispered at Pris, following her down the corridor. "You'd think they'd at least talk to each other for christ's sake."

"Mostly they're deaf," she said over her shoulder, "and some of them don't even know they're sitting next to anybody, anyway."

He never had a problem finding Esther's room because she'd brought her Christmas decoration with her. It had hung on her old front door long enough to lose all its color. A gray Rudolf with a gray nose and a gray bow around its neck. She'd put it up one December a couple of decades ago and never taken it down. Until she moved here.

He and Pris hesitated before they went in, the way you did when you were getting set to face something painful, and then he was seeing the wispy-haired woman who used to be his mother slumped on the raised hospital bed, asleep, her mouth wide open.

For a second he felt an absurd sense of relief because this husk of an old woman bore no resemblance to Esther. This was no tyrant, no dictator of pain or pleasure, terror or relief. And then as if she sensed them, she opened her eyes and her mouth snapped shut. She squinted at them, frowned, and as recognition dawned she seemed to grow larger right in front of his eyes.

"Hmmph," she said, "might as well be a dream, for all I see of you." And in an instant, the old imbalance had reasserted itself. Esther was still there in that wrecked exterior. Still alive, still kicking, still capable of damage.

"You're late," she said to Pris.

He went over to the bed, bent down and kissed her forehead, even though he'd learned early that she was in the wrong line when they were handing out the capacity for affection. She had a way of accepting it without reciprocating one iota. No kissing back, no hugging beyond an occasional brief sterile press.

As soon as his lips touched her dry forehead, he was catapulted back to the morning his father died, her kitchen, three a.m. He'd gone there thinking she shouldn't be alone, thinking she needed comfort. After all, she'd just lost the man she'd lived with for forty-eight years.

He'd found her grooming the little Lhasa Apso his father had hated.

"You shouldn't have come," she told him, "what good is it if everyone loses sleep?"

"I wanted to make sure you were okay," he said, and then he'd hugged her, thinking that's what was called for. After all, it's what people did when they were hurting, reach out to each other. But there'd been no response, no warmth from Esther. Not even a goddamn hint of emotion. And maybe the reason it stood out for him, why he remembered it so sharply was because *he'd* been the one looking for comfort that night, and there'd been none.

She squinted at him now as he stepped away from the bed. "You've been far away, Nathaniel? China maybe?"

"Not quite that far." She was half the size she used to be. There were whiskers on her chin, something she'd never have allowed a few years ago. One foot was sticking out from under a standard-issue, woven, white blanket, and somewhere between now and the last time he'd seen her feet, her toes had gone even more crooked and gnarly.

"Someplace with no phones then," she said. Her bony shoulders rose, fell. "Ahh ... what's the difference." She sighed and pointed at a small rose-colored upholstered chair. "You're here. Sit."

He held out the carnations.

"Very nice. Some day, maybe before it's too late, I'll be worth a few *roses*, huh?"

Pris cleared her throat. "You know these will last longer, Ma. Isn't that what you told your roommate when her son sent roses? That roses are silly and carnations last longer?" Pris grabbed the flowers out of his hand and for a second he thought she was going to dump them headfirst into the wastebasket. "I'll get a vase," she said tightly, and left the room.

"Kimberly," Esther said, "she never comes. And Roberta." She made a motion with one hand like she was shooing away a fly. "No great loss there." She looked at him. "And to think you could have married that other one. That beautiful girl. The pianist."

It was a refrain she'd been using variations of for twenty years. "You're a lucky girl, Roberta," she'd say over the Thanksgiving turkey, "a pianist, a girl with the loveliest hands I've ever seen almost got him. But he picked you." And then she'd shake her head. "Love." She'd shrug. "There's no explaining it." Or opening presents on Christmas eve, "Guess who I ran into last week? That girl you almost married. The pianist. And you know, she's as beautiful today as she was at twenty-one." Looking at Roberta, "Some people just don't age, you know? If only *we* could be that lucky."

No wonder Roberta got the runs every holiday. Everything she kept inside coming out the wrong end. And over Julie McKenney, of all people, whose only pianistic achievement as far as he could remember was being able to play chopsticks in every key. Though one thing she did have going for her, her willingness to let him finger fuck her at her kitchen table every Monday afternoon when they were supposed to be solving algebra equations. At least until her father walked in one day and found his daughter in a fairly advanced state of ecstasy, called him a fucking pervert, and threatened to kill him if he ever saw his dirty Jew face around there again. As if he'd *forced* her to pull down her panties and spread her legs and beg, *faster faster faster*.

Down the hall someone yelled, then yelled again. Esther didn't seem to notice.

"So how do you like being waited on hand and foot?" he asked.

"Now you're here," she said, ignoring the question, "we can get something settled. You're sister there can't seem to arrange anything right. So you call the person in charge right now and find out about leaving. Today would be fine, because if I never saw another person from this place again, it would be too soon." She leaned toward him a little. "Colored, that's what's here. And not just cleaning the floors either." She aimed a thumb toward her chest. "Me, cleaning me. Washing me down there." She pointed in the general direction of her private parts. "A colored person seeing your mother down there. What do you think of that?"

It was true. He didn't know what to think of that, and then Pris walked in with the carnations in a glass vase and set them on top of a bureau.

"And they took my watch, you know," Esther said, "my diamond watch, the one I was going to leave to Kimberly." She shrugged. "Though for the life of me I don't know why. Maybe if she came to see her grandmother once in a while … it wouldn't kill her, you know."

Pris sighed. "She was here just a couple of weeks ago, Ma." She looked at Nate, crossed her arms. "We go through this every day." She looked back at Esther. "I already gave Kimberly the watch. You told me to, remember?"

Esther didn't even glance in her direction. "All your life," she said, "you do for people and look at the thanks you get." She pointed a bony finger at him. "You just wait. You'll get a taste of your own medicine and I'll enjoy every second you're miserable."

At the end of the bed, Pris shifted from one foot to the other.

"I think talk like this isn't going to get us anywhere," Nate said. "You agreed to come here because being alone at home wasn't working out. And this was by far the best place we could find. You get good care here. The staff pays attention. And Pris comes almost every day to check on you."

Esther stared at him for a good ten seconds with a look that was almost feral. Then she turned her face away, toward the window, and he was ten years old again, a howling wind opening up inside him because he'd wounded his mother. He was always wounding his mother. It was impossible not to. No matter what he did he ended up wounding his mother.

He looked at Pris. She looked back with a blank expression. He knew what she was thinking, and right now a drink seemed like a good idea to him, too.

"Is there anything you need, Esther? Anything that would make things better?" He'd stopped calling her Ma years ago, but for some reason he hadn't figured out yet, even *Esther* came out hard.

She didn't reply. She would ignore them for as long as she felt they deserved it. Christ, this was insane. They were like atoms, charged atoms. The three of them locked into some fucking unbreakable attraction, which nothing … not desire, not rejection, not, he feared, anything short of death was going to alter.

He blew out a slow breath. Once, in this very situation, he'd walked out. On a day when life was feeling too simple, too normal for his own good, when every action seemed logically to lead to an equal and opposite reaction. If ignoring him meant she didn't want him there, then leaving was a reasonable thing to do, wasn't it? And then a little less than three hours later he'd got the call that she was in ER with a heart attack. His fault.

"View's not bad," he said, looking out the window. Pris shrugged. Her mouth was tight. There were tiny vertical lines he'd never noticed before around her lips, two deep lines across her forehead. She looked like she'd aged ten years since they'd walked in.

He tried again. "Where's her roommate?"

Pris looked over at the empty bed. "She asked to be moved."

"Thank god for some things," Esther muttered, "common people. Coarse as they come."

Down the hall there was the sound of a metal tray hitting the floor. It was ludicrous, the three of them still doing this tight-assed dance after fifty years. Esther, with her chin whiskers and her gnarly toes, still calling the shots, and the two of them as helpless as if they were still pissing in their pants. He looked at her foot sticking out from under the blanket, remembered how she used to paint her toenails with bright red polish. The way she'd sit at the kitchen table with one foot on the edge of an adjacent chair, toilet paper stuffed between each toe while she stroked on the color. Once, in third or fourth grade, he'd brought a friend home after school. There wasn't a rule against that, but they hardly ever did it because you never knew how Esther was going to take things. You needed to be careful. You never pushed too hard on whatever tentative balance there was.

But this friend had been a new kid, from New Mexico or California, somewhere out west, and for whatever reason they'd hit it off. They'd bragged to each other about their model plane collections, and the kid had shown him his. It was okay, but it was half the size of his own, and his desire to show off had gotten in the way of caution.

They'd walked into the kitchen, he and this kid, and Esther had been there painting her nails, her skirt hiked up above her knees, and he didn't know if the kid was gawking or not, though he doubted it from the look on his face when Esther started. "What do you think *you're* gawking at?" That had been the first thing out of her mouth. "Who *are* you anyway? Who invited you to walk into my kitchen and *gawk* at me like that?" And then, since she wasn't watching what she was doing, she'd made a bright red slash of red across her toes. "Now see what you made me do!" She'd started crying then, standing up so suddenly that the nail polish bottle tipped over on the formica table top. He could still see her standing there waving the tiny brush, her face contorted and ugly, the toilet paper between her toes, the pool of red polish on the table. "What's your name? I'm going to call your mother and tell her exactly what you did. I'm going to tell her you sneaked into my kitchen uninvited and looked at me where no one has a right to look!" That was the last thing he remembered her saying. It had gone beyond that, but he was in his I-wish-I-was-dead mode by then. He didn't hear the rest.

He took his eyes off her foot. God, he hated it. Both her feet. And other things, too. The way she bit down on her knuckle when she got mad. The little crunching sound she made in her throat when she drank her morning coffee. The awful peanut butter cookies you had to eat at least three of to avoid insulting her. And the way she held everything together with rubber bands — her checkbook, her wallet, magazines, cereal boxes, cheese, ice cream containers. Everything. Things that damn well held themselves together for everyone else except Esther. And that sweet perfume she'd used as long as he could remember. He especially hated that. He glanced back at her foot, stuffed his hands in his pockets, stifling an urge to reach down and cover it with the blanket.

He made himself look away, up at the ceiling. There was a barely visible brown stain above the other bed and he ran his eye around its irregular edge three times. Still, he couldn't stop thinking about her foot. Son-of-a-bitch. So now what? Had he developed some kind of obsession with his mother's fucking foot?

Trying not to think about it didn't work because he couldn't think of anything else. He blew out a loud, impatient breath and Pris glanced at him. She had a carnation petal on her blouse, directly above one nipple. A bright red pastie, and it sent a sudden rush of giddiness through him.

He aimed a thumb toward the empty bed. "A commoner," he said to Pris, "the lady who asked to be moved? She was a commoner. Unlike us." He stood up a little straighter. "Royalty."

There was a beeping sound from across the hall. The nursing home dog trotted by the door, its collar jingling. He turned around and caught sight of its tail just before it disappeared. Even a dog knew better than to come in here. He bowed stiffly in Pris's direction, "Your highness, any beheadings this afternoon?"

She stared at him.

"Hey, did you hear the Duke dropped his pants this morning and mooned the crowd from the balcony? Cheeky bloke."

Her lower lip trembled.

"Are we somewhat amused?" he asked her.

She pressed her lips together. "No, we are not somewhat amused."

"Somewhat abused? Did you say we are not somewhat abused? Are you somewhat mad?"

Her hand went to her mouth and she snorted into her palm, shook her head. "Somewhat mad for abuse," she said, "otherwise what in hell am I doing *here*?"

He frowned. "Tell me … are we dining crowned or uncrowned this evening?"

She raised her eyebrows. "You dare to frown on the crown?"

"Only out on the town," he said, "you know how the crowns attract the attention of the hoi polloi."

"And what is the use of royalty," she said, "if it is not to attract the attention of the hoi polloi?"

He held up one finger. "Ah, but surely we have other uses. Coins, for instance. We look well on them."

She nodded. "And we wave well." She held up one hand and twisted it insipidly.

"Plus we almost single-robedly eviscerated the ermine population."

"And if we'd had our way, executioners would still set the trend in hoods and beefy topless leather fashion."

"Polo," he said, laughing out loud.

"Corgis."

"Stiff upper lips."

"Hemophilia."

"Inbreeding."

"Stop it! Stop it!" Esther's face was bright pink against the pillowcase. "This is what I deserve? Two ridiculous clowns!?" She plucked at the blanket. "Mock me, go ahead. I lie here being tortured, suffering and alone day after day and then you come, my own children, and mock me?" Her voice went shrill, she pointed a finger at them. "If your father was still alive this would kill him!"

It sent them both over the edge. It was the first time he'd seen Pris out of control without a drink in her hand in years.

Two nurses appeared in the doorway.

"Get them out of here," Esther started yelling. "Get them out, get them away from me!"

He tried to say something, but words were impossible, so he just grabbed Pris's hand and pulled her toward the door. The nurses stepped aside, and he and Pris laughed their way between them and out into the hall. An old woman going by in a wheelchair looked up at them and chuckled.

They had to lean against the wall three times before they finally made it outside and into the car, where they sat until a bird could fly by without sending them off again. He felt weak. Light. Pris's cheeks were red, her eyes bright. She didn't look old anymore, and a couple of times he wanted to put his hand on her cheek, to let her know he cared, that he wished things had been different, better.

They sat with their backs against their respective doors, facing each other. Pris shook her head. "I'll never be able to go in there again."

"She won't remember any of it in a couple of days."

"You're right. I forgot." She giggled.

But it was all out by then, and all they could do was smile at each other.

CHAPTER FOUR

Driving home from Duxbury on 139, the sun was murder. Right in his eyes, blinding him to the brake lights on the cars in front of him, to whether the traffic lights were green or red, until finally, he couldn't take it anymore. He swung off at the next intersection and made his way to Dorchester driving south, down to Brockton and Route 24. He was in no hurry to get home anyway.

He hadn't had anything to eat since the Danish, and he had a dull ache in his stomach. He'd wanted to take Pris out to dinner, but she said she had to get home. To what? he asked, as if he didn't know. As if he'd actually thought a half-hour of laughing could change her, take away her thirst.

His stomach growled. That was the thing about hanging around an alcoholic. They never got hungry, never wanted to stop drinking long enough to eat.

An hour later, he pulled into his usual Burger-King and got in line behind a maroon mini-van full of kids, its rear window covered with stickers from Knott's Berry Farm to Mt. Washington.

His stomach never used to bother him, but it bothered him a lot now. It hurt when he didn't eat and it hurt when he did.

The maroon van took forever to order, took forever to distribute the food the girl handed through the sliding window, took forever to come up with the money to pay her; and when he finally got handed his two whoppers, his large fries, and his extra-large coke, the pain in his stomach was big enough so he knew the food was only going to make it a whole lot worse. But by then he was too hungry to care.

He found an empty spot in the parking lot and unwrapped it all. He knew it was the worst thing he could be eating, that tasting good was the only thing it had going for it. Burgers and fries, fries and burgers, three, maybe four days a week. Pizza. Chinese. Bad Thai. Fried chicken. Now, all his meals came out of a container. He picked up one of the burgers and bit into it.

It wasn't the hole he was burning in his gut that bothered him, though, it was what he'd discovered about himself lately. All his adult life he'd thought he was a relatively capable human being. He'd taken care of a family for two decades plus, bought and sold cars, put things together — stereos, bicycles, an imitation redwood picnic set that had come out of the box in at least sixty pieces. He had a two handicap in golf, could open a bottle of wine, sail a dinghy, tread water. He could hit a tennis ball over the net.

But now he knew it was all sham. He wasn't competent at all. It was as if during all those years only his outsides had changed, but inside he was still nine years old. He had no common sense, no will power, no self-control. He was incapable of keeping a job or a wife. He couldn't go to see his crazy eighty-nine year old mother without causing her unnecessary grief. He couldn't even manage a simple thing like feeding himself right. God, how could anybody be so pathetic?

He took another bite of the burger, popped some fries in his mouth, rinsed it down with Coke.

He watched three teenage girls walk by. They looked about seventeen, but were probably younger. It was funny ... kids seemed to grow up faster and adults seemed to grow old slower than they used to. Then one of the girls stumbled and almost tripped and they all went hysterical, grabbing onto each other, so that he could hear them laughing even after he couldn't see them anymore. He thought of Pris and himself and smiled.

When he was finished, he rolled the napkins and the wrappers into a ball, stuffed it inside the bag along with the empty Coke can, got out of the car and walked over to a trash container. He looked at his watch. A little before seven. He'd told Roberta he'd be over at eight-thirty, that he needed to talk to her and wanted Kim there, too. That it wouldn't take long.

And after it was over, after he'd let them know Kimmy's future was up for grabs, then maybe he could go home and put himself into a coma. One that would last long enough for his luck to change.

He looked across the intersection at Doug's Video, wondered if, failing the coma, a couple of *Dirty Harrys* would do the trick. Or maybe a Sly or a Van Damme, anything sufficiently shallow to stimulate only the most primal portion of his brain stem.

He left the car at Burger King and walked across the intersection.

Doug's family were old neighbors. He'd watched Doug grow up. He was, what ... six years older than Kim? A good kid who never got into trouble. Still a good kid. The store was low on choice, but big on service, and the rental was a little cheaper than the Blockbuster near the Mall.

He opened the door, gave the sign in the window a sideways glance.

"Hey there, Mr. M. How's it going?"

He nodded. "Okay, Doug — how about you?"

"Great. I ran into Kim yesterday. Boy she's all excited about Wellesley." He shook his head. "Bet that's going to put you in hock for a while."

Nate nodded. "More than you know." He looked at the sign in the window again. It had been there a while, and sometimes he kidded with Doug. *Hey, maybe I'll take that job, huh? Since I'm here so much anyway. Does it come with an employee discount?* And they'd both laugh.

He thought about what it would be like to have someone he worked with at Kitt-Boland, maybe someone who used to work *for* him, come in. What it would be like to put their videos in a bag, give them change, wish them a nice day.

"Can I help you find something, Mr. M?"

"Well…" He looked around, thinking how it was something to do. It was money. And tonight he'd be able to tell Roberta he was doing something to tide him over until a real job came along. He nodded, tried to sound off-hand, a little surprised, like what he was going to say had caught him off-guard, too. "Yeah Doug, as a matter of fact maybe you can." He pointed at the sign. "How about a job? I'm on a kind of sabbatical and I'm going crazy with all this spare time. 'Specially on the weekends. And that's what you need covered, right, weekends? Course I've never done retail … oh, a long time ago when I was a kid." He scratched his head and told himself to shut up. "Morrison's, I think that was the name. It was a dry goods place downtown. Guess you don't see dry goods stores now, huh?" He shrugged. "So I'm applying. For the job." He nodded. "This job."

Doug didn't say anything. But he got a look on his face, a sort of loopy pleased look that seemed to be causing him a lot of effort. And at the same time, a vacuum opened around Nate. He would have given anything to be able to walk into the store all over again, rent a goddamn video like he always did, and get the hell out. What had he been thinking? What the hell had he been thinking?

Doug cleared his throat. "Well, the thing is Mr. Madigan, it's only an entry level job paying minimum wage. I … uh, and there's a lot of monotony to it, you know? But then at the same time it can be tricky. I mean, it's working with the public. You know … it's … it's not a specialty store, it's strictly mainstream, so it's a job for someone who's up on the culture, if you know what I mean, someone who's seen every movie Sean Penn's ever made, for instance." He laughed a little.

There was an endless awkward five seconds of silence, and for the life of him Nate couldn't think of a thing to say to fill it.

"Of course you could think it over, Mr. M, and then we could talk about it again."

He nodded. "Sure, Doug. Just something that came into my head. Probably not such a good idea." He laughed a little. "'Specially when it comes to Sean Ben."

"Penn," Doug said.

"Penn, right." He started backing toward the door. "So ... I'll see you later, Doug. Take care now."

"You too, Mr. M."

He made it out of the store, then across the intersection without getting hit, got into the car, slammed the door. The smell of the fries and the burger still hung in the air. He felt so hugely foolish he could have torn the steering wheel out with his bare hands.

Tricky? Is that what the little fucker had said? *Tricky?*

CHAPTER FIVE

There were four messages on his machine when he got home. One from Kimmy who wanted to know if he could help finance her graduation party. One from a guy who still worked at Kitt-Boland, telling him that the job he'd heard about in Maine wasn't going to happen after all. "So tell me something new," Nate muttered. One from Roberta who wanted him to know he had to finance Kimberly's graduation party. And one from a woman he'd met in line at the unemployment office. Rose. She was a cost accountant, a little on the pudgy side, but she had pretty eyes and a nice smile. She had a dachshund named Max and she liked jazz. "I hear," she said to his machine, "that it's okay now for women to call men. And since you didn't call, I thought I'd let you know that I'd like you to. You don't meet all that many promising people in line nowadays. So maybe I could offer you some lunch on Saturday ... they say lunch is better than dinner for these things ... and I make a truly masterful German chocolate cake. RSVP. Bye now."

It was something that would have made him feel better, maybe even excited, any other day. But today nothing was going to go right, and it wasn't over by a long shot. He looked at the clock. Just a little more than forty-five minutes until he had to walk into the teeth of the dragon and he didn't have a clue what he was going to say.

Did he make it an announcement — "Okay, I'm sorry as hell to have to say this but I'm out of work and you'll have to call off your plans. The new tires for the car, painting the garage, Kimmy's graduation party. Oh ... and Wellesley, too."

He sank down into the sunken center of the barrel chair he'd been sitting in too much lately. The springs groaned. What had he done, for christ's sakes, to deserve this?

He put his head in his hands and the faint smell of stain went up his nose even though he'd scrubbed his hands at the laundry sink in Pris's basement. The hamburger and fries, they were there, too, and the combination was nauseating. He got up and went into the bathroom, turned the shower on high, shed his shoes, his socks, his pants, his shirt. He sudsed himself twice, then stood under the water even after it went cold trying to wash away the greasy feeling that things were never going to sit right again.

He shut the water off, walked into the bedroom dripping. Both towels were dirty, and he pulled them out of the pile of clothes in the corner, smelled each of them, tossed one back and dried himself with the other. He pulled on clean underpants, a pair of semi-clean jeans, took a denim shirt out of the closet. He combed his hair, looked at himself. He'd never felt so low in his life.

Outside, the day had disappeared into night, and as he watched, a light went on inside the house across the street. There was the sound of a plane overhead, a motorcycle putt-putting then going silent, a door banging, someone calling 'Jimmy,' a dog barking on the next block. It made him remember the way he used to feel when he was a kid, moving through a sifting dark toward home, walking back from Billy Picardi's house. Billy, with the train set that took up half the basement, the Howdy Doody tent in the front hall, the Woody Woodpecker doorbell. As if life wasn't a serious thing that bit you in the ass on a regular basis. As if kids should take up space. He'd walk the whole length of Crosby Street in the growing dark toward home, the gritty feel of the asphalt under his Keds, a kind of inescapable gravitational tug pulling him home, while the glow of Billy Picardi's house faded away behind him. And by the time the yellow lights of his own house came into view, the air would be black and he'd be invisible in it, and wanting to stay that way.

He grabbed his keys, shed the memory, got into the car, closed the door and sat there looking up at the black edges of trees and roofs against the somewhat less dark sky. That's what he needed now. Someplace to be largely invisible.

He drove toward Newton on streets that had lost their familiar feel. And the closer to the house he got, the stranger it all felt. He passed the drugstore that wasn't his drugstore anymore. The pizza place where Nick used to greet him by name. The copy store he no longer used. The supermarket he didn't shop at. He turned down the street he didn't live on anymore, stopped in front of the house that was no longer his. In *front* of it because it didn't feel right pulling into the driveway, because pulling into the driveway said *I'm home,* while parking in front was *Don't worry, I won't be here very long.*

He hesitated long enough on the sidewalk to notice how neat everything looked, how well-cared for. It seemed things had improved since he'd left. There were professionals taking care of the yard now, sealing the driveway, fixing all the things Roberta had been waiting years for him to take care of. He looked at the trimmed shrubs that used to block the front windows, the new garage doors, the fixture next to the kitchen door that someone had reattached. And then he found himself with his hand on the kitchen doorknob, about to walk right in, an instinct not buried deep enough yet to suppress without a conscious effort.

He walked back around to the front door and rang the bell. The door flew open. "Daddy!" Kimmy threw her arms around his neck. She smelled of soap and fruit, strawberries and cream, and if he could just stand there holding her in his arms for the rest of his life then everything else wouldn't matter. "Did you get my message?"

She was bouncing a little, a habit she had when she was happy. And she'd done something to her hair since he'd seen her on Tuesday. It was shorter, curling forward onto her cheeks like a Dutch girl's cap, bouncing, too. He liked it.

"I like your hair, buddy. And, yeah, I got the message." He made his voice go high ... 'hey dad, send cash so I can party.'"

"Oh Da-ad. It's just that Mom figures if we have it here then she won't have to worry about me. But it's gotta be huge. I mean, everybody already knows about it. Half the class has already said they're coming."

"So maybe if half of them each bring a bag of chips, and the other half each brings a jar of salsa, all I'll have to be good for is some apple juice to wash it all down?"

She made a face at him. "I've already called about renting a tramp, and a regulation size volleyball net. The Percys said we could use their basketball hoop because they're not going to be home, but Mom said no because everybody going back and forth might damage those precious bushes Mr. Percy's always fussing over. I mean, does she think we can't tell the grass from the rhododendrons?"

"She's right, K," he said. "Stay in your own yard. Herb puts pictures of those bushes in his Christmas cards."

She shrugged. "I guess."

"I saw Grandma today."

"That's good. Because when I saw her last time she went on and on about how you never go."

"Well, she said the same thing about you."

"What do you mean? I was just there two weeks ago!"

He shrugged. "The memory thing. Anyway, she looks pretty good, considering."

"She hates it there."

"Wouldn't you?"

She shrugged. "I guess so. But I'm not ninety-two."

"Eighty-nine."

They looked at each other and laughed a little.

"C'mon." She grabbed his arm. "Mom has to get up early tomorrow to catch a train to New York. She's meeting someone about her cookbook and she wants to go to bed early tonight."

"Has she finished it?" He followed her inside.

Kim nodded. "Somebody may actually want to publish it." She turned toward him. "A potato cookbook. Can you believe it?"

"It'd be great. I hope they buy it." Maybe, he thought, it could become a best seller and then Roberta would end up financing the Ivy League education.

There was the sound of the dishwasher starting up in the kitchen. Kim led him into the living room. He sat down on the couch. There was something different in here, too, but he couldn't put his finger on it.

Ozzie appeared from nowhere and rubbed against his leg, purring. He scratched between her ears and the purring edged up a notch.

"Hello, Nate."

He started to stand up, changed his mind and sat forward instead. "Hi Roberta." He couldn't think of anything else to say. There was a small uncomfortable silence and then she sat down. Like Kim's hair and the room, she looked different, too, but like the room, he couldn't put his finger on what was different about her either. Unless it was her hair. He tried to remember if it had always curved forward toward her chin.

"We're having a nice spring so far," she said, "weather-wise, I mean, aren't we?"

He nodded. He had no idea what spring was being like weather-wise. Vaguely warmish and rainy he supposed, like most of them.

Kimberly bounced a little in her chair. They all looked at each other.

"So, Daddy, what's up?"

He interlaced his fingers. He looked around. "There's something different in here, isn't there?"

"The rug's new," Kim said. "The old one was all stained from when Tye was a puppy."

He nodded, and they fell into another silence, all of them looking at the new rug as if it were the most fascinating thing they'd ever seen.

Tye had been run over last spring, just after Roberta told him their marriage was over.

"And I had the walls painted," Roberta said.

He looked up from the rug. "Oh, right. You'd been wanting to do that for a long time. It looks good."

She nodded. "I like it."

"Good. That's good."

She looked at him. They were both looking at him. He cleared his throat. "I uh ... I have some ... there's been a change. In my circumstances." He cleared his throat again. "I ... they, well, there's been some reorganization at work." He looked at his hands. "My position was ... dislocated."

Kimmy stared at him for a second, then she frowned. "Does that mean you have to move?"

He shook his head. "No."

Roberta sat forward. "They fired you?"

"Well ... no. They didn't *fire* me. They did away with my position ... and it may just be temporary. You know ... they may bring it back. When things pick up." He looked at Roberta then at Kim. "And then again, they may not. So I've been looking for something else. I mean, I can't wait around for them to call, so ..." A car with a muffler problem went by the house. "Trouble is there's not a lot out there right now."

"How long?" Roberta asked.

"How long what?"

"When did they let you go?"

He shrugged. "Couple of weeks ago." Somehow he couldn't tell her the truth.

"Did you get a severance package? Can you collect unemployment?"

He nodded. "Oh, sure."

"What about your benefits? Are we still covered? They didn't cancel your insurance, did they?"

"No. Of course not. Don't you think I'd have told you? That goes on for twelve months. After that we can stay in, but I have to pay. Although I'll have another job by then, so that's not anything to even be concerned about."

"Then it doesn't make any difference?" Kimmy said. "I mean, you get paid by unemployment. And you'll get a new job. So it's no big deal." She smiled, looked from him to her mother back to him.

He made himself look straight into her eyes. "It's kind of a big deal, K. Unemployment only pays a fraction of what I was making. And although I'll get another job ... maybe even a better one ... there's no way of telling when that will happen. It's turning out to be a little —" he shrugged, "tougher than I thought it would be." The clock on the mantle made a whirring noise. "It looks like we're going to have to make some adjustments."

It got quiet.

"What adjustments, Nate?"

He looked at Roberta. "Put off any more house repairs for a while." He cleared his throat, and this time he had to make himself look back at Kimberly. "And, Kimmy, I think you're going to have to put Wellesley off a year."

For a moment, it was like she'd turned to stone, and then she shot straight up. "You mean I can't go to college?"

"Of course you can go to college. You'll just have to do your freshman year at UMass."

"UMass?" The way she said it made it sound like he'd told her she had to spend a year in North Korea.

"It's the last thing in the world I expected," he said. "I wish like hell you didn't have to change your plans, honey. But a lot of your friends are going out to Amherst in September, right? It won't be that bad."

She stood there looking down at him. He'd never realized how much she looked like Roberta and it caught him smack in the gut.

"I just want you to know," she said, her voice high and shaky, "that this has been the worst year of my life thanks to you." Then she ran past them out of the room, kicking Ozzie's rubber ball in the process. The ball hit the doorframe, ricocheted back toward the middle of the room and rolled to a stop near his foot. He stared at it.

Everything seemed to gray out ... the level of light in the room, probably the color of his blood. His throat went tight.

After a while, Roberta sighed, sat back. "She'll get over it, Nate. She'll realize it's not the end of the world. It might take a little time, though."

He just looked at her.

"Oh, c'mon. It's not as if it's your fault. You didn't quit on purpose." She narrowed her eyes and leaned forward a little so her hair, those two new curves, he was sure now they were new, leaned forward a little, too. "You didn't, did you?"

"What do you think?"

She sighed again, then she and her hair leaned back. "She'll survive. We'll all survive."

For a second, they stared at each other.

"How come you're not reading me the riot act?"

She shrugged. "I don't know. Maybe because you don't look like you could take it. You don't look well, Nate."

He looked down at his hands. "I'm fine. This was just so damn hard."

She crossed her hands over her stomach. It didn't look as big as he remembered it. He looked at her face, realized she'd lost weight.

"Remember when she was a Brownie," Roberta said, "and you two spent all that time building a car for the Pinewood Derby? And she was absolutely certain she was going to win even though we told her there was a chance she might not. Though I think you were as convinced as she was."

He nodded. "And then she came in sixth." He shook his head. "I still remember the look on her face."

"She cried herself to sleep, had a tantrum at breakfast the next morning, and I remember watching her on her way down the street to get the bus, and the McShanes' dog came running up to her the way it always did ... remember the little terrier they used to have?"

"Shamus, yeah."

"Shamus came up to her, all wiggly and friendly, and she kicked him! Well, she didn't really kick him, but she kicked at him, kicked the air. And he got the message. Took off with his tail between his legs." She uncrossed her ankles, crossed them again. "Anyway, she got over that, after a suitable period of time, and she'll get over this, too. Actually I've always thought UMass was a better choice." Then she seemed to think of something that took the ease out of her posture and she sat forward again. "There *is* enough money for UMass, isn't there?"

He nodded. "That's the severance." And all of a sudden he thought if they kept talking about it he was going to cry. He cleared his throat. "Kim said you're going to New York tomorrow about your book."

She put her lips together and her head went up and down, as though it wasn't something to talk about out loud. She had these little things she did … tossing salt over her shoulder, knocking on wood, getting upset if you tempted fate by saying something like, *I haven't had an accident in ten years.* He'd stopped paying attention to it. He'd stopped paying attention to most of the things she did or said.

But right now he was feeling confused, because he was feeling like a warm quilt had been draped around him. He was home. It felt familiar again. And Roberta was looking and acting more like the girl she used to be, the one he'd almost forgotten.

"Which reminds me, Nate." She stood up and he felt the warm quilt lift. "I have to leave at a ridiculous hour tomorrow to get to New York on time."

He stood up, too. His body felt like it had become disjointed during the past half-hour, all his parts at awkward angles. But it must have been something internal, because Roberta continued to regard him with the same even, almost pleasant, look.

"You'll find something, Nate. And don't worry about Kimberly. Give her some time to get used to it. I'll talk to her, too."

He nodded. He wanted to say how grateful he was that she wasn't screwing him to the wall, which is what he'd expected, what he'd been prepared for. Thank her for being understanding. No, not just understanding, supportive. Jesus Christ. Roberta, understanding and supportive. How in hell had *that* happened?

But all he said was, "Thanks, Roberta."

And then it hit him somewhere between the living room and his car, after she closed the front door and left the walkway light on until she heard his car door slam, that she hadn't *gotten* anything. That what had happened was she'd *lost* something. She didn't care anymore. She'd lost whatever emotions she'd still had for him. The jealousy, the anger, the pain, the resentment, the disappointment. They'd meant something beside just a hard time. They'd meant she cared enough about him to feel something. Now though, she wasn't feeling anything. He could have been the postman sitting on the couch telling her his hard luck story. She'd have offered *him* her condolences, too.

He felt the sink-hole that was inside him get a little deeper. He shivered. And driving home, he thought he had a pretty good idea what an infinitesimal dot of dull light might feel like moving through the immense void of space.

CHAPTER SIX

It came to him sometime between three and four in the morning, after tossing and turning most of the night. So he got up. Because he knew if he didn't, if he fell asleep and woke up in the morning with the sun in his eyes, he was going to see it for what it was. Cowardice. Delusion. At best a very bad idea.

It took him an hour to put everything in order — write the letters; collect the passbook, the insurance policies, the info on the 401K, the stock certificates. The passbook would cover the graduation party and the one-year state tuition. The rest of it was useless until he was dead or it was too late to matter much.

He'd use his credit card to take him wherever it was he was going.

He wrote a note to Mrs. Cready: *Sorry, but I've been called away suddenly....* He was paid up through the end of next month, and she could send his first and last to Roberta. He included an envelope for that. *And by the way, hope the peony pulls through.*

It took him two minutes to write the note to Roberta. *Going where the jobs are. Will keep in touch. All worldly possessions enclosed.* Then it took ten minutes to find an envelope big enough to put it all in.

He wrote a note to Pris. *Got to get away. Sorry to leave you with Esther. Give Ray a call.* Even though he knew she wouldn't.

The sun was just beginning to lighten the sky by the time he finished the letter to Kim. *You've always been the most important thing in the world to me. Sorry I've let you down.* Blah blah blah.

He left Mrs. Cready's note leaning against the front door, made two trips between the house and the car, and then sat behind the wheel trying to decide which direction to take. South had never appealed to him much and he hated the idea of earthquakes so scratch westward ho. He was already about as east as you could get, so that left only one point on the compass.

The dog wasn't barking yet, just standing there in front of its dog house in the half-dark looking back at him. Not such a bad-looking dog. A black and white version of Lassie. He used to watch Lassie. Lassie and Jeff and Mom and Gramps. A family under pressure, with no father, no extra money, but making it because they all loved each other so much. Is that where he'd learned his idea of reality? From a ten-inch black and white cathode ray tube? Was that why life had always felt like a set of clothes that didn't fit?

The dog scratched itself, keeping its eyes on Nate the whole time. Then it lay down with its head on its paws, looking from Nate to the house where its owner still slept, then back at Nate. It was waiting, too. For something that would never happen. For the person who owned it to come outside, unhook it from the chain, and take it for a walk. Take it out of the five-by-five world it inhabited day after fucking day.

He sat there thinking what it might feel like, hitting the end of that chain four hundred times every twenty-four hours. Which led to his second bad idea in just two hours. But he decided he wouldn't give himself time to think about this one either.

He got out of the car, crossed the yard, stepped over the sag in the fence. The dog sat up, its ears perked, its head cocked. He stopped about three feet away and stood there. The dog didn't growl, didn't move, except for its tail just a bit.

"Want out?" Nate asked.

The dog's head cocked in the other direction.

Nate put his hand out and the dog's nose moved slowly toward it, sniffed.

Nate undid the chain from the dog's collar. "C'mon," he said.

At first the dog didn't move. Then it took a couple of steps, a couple more, stopped at the edge of the grass that ringed the dirt circle and trembled slightly, as though it was about to fall off the edge of the world.

"C'mon," Nate said, "it's okay."

The dog sniffed the grass, placed one foot gingerly onto it, then another, then did a little leap. It trotted after Nate, hopped the saggy fence, and jumped into the back seat of the car when he opened the door as though it was something it had been practicing in its mind all its life.

Nate headed for the Mass Pike, the dog panting and pushing its nose into the front seat every once in a while. He stopped at the toll booth, grabbed the ticket from the machine, and the dog lost his balance at the sudden stop, came half-way into the front seat then back-pawed away.

"Sorry there..." Nate said, looking at the dog in the rear view mirror, realizing he didn't know the dog's name. He got on the Pike heading west just as a jet crossed the highway heading low into Logan. The early sun caught the plane's belly, turning it gold. "Logan," he said, glancing at the dog in the rearview mirror. The dog's ears went up.

It was too early for much traffic and they made good time. They passed Palmer, as far as he'd ever been on the Pike, the time they'd gone to Roberta's nephew's graduation, five, maybe six years ago. And then suddenly they were in New York and he felt a surge of elation because now that all the signs weren't green and the names were unfamiliar, it didn't seem like he was just taking a drive, aiming himself in a direction that would eventually double back on itself and take him right back where he'd started. Instead, he was experiencing an edge of that old feeling he'd known a long time ago. When getting in the car and taking off was more than just driving. When it meant anything could happen because the world was full of possibilities. That's what it felt like now. That anything could happen. And with every mile, a little bit of weight evaporated from his soul. This was running away as it should be.

Which made him remember his other attempt at escape. Two days to go before Billy Picardi's birthday party. Games, prizes, and something no one had ever heard of before — a taffy pull. Plus, there'd be one of Mrs. Picardi's cakes. Not the little square Jiffy cakes he and Pris always had ... vanilla on vanilla with disgusting strawberry jam between the two thin cut halves unless they got lucky and the jam jar was empty.

Why did she do it, he wondered, when she knew they both hated the stuff? Was it possible she did it *because* they hated it? Was she that despicable? Or was it only *her* taste she wished to cater to, and he pictured her dipping her spoon into the jar and filling her mouth with the putrid jam, making that smacking sound with her lips that still gave him the chills.

Now Mrs. Picardi, on the other hand, made her cakes from ingredients she kept in big shiny glass jars on the kitchen counter ... flour sugar chocolate. She measured and she stirred and she ended up with flour in her hair. She filled pans and stacked layers and covered the whole thing with icing she boiled and that somehow stood up in soft peaks and tasted like ... like heaven. And she was constantly putting all kind of things in the oven ... cookies, brownies, cupcakes, something she called pizzelle that he and Billy could eat by the dozens. Pizzelle. He could almost still taste it. Why hadn't he ever had a pizzelle since then?

Mrs. Picardi thought Jiffy cakes were horrid. And that's what she'd told Esther when they ran into each other at the A&P two days before Billy's party. "Good thing I remembered I was out of cake flour or I would have gone to make Billy's cake and got myself in a pickle," she'd said to Esther. Then, as she took down a box of Swans Down cake flour, she'd looked directly at the Jiffy boxes. "Can you imagine anyone actually using that horrid stuff?"

Esther's umbrage had fermented into something lava-like by suppertime.

"I'll tell you," Esther told the three of them, "if she thinks she can talk to *me* like that, she's got another thing coming."

The cabbage soup had gone from clear and steaming to cold and cloudy through four retellings of Mrs. Picardi's insult. Each one more full of venom until finally she'd leveled him with a look across the table. "And I'll tell you, young man..." one finger poking the air between them, "...that's the last time she'll ever insult me, and you can forget the fancy birthday party with the fancy cake because you're not going."

If she'd emptied a vat of ice water over him, it would have had the same effect.

"Oh, Esther..." his father said, not looking up from his soup.

"'Oh, Esther? Oh, Esther?' which means what? That you're siding with that woman?"

His father cleared his throat. "I just think that it's..."

"And does anyone care what *I* think? Does anyone care that I've been insulted?"

"But ... but, I wrapped up Billy's present," Nate said. "I wrapped up the potato gun already." Surely she would see how that made what she had said impossible.

She half-stood and he had to force himself not to flinch, but all she did was lift the ladle out of the cold cabbage soup and refill his bowl. "I returned it this afternoon," she said. "And the next time I spend all day making you dinner, make sure you take more than one piece of cabbage."

That was the moment, with the stench of the soup up his nose and silence settling over the dining room, that he knew what he had to do.

It came to him in a piece, as though he'd been thinking about it for years instead of seconds. He'd take the path to the tracks after school and hop a train. That's what kids in books did. They had adventures. They never looked back. Sometimes even, they found a new home. A better one.

Except lying in bed that night, he'd thought, what about Pris? He'd leave her all by herself, and how could he do that to her? How could he leave her all alone with Esther?

"I'm running away," he told her the next morning on their way to school. "Today. You don't have to, but you should come, too."

"But Mom..."

"We'll never have to see her again," he said. "It won't matter."

"They'll just come after us," Pris said, "and then she'll kill us."

"Not if she can't find us. Not if she doesn't know where we are."

Pris's eyes got wet. She was such a baby. Why couldn't she ever stand up for herself? Why was she always so scared? "But Nate ... maybe she'll change her mind. Maybe she'll let you go to Billie's after all."

"Didn't you hear what she said? And now she won't even let me play with him. Ever. My best friend!"

That was the last thing either of them said until they met at the bottom of the school stairs at 3:05.

"Are you coming?" he asked her.

She nodded, her face all pinched and blotchy like she'd been crying all day.

His plan was to hide in the woods at the last curve before the station. It was an easy run from there as the train slowed to a stop, and he didn't want to risk anyone seeing them at the station, didn't want to leave any clues. There was another train at six, and it would be good and dark by then, but Pris had a ballet lesson at three-thirty, so they had to be on the four o'clock for sure.

"I'm cold," Pris said, shivering.

"It'll be warm on the train."

"How'll we get tickets?"

"We won't. We'll sneak into a box car. We'll save our money for later."

He wished she'd stop looking at him with her doggy eyes. It already wasn't feeling like it was supposed to, and her looks weren't helping.

When they heard the train whistle at five minutes of four, Pris started to cry, and everything inside him crumbled.

"She's gonna kill me," Pris said, as they walked home. "She's gonna kill me for missing ballet."

"It's my fault," he said. "I'll tell her, and you won't get in trouble."

"It won't make any difference." She wiped her nose on her coat sleeve.

By the time they got home, it was almost dark. He'd given Pris his gloves, but she was still shivering.

"I'll go in first," he said, when they got to the back door. But when he went to open it, the cold metal knob didn't turn. It was locked.

The front door was locked, too.

The kitchen light wasn't on the way it usually was. Only the light in Esther's bedroom.

"We can climb in my window," he said. "C'mon."

But when he tried to slide it up, it wouldn't budge.

"She locked that, too," he said. And they just looked at each other.

They waited in the garage, sitting close together in the dark under some burlap bags, until their father's car turned into the driveway.

Their father didn't even try to go inside. He just got them into the car, calmed Pris down, checked to make sure their fingers and toes weren't frozen. And then, as impossible as it seemed, he backed out of the driveway, drove downtown, and parked in front of Howard Johnson's. They'd never eaten there before, only had ice cream cones from the fountain, but that night they ate things they were never allowed to have. Fried clams with spicy tartar sauce, milk shakes, French fries drowned in ketchup, drippy ice cream sundaes. Their father told them about when he was a kid, how he'd run away once and gotten half a block away before a farmer's flock of geese surrounded him and chased him all the way home. They laughed. They were there an hour, no more than two, but it was a dinner he would never forget. A feeling he could never get enough of.

Their father left the table while they finished their sundaes and they watched him in the phone booth, mostly talking, his jaw hard, glancing at them once across the restaurant and flashing them a tight smile.

When they got home, the doors were unlocked and Esther was reading in the living room. She said hello. Then she wrinkled her nose and sniffed. "I see you've already had your dinner. God knows. So I shouldn't have bothered waiting." But that was all she said. He didn't go to Billie's party. It was the only time he tried to run away. But when he thought about it now, he realized he was never really home again after that.

A sign for Seneca Falls flashed past, and he decided he liked the sound of it well enough to investigate.

An hour later he stopped at a mini-mall outside town and bought a leash, a bowl and food for Logan, got directions to a state park and walked the dog for a couple of hours. A sign said that according to Indian myth, the Finger Lake area had been created by the Great Father, who saw the beauty of the land and laid his hand on it, leaving the imprint of his fingers.

"Jeez, Logan," Nate said, watching the dog make his way from tree to tree. "Hallowed ground, and all you can do is lift your leg?"

He found it eased him ... Logan crisscrossing with his nose against the earth, the clear air, the way people walking on the paths seemed to be in no hurry. He could almost entertain the thought that they were like him … jobless, homeless, loveless, but taking it better. Which meant maybe there was hope for him, too.

He drove into town, found a place to park, and they walked the Canal Harbor, past store windows, stone benches, forsythias not yet come into bloom. Logan was being the perfect leash dog, no straining, no balking, as though he was under the same spell. Feeling freedom, or at least the illusion of it, and entertaining it as a permanent condition.

He stopped to eat at an outdoor café, where two other dogs were already leashed to diners, and he ordered a club sandwich and a glass of milk for himself and a burger and a dish of water for Logan. He ate Logan's pickle and ordered a second glass of milk.

He stayed after the waiter had cleared the table, the only diner left outdoors. He was far enough north now so there was still a brittle feel in the air, a hint of winter already forgotten in Boston as the sun began to settle on the tops of the trees. Logan was lying at his feet as though he'd always been there, which was almost what it felt like, and he leaned down and scratched the top of the dog's head.

"You know who would have liked you?" he said, "my father."

Logan looked up, then sighed and settled his head back onto his paws.

He looked at the treetops, going black now against a mauve sky. In most families it was the kids who wanted a dog. But in his, it had been his father. But of course Esther wouldn't budge. Wasn't it bad enough she had to clean up after the three of them, and now she was supposed to clean up after a dog, too? Hair? Dander? Food and water drooled all over the kitchen floor? What did they think she was, a maid to a dog?

And then what had she gone and done just one week after his father got the diagnosis? Come home with that goddamn Lhasa Apso. A little shit of a dog who loved only Esther, who ate tenderloin tips Esther hand-delivered one at a time, who'd just as soon bite everyone else as look at them. Including his father, who didn't have enough trouble already.

He'd figured it out eventually. Esther was thinking ahead. She deserved consolation, didn't she? A little comfort? A few moments of happiness here and there, especially with a man in the house too sick to even carry on a simple conversation? And what about when he was gone. Didn't she deserve a little companionship then?

Out of the corner of his eye he noticed the waiter hovering near the door to the inner dining room, probably wanting to close the patio and get away from the nip in the air. "Okay, Logan," he said, "let's go." He left a big enough tip to make up for the lingering and walked back to the car.

It was dark now, and he opened the back door for Logan, got in himself, started the car and waited for the temp to rise. Then he cracked a window, pushed the heat knob until warm air flowed, put his seat back all the way and settled his back against the door, his legs stretched out into the passenger seat. He didn't feel like driving yet. He kept thinking about his father, seeing him, but not really seeing him, only imaging the photos that had always been in the old album. As though all his other memories of the man had evaporated.

Theodore Madigan. Theo. Sometimes Ted. Esther's husband. Nate and Priscilla's father. An Irish Catholic who never went to church. Married to a German Jew who never lit a candle, whose kids went to Saint Bartholomew's Catholic School. Why? Because it was three blocks away from the house? When the elementary school all the other kids went to was only four in the other direction? His father couldn't have demanded it. He never demanded anything. Even when he was nothing more than an emaciated face on the pillow with the hospital sheet pulled up snug under the bones of his chin. *Can I get you something, Dad? Some water?* A shake of the head. No. Nothing.

But who had he been beside those things? Who, for Christ's sake, had Theodore Nathaniel Madigan been?

He glanced into the back seat, seeing Logan's dark outline sitting erect, ears up, the distant light from a streetlamp reflected in his eyes.

"He stopped to pat every dog he saw," he said out loud. "But he liked the big ones best ... shepherds, Airedales. That's why he would have liked you."

They'd seen a Great Dane on one of their Sunday afternoon walks, and he'd thought his father was going to stand there all day ... looking at it, patting it, asking the owner all kinds of questions, as though they were about to go out and get one for themselves that very afternoon.

Logan sighed, made a couple of awkward turns and settled down on the seat.

He knew his father had started off as an apprentice to a furniture maker. But then there was the Depression, and no one was buying furniture, so he went off to plant trees with the CCC.

1938. His father planting trees in Montana. And there he found Esther Neuburger. Along with her three sisters. All of them sent from Germany as little girls to live with an uncle on a farm in Montana of all places. A farm that ended up supplying Theodore Madigan's CCC camp with sweet potatoes.

But why? Why were the girls sent? 1927 was in his head, though he had no idea why. Which would have made Esther six. None of them older than ten. Four little girls all that way alone? What happened in Germany? Sickness? Death? It couldn't have been anticipation of what was going to happen there. Not when it was still a decade down the road.

So that was it? That was all he knew about his parents before they turned into the people he remembered? With everything that had gone on around them — Hitler, the war, the depression, the Atom bomb — and that was all he knew? Because they never talked. About anything. He didn't even remember how he knew what he knew.

It wasn't as if there'd been a lot of people in and out of the house to hear it from. Esther had her sisters. But Auntie May had never set foot in their house far as he could remember. And Dolores had never said more than hello, goodbye. Auntie Miriam, though, he remembered her. Different from Esther and Dolores — in looks, personality. Thinking back, maybe the only sane one. And trying to remember, he was suddenly back in the old dining room, frozen, hearing their whispered voices in the kitchen.

Saint Bartholomew's, Esther? Saint Bartholomew's? They're Jews, for Christ's sake. You're their mother. You're a Jew. That makes them Jews. And you send them to the nuns. To the priests? Why? So they'll grow up knowing nothing of their heritage?

Leave it alone, Miriam. It's none of your business. They're my children, not yours. Mine. And I'll do what I want.

For the first time in years he remembered how it had hit him like a smack from a bat. He was a Jew? A Jew *and* a Catholic? But everybody knew you couldn't be both. What if the sisters found out? What if the priest could see the knowledge of it in his eyes and passed over him next Sunday at communion?

It had consumed him for days, maybe months, and then, when nothing happened, it had become the first chink in his religious armor. The beginning of his slide toward fallibility. Because if *that* didn't matter, did anything?

The more he thought about it now, the more the questions piled up — history, ancestors, circumstances he knew nothing of. But Esther didn't talk and Miriam was dead years ago in a plane crash, so it was probably too late for answers. Though why should it matter when he'd gone without them all these years?

Maybe his fault. A case of arrested curiosity.

Did his father have friends? If he had, Nate hadn't met any. Hobbies?

He worked, he came home, he read the paper. He came to Nate's baseball games, but didn't hang around after the final run. He'd shaken Nate's hand when he left for college, and maybe he'd held it a second longer than Nate expected.

He couldn't remember Pris and his father ever even speaking to each other. But they must have, right? At least he'd had the Sunday walks, just him and his father. But what did Pris have?

He remembered his father's hands, thin and long-fingered, that he used to smoke on the walks, a pipe, which he left outside in the garage because Esther wouldn't abide him smoking in the house. The walks were a kind of amorphous *thing*. Only little bits hanging in his memory — the dogs, the smell of the pipe. Except for one walk and the feeling that his father was propelling him out of the house and down the street. Mad, his father had been mad as hell, showing it in everything he did — the way he struck the match, tossed it, strode forward, with Nate having to trot to keep up. *Damn crazy blood.* That's what his father had muttered as they turned onto Kingsbury.

It had something to do with Auntie May dying. Or that's how he'd fused it in his mind. His mother in bed for days, his father angry, Auntie May dead. Crazy blood. It could kill you. It had killed Auntie May and it could kill him, too.

They hadn't talked until the very end, just a few minutes from their own street, the pace slowed to almost normal. He had to know. It had crashed around in his brain the whole time, trotting along, and finally he'd blurted it out. *Do I have crazy blood?* And his father had stopped, so Nate had to stop, too, and turn around. His father shook his head. *No.* And then he'd repeated it. *No.*

He'd decided to believe him.

Logan stirred, and Nate was suddenly aware of the door handle pressing into his back. He shifted around until he was facing forward. So that was it. That was all he knew, all he remembered.

Somehow, his father had managed to leave almost nothing of himself to anyone. A chill went through him wondering if Kimmy would some day be thinking the same thing.

And what about Esther? How in hell had *that* ever happened? How had that quiet man who never raised his voice, never acted irrationally, almost never did anything other than what you expected ... how had *that* man stayed with Esther all those years? And how, when you thought about it, had he barely intervened when he must have known what was happening to his kids. And he must have known. He must have.

Logan let out a sudden yip and Nate jumped. The dog whimpered in his sleep, dreaming what ... that he was back on the chain?

"Logan," Nate said, and the dog went quiet, sat up, shook its head.

So things still haunted, even after you'd left them behind.

"Well, fuck that," he said out loud. If this was escape, then escape was what they were going to do.

Back on the highway, he passed names he kept quietly repeating because they felt good on his tongue. Canandaigua, Batavia, Schenectady, Utica, Oneida, Syracuse. The whole path that would someday be Interstate 90 walked off three hundred years ago by natives who had no idea what was approaching from across the sea.

Then just short of Buffalo, when he'd had enough driving, he started seeing signs for Niagara Falls.

CHAPTER SEVEN

Mina Malloy pulled into the Big Bear parking lot and stopped in her usual space at the farthest corner from the entrance. Partly for the exercise, because she was getting pudgy, nothing zipping up without a struggle anymore, but mostly for the comfort of the long walk and the few extra minutes of anonymity beneath the late afternoon shadows. Before the harsh lights, the unwanted contact, the potential for unforeseen danger.

She pulled a carriage out of the rack and pushed it through the automatic doors, past the displays of orchids and gerbera daisies on her right, bins of rolls and bagels on her left, past the produce aisle, then down the baking aisle, where she grabbed a Duncan Hines chocolate cake mix, a bag of milk chocolate chips, and a box of birthday candles even though she knew there were probably candles at home, but where, she had no idea. And then her eye fell on a display of containers full of chocolate sprinkles and she grabbed one of those, too, because Scotty could never get enough chocolate. Which reminded her. Don't forget the ice cream.

She headed for the meat counter, hamburger for the sloppy Joes. "And buns," she said out loud.

A woman going by glanced at her and Mina looked down, pushed on. Careful careful.

She pulled a pint of chocolate ice cream out of the freezer and a pint of Oreo cookie crunch for Lydia. Nice to be able to buy it ready-made now, less messy than breaking the Oreos into the ice cream the way they used to. "We invented it, Mom, and we didn't even know it!" That was her Lydia, Oreo lover and perpetual ray of sunshine, the only redhead in the family since Great Aunt Betsey. Though Lydia's red hair was wild and curly and Great Aunt Betsey's tight as a cap, at least in the pictures. Funny, redheads were supposed to be fiery-tempered but that wasn't Lydia, though for sure she had her stubborn moments.

No amount of cajoling had ever got her to let go of that scrap of a blanket she dragged around every single waking hour until it finally turned to dust. Mina used to have to sneak in at night when she was fast asleep to pry it out of her hand and wash and dry it quick. Hoping all the time Liddy wouldn't wake up. Pinkie, she called it. Even though it was yellow. A crib blanket ending up no bigger than a hankie. All strings and holes.

With everything in her cart, she looked for the checkout clerk who never spoke, who barely even looked up. But he wasn't on. Only one line open, so she had no choice. That thin woman with her hair pulled tight back from her face and piled high on her head like a plastic fountain. Platinum. So obviously fake. Who had platinum hair these days. And chatty to boot.

"Looks like someone's having a birthday!"

Mina nodded.

"Hubby?"

She shook her head. "Son."

Blondie had to pass the ice cream over the sensor twice before it made the proper beep. "Now isn't that nice. How old?"

Mina opened her wallet. "Four." Four! Why on earth had she said *four*!

"Four?" Blondie squinted at her, and Mina knew exactly what she was thinking ... *you have a four-year-old kid?* "My friend has one about that age," she said. "He goes to pre-school. Does yours?"

The total popped up on the little black screen and Mina took out a twenty and handed it to her without answering.

"All mine are grown and gone," Blondie said. She counted out a quarter, a dime, three ones, "and I'm just as glad. Kids today got too many problems."

Mina took the change, the receipt, scooped both bags in one arm, and fought the urge to run for the door. She'd have to remember not to come back on Thursdays. Blondie was just the kind of person who could do her in.

It took her half way back to the house to get rid of the feeling the conversation had settled in her chest, and to get a little of the day's excitement back she started flipping through Scotty's birthdays, picturing the images in the album.

The chubby one-year-old with the paper hat slipped to one side and the sweet smile aimed at Ben.

The six four-year-olds sitting around the table. Callie from next door crying because she wanted all the presents for herself. Tim, Scotty's best friend and the neighborhood cut-up, sticking a finger in the icing.

Nine-year-old Scotty waving the GI Joe he'd wanted so much. Oh how she and Ben had fought over that stupid thing. And now she wondered why she'd been so fussy, so bothered. "He'll grow up to think it's perfectly okay to play with guns," she'd argued. As if a future no one could begin to predict mattered more than the nine-year-old right in front of her.

Then the bowling party when he was twelve, that was her favorite, looking at his face and seeing the boy he'd always been and just a hint of the man he'd become some day.

She pulled into the driveway, all the way around to the back of the house, and stopped near the back door.

Curled up on the back step, Mrs. Dalloway raised her head and looked up, lids narrowing her green eyes to slits, then she came up on all fours, stretched her tail high, front legs straight out. A yoga position Mina used to be able to do.

She carried the bags inside, Mrs. Dalloway slipping past her legs, and let them down on the kitchen table. Four o'clock. Two hours to get dinner, make the cake.

She put the radio on, tuned it to Canadian news ... a small plane down in British Columbia, a spring snowstorm, Quebec making secession noises again. She liked listening in on what was happening in another country. It gave her a safe sense of otherness. They were people she'd never have to know, never have to see, but doing exactly what she was doing — waiting for children and husbands to come home, making dinner, suffering and laughing and being.

She got the cake into the oven, made the sloppy Joe mix and set it to simmer, put the good plates on the table, the ones she'd bought with the money she made working at the farm. Ben thought she was crazy. "Why would someone choose to get out of a perfectly good bed at four in the morning to go feed some cows that don't even belong to her?"

He couldn't understand that it was a comfort. The cows, the smell, the regularity of the milking and the mucking. Beautiful and ugly, with their big soft eyes, their fly-ticked, shitty hides. And oh so solid when you needed something to lean against.

Ben didn't need to lean on anything. Took the minutes as they came. No railing. No caving. Able to hold himself up through it all. Though she'd never trusted him to hold her up, too.

She was standing at the window watching two crows flap from pine to pine against a darkening sky when the oven timer dinged. She took two potholders from the hook and lifted the angel cake pan onto the dull-red tiled counter. Perfect. The edges just about to pull away from the sides. She pushed a spoon into the butter she'd cut up in the bowl. Almost soft enough. Took confectioner's sugar out of the fridge, the vanilla down from the cupboard, plopped two squares of bittersweet and half the bag of milk chocolate chips into a pan on the stove. She turned the gas burner on low.

While she waited for the chocolate to melt, she smoothed the top of a potholder. Fraying. She'd have to re-sew the edges. How Lydia had labored over them, her first Home Ec project. Pieces of material snatched from an old dress of Mina's, Ben's old ties, Scotty's ragged jeans, her own summer dress from when she was three.

She picked up the potholders and hooked them back onto the wall. Transmogrification. Was that it? Everything in existence always in existence. Just changing form. Dress to potholder, potholder to rag, rag to decay, decay to earth, earth to cotton, cotton to dress. But what of the essence that was Scotty, Lydia, Ben, Mina. Where did *that* go? What did *that* become?

Out of the corner of her eye she saw Mrs. Dalloway jump onto the redwood rocker in the corner. "That used to be mine, you know. I hardly get to sit in it any more since you took it over."

Mrs. D. gave her a disinterested glance and settled down, closed her eyes.

"You don't even care, do you? You don't give one single thought to why or how or when..." She stirred the chocolate, turned the heat off. "Where do you think it comes from, Mrs. D., this thing we spend so much time on? This asking why? When there never seems to be anything that even approaches a satisfactory...." But then she clamped her mouth shut. What the heck was she doing? This was a happy day. Scotty's day. And next month it would be Lydia's, then her own in September. Ben's, just before Christmas. He'd be 62.

"My wife here picked wisdom over pizzazz." That's what he told people. He was too conscious of the age difference, and what was twelve years ... nothing really.

The clock in the living room cuckooed five times, and she took a can of potato sticks out of the cupboard. She'd wear her good blue flowered dress, the one she saved for special, decided to wash and change while the cake cooled, walked down the hall past

Scotty's room, Lydia's room, to her and Ben's room at the end, and the warm sweet odor of chocolate everywhere.

CHAPTER EIGHT

The candle flames flickered, lapping down into the tiny wells of melted wax, and Mina leaned forward and blew them out one by one, then sat there in the half-dark not moving, letting her eyes wander over all the familiar surfaces that had taken on a provocative strangeness now that they were moon-silvered. She cut herself another slice of cake, spooned the ice cream over it ... a little chocolate, a little Oreo cookie crunch, both of them soft and runny now. Nine o'clock at least. But it was going to take so much effort to carry the cartons to the freezer, too much for just now.

"Try a little, just a taste." She'd hold the spoon near his lips, coaxing. The only thing she could think of to do. The thing she'd been doing since the moment he was born. But it was too late. All futile. And too impossible. So that by the time it was Lydia's turn, Mina had passed into some other world where feelings didn't work anymore. And Ben, poor Ben. Nothing left for him. Nothing. He'd reach for her and she'd imagine his hand going straight through hers like it was nothing but thin air. All her skin, muscle, bone rubbed away by the friction of grief.

Mrs. Dalloway mewed near her ankle and she reached down and absent-mindedly rubbed the cat's arched back.

She'd gone to his house once, the president of Dow Chemical, hearing he vacationed in Nassau. She'd bought the last-minute ticket for a price that at one time would have put her in shock, but she was shock-proof by then, and rich, and there were things she had too much of to keep them all to herself. Rage. Frustration. Sorrow. Vengeance. And who better to share them with.

Or maybe she just wanted to look him in the face. To see if the knowledge of what he'd been part of was visible — some underlay of angst, a scrim of sorrow deep in the eye, guilt lines around the mouth. *Contrition*. She would have preferred that to the big fat check. *I am so deeply sorry over what we took from you. A son. A daughter. A husband. Unimaginable.* Yes, that's what it was. Unimaginable.

Once she was on the island, she took her time. Rented a house, got to know the service people — the maids, the baby sitters, the deliverers of the gracious life. And while she waited, she thought how ironic to be here, where she and Ben and Scott and Lydia could never go because there were shoes being outgrown and always a transmission to replace, a new hot water heater needed, or a roof, braces.

Ah, the braces.

He wanted them, Scotty, despite everything. Aching proof that he believed he would smile in all the photos — yearbooks, graduations, keg parties she'd never know about — looking into the camera with straight, even teeth.

So she took her time and then one clear February morning, when the news was right, she walked along Cable Beach, glancing up at the lovely private beach houses until she found the one with the blue dolphin flag waving from the patio.

The woman sitting on the deck was thin, blonde, born with money in her genes. Golden smooth skin, hair careless and perfect, the bones under her skin so fine that Mina felt way beyond her own bulk standing below on the beach looking up.

"Good morning," the expensive woman said, unaware she was under siege, thinking all the people passing on that private sand were beyond suspicion, and that she was safe, protected from any hint of danger.

All the words she'd thought and never uttered flew into Mina's mouth. *Your husband and all his kind killed my children, killed my husband, killed me, though for some reason I'm not quite dead yet. Him and those like him who lied to us all those years, told us not to worry, told us the paleness meant nothing, the sores meant* nothing, the thin hair and the fragile skin, and the vomiting in the night meant nothing, told us the dead dogs meant nothing and the aborted fetuses and the smell and the tiredness and the bleeding. All nothing. Did he truly believe it? Did the cancers mean nothing to him? The dead children we'd hold in our arms some day? And what about the ones who didn't quite die, who gave up limbs and breasts and ovaries and hope?

She'd opened her mouth to scream it all, and then there was the little girl — blonde, sun-streaked hair, red dotted bathing suit, still chubby with toddler-hood. Looking down at Mina through the wood rails, smiling, full of trust and delight, and Mina had pressed her lips together and walked away across the beach, all her poison still inside.

Nine, ten, eleven. The cuckoo went silent and she still sat there in the silvered shadows, the ice cream gone liquid, the creaks of the house quiet. Soon there'd be the crickets at night. They had come back, after all the silent summers, just like she'd come back.

She pulled the candles out and replaced them with new ones, reached for the matches. Twenty-four, plus the five on the two pieces she'd eaten. She had to blow the match out on number seven, when it burned too close to her fingers, and lit the rest with another candle, then got up and lit the two kerosene lamps on the sideboard, too, tired of the moon, the way it gilded.

There was a story for every year. The family trip to the Grand Canyon the summer Scotty was thirteen. Being elected class treasurer his first year in junior high. The four inches he grew from fourteen to fifteen, just like Ben had. The cracking voice, the peach fuzz, the way his face turned red when a pretty girl walked by. He played hockey all through high school even though she hated the game, but Ben was on Scotty's side, even after he got a concussion the night after those boys died in the middle of the night on Route 77 and feelings went all out of control over a bad call. His SAT scores were better than they'd hoped, 688 Math, 590 Verbal. He got into NYU, Hunter, and UNH, picked UNH, started out a business major, but switched to chemical engineering. An irony. He met a girl named Christine his junior year, and the first time he brought her home, Mina knew she was shaking hands with her future daughter-in-law. The wedding, small and tasteful; the in-laws, unobjectionable. Mina and Ben paying for the photographer and the music, Lydia catching the garter, which was perfect because by then Lydia was engaged to Tim, a violinist at the music school. They played duets, Lydia on the piano. She had beautiful arms, strong fingers, and her mass of red hair caught the lights when she played on stage....

But this was Scotty's story.

Scotty and Christine had a baby boy they named Benjamin, then a girl, Caroline. Caroline looked just like her Aunt Lydia, red hair and all. They lived in Canton, only ten miles away, so she and Ben could visit often, take their grandchildren for outings and overnight visits. Christine's parents lived a thousand miles away and weren't all that crazy about being grandparents anyway. No competition.

They'd all come tonight for Scott's birthday. Caroline and Benjamin. Lydia and Tim. Lydia was pregnant, and, of course, it was guaranteed that the baby would be musical.

She stared at the subtle movement of the bright white candle tops, their pale auras. There was danger here, she'd once been told. A psychiatrist she'd gone to faithfully every week for a year. "We all flow away from pain, Mina," he'd said, "and the mind supplies its own narcotics for that. But this narcotic you're choosing is as seductive in its way as heroin. And as destructive. How will you know when you reach the point where the fantasy is more real than your actual life?"

But didn't he see? There was no more life in her life. It was the fantasy that had depth and color and possibility and complication. She crossed her arms, hugging herself. And warmth. A second of it was more real than any year she'd spent since 1985. That's why she'd quit Dr. Schultz. Because she knew better than he where the real danger lay.

Mrs. D jumped into her lap, purring softly, and Mina unfolded her arms, pressed her fingers into the cat's fur, and gradually the knocking registered.

She blew out the candles that hadn't already burned down into the icing, got up and went to the door, something she never did, but she'd been careless, forgotten to pull down the ugly opaque shades, and if it was someone official, not answering wasn't going to make them go away.

The moon lit up the outside like day. The man nodded. "Sorry to bother you, I know it's late. But I saw your light and there doesn't seem to be anybody else here at all. He pointed off in the direction of the barrier fence, "My car broke down ... I wonder ... could I use your phone?"

She let him in because of the dog. Except for the coloring, it looked just like their McDuff, black instead of white, but with the same fine long nose, the same bounce.

"I just got gas about an hour back on the highway. But of course it had to wait to break down until there were no gas stations, no ... anything." He looked beyond her to the table, the cake, the wrapped present. "I'm sorry. I'm interrupting."

She shook her head. "It's over. You're not interrupting anything."

"If you just point to the phone, I'll use it and be out of your way."

"I don't have a phone."

He stood there. "Oh." He looked at the dog, back at her, took a step back toward the door. "Maybe a neighbor then...."

She shook her head. "There are no neighbors. Only me."

He seemed to go speechless for a second. "Oh." He sighed. "Then I guess I'll just head back to the car. Sorry to bother you."

"What good's that going to do, if it won't run?" she said to his back.

He turned around, shrugged. "Well, I'll fiddle under the hood. Maybe I'll get lucky."

"It's coming up on midnight," she said. "Sit down. Have a piece of cake. I'll make some coffee."

He put his hand up. "No really, that's not necessary."

"It's a big cake. I'm just going to throw it away, so you might as well eat some of it." She pointed at the table. "Go ahead. Give your dog a piece, too." She bent down, patted the sleek black head. "What's his name?"

"Logan," he said. "I'm Nate Madigan."

Just then, the dog jumped and let out one sharp bark in the direction of the hallway.

"Must have seen Mrs. Dalloway," Mina said, "my cat. I'm Mina. Mina Malloy."

He nodded. He looked uncomfortable. But the dog seemed happy enough.

"Take any seat," she said. He looked at the unused plates, then took the chair at the end of the table. She stared at him for a second before she went into the kitchen, recognizing that, yes, he was lost, but more than just that. *Gone astray* popped into her mind, maybe *bewildered*. And suddenly the song was playing in her head ... that first recording with Mel Torme, the thick old 78 she dropped and cracked in half, even though she always tried to be so careful with Ben's precious collection, and she could still see him standing there holding the two pieces, gently, as though they'd already suffered more than he could bear. *Bewitched, bothered and bewildered, am I-I-I...* Was it Rodgers and Hart? Or Lerner and Loewe? She always got them confused.

"What kind of car is it?" she called from the kitchen.

There was no answer, and for a second her mind stumbled into darkness. Hadn't someone knocked at the door? Hadn't she let him in?

"A Volvo. It's an '82 Volvo. A sedan," and the darkness dissolved and with perfect clarity the lyrics settled into neat stanzas ... *I'm wild again, beguiled again, a simpering whimpering child again....* She spooned grounds into the coffee maker, humming. *...couldn't sleep, and wouldn't sleep...* Rodgers and Hart, yes. Or at least she was pretty sure. *...I'll sing to her, each spring to her...*

CHAPTER NINE

He couldn't get rid of the feeling he'd stumbled into a starring role in a Twilight Zone episode. His intention had been to stop at a motel hours ago. If he'd done that, he'd be asleep right now. The car wouldn't have broken down until tomorrow morning when service stations were open and everybody you met had a phone.

But he'd gotten it into his head to see the Falls lit up. Stupid stupid. A million postcards, but he had to see the real thing. And for a while it had been worth it, until he took a wrong turn, got lost, and the car began to stagger. And now he was here, wherever the hell *here* was. With Mina Something. Mallo. McCoy. Malloy.

Then the air suddenly filled with the heady smell of coffee and his anxiety ebbed just a bit.

He looked at the unopened present across from him on the table. At the cake. At the clean plates and the little pile of burned-down candles. A party nobody bothered to attend?

"Here you go," she said, reappearing from the kitchen and setting a mug down in front of him. "Sugar? Cream?" Logan raised his head off the floor.

"Black's fine. Thank you."

"How about your dog? Has he eaten?"

Nate nodded, and she sat down at the opposite end of the table and just looked at him. His mind went blank. "Nice house," he finally said.

She looked around as though she'd forgotten where she was. "This?"

He nodded.

"I hate this place."

"Well ... I guess it's a little ... isolated. I mean, with no neighbors." He wondered if they'd all moved away because of her. Or maybe she'd made them disappear, turned them into toads, crickets, slimy worms. She had a look of haunting ... dark glittery eyes, purplish circles beneath, longish dark hair pulled back at her neck, a shapeless dress covered with a shapeless pattern like something one of his aunts would have worn. The word 'witch' came to mind.

"Good coffee," he said, intending to bolt it down quick and make his exit.

"Spring water."

He nodded, not sure what that meant. Logan sighed beside him on the floor.

"Ben, that's my husband, used to say I couldn't make a decent cup of coffee for a million bucks. And all the time it was the water." She gave a sarcastic chuckle. "Water, hah. Benzene dioxin arsenic chlordane ether DDT mercury naphthalene phosphorous toluene." She took a breath. "And those are just the ones easy to pronounce. Naphthalene ... that's the one they dry clean your clothes with." Her eyebrows went up. "If you knew what it could do, you'd wear them dirty. Can't figure out if it smells okay because we associate it with clean or the other way around. I actually used to like the smell of it. How about you?"

He swallowed, thought for a second. "Not a bad smell."

"Now I can't come anywhere near it or I break out in a rash. Would you believe a couple of doctors told me it was all in my head?" She tapped her head. Then the sarcastic chuckle again.

Nate set the mug down. "Well, it's late and I've bothered you long enough." He stood up. "I appreciate the coffee."

"And where exactly do you think you're going? You can't walk anywhere, it's too far. And I can't drive you because I go nowhere after dark." She looked at Logan. "He's comfy enough."

"We'll be fine in the car."

"Nonsense." She stood up, pointed toward the hallway. "Got a perfectly decent futon in there that's never been used. I had to carry everything in myself and all I could handle was a futon. But I have one in my bedroom and it suits me fine. So that's settled. You'll sleep in there." She picked up a knife and cut three pieces of cake. "I shouldn't," she said, "but we never get company so I'll splurge." She put each one on a plate, got up and brought one around the table for him and set another on the floor for the dog.

Nate sat down again.

"We had a collie," she said, standing there with her hands on her hips, watching Logan wolf the cake in two grabs. "But he was white and black, named McDuff and oh how the kids loved him. He took turns sleeping with them. One night he'd jump in bed with Scotty and the next he'd spend with Lydia, and they always knew the schedule. He did, too. Never got mixed up. Then all of a sudden he couldn't walk anymore."

"Got old," Nate said, looking up at her.

"He was three."

"Oh."

"First his legs went, then his bladder, couldn't eat." She looked at Nate. "Cancer of the brain."

Nate shook his head. "That's awful."

"Well," she said, walking back to her chair, "Duff was a swimmer. Always in the stream. Loved to dig holes." She leveled him with a look again. Her looks seemed to have weight. "Least he died quick. The rest of us weren't so lucky."

Logan moved the cake dish across the rug, licking it clean, as a bunch of images ran through Nate's brain ... zombies, vampires, night of the living dead. He'd been up almost twenty-four hours, except for the one-hour nap at the state park. His lips felt numb. Hallucinations were next. Or maybe they'd already started.

"We should have put two and two together." She took two bites of her cake. "But we didn't. Nobody did. I mean, a lot of it was right there to see, but you know what I think..." she leaned toward him as though she was going to share a secret she didn't want anyone else to hear. "...I think for a long time we didn't want to know. I mean, how can you want to know something like that? We're too good at seeing only what we want to see. Blocking everything else out." She ate another bite of cake. "Don't you think that's true?"

He nodded, taking a forkful of his chocolate cake, too exhausted to even try to make sense of any of it.

"It's late," she said, as if she could read his mind, "and you're tired. Where did you say you were from?"

"Boston," he said, though he didn't remember mentioning it.

She crossed her arms and sat back in her chair, closed her eyes. "Federal Metal, Lewis Chemical, Salem Lead, South Bay Incinerator, Laidlaw. Not to mention that harbor." She opened her eyes. "Got so bad you could almost walk across it. Straight to that island, what's it called?"

The only island he could think of at the moment was Nantucket.

"Georges Island," she said, "the one with the old fort."

Had he ever even heard of Georges Island?

"But it's cleaned up some now, the harbor." She nodded, a nod of grudging approval. Then she shook her head. "All through the '80s, though, it was something — lead, mainly." Then she stood up. "I've got nice clean blankets and pillows. Bathroom's down the hall on the right, one door before the guest room. You can flush the toilet with the water in the pail, use the spring water on the counter for washing. I'll get you a new toothbrush. Use the spring water for that, too."

She turned and disappeared into the kitchen and he stood up, hesitated, then took a step toward the front door. Why on earth had he ever gotten out of the car?

"Here," she said behind him, and he turned away from the door and stared at the toothbrush she was holding out to him.

Had he been drugged? Was there something in the coffee? The cake? But he had barely touched the cake. He reached for the toothbrush. Yellow. Ipana. He pointed it at Logan. "I ... uh ... I should take him out." He set the toothbrush on the table.

"I'll do it," she said, "better if he goes in the back. C'mon, boy." She clucked her tongue and disappeared into the kitchen again with Logan trotting after her as if they were life-long best buddies. He heard the back door open, close. He heard her singing.

"Christ," he said under his breath. He moved toward the front door again, put his hand on the knob and started to turn it, then let go. Was this what drove people into the lavatory to choke to death on the dirty tile floor instead of choking to death in full view and the possibility of rescue? This thing that was stopping him from just getting the hell out ... a hesitancy to what ... make a fuss? Be impolite? Dammit, weren't you supposed to ignore Dear Abby in favor of the hairs on the back of your neck?

But, shit, how could he leave the dog.

The back door opened, closed. "He didn't make me wait a second," she called from the kitchen. And there was Nate, fussless and polite, standing by the table with the toothbrush in hand when she reappeared. He turned toward the hall when she pointed, turned right at the bathroom door, unwrapped the yellow toothbrush, tried the tap which produced no water at all, brushed his teeth with the spring water, washed his face and hands, flushed the toilet with the water in the pail, and counted to fifty before he stepped out. Logan was waiting in the hallway, tail high and wagging, a look on his face like *isn't this fun?* Weren't dogs supposed to sense things? Danger? Calamity? Weren't they supposed to curl their lip and snarl at people with evil intentions?

"All set." Mina Malloy stepped out of a doorway at the end of the hall, which made Nate jump and made Logan wag his tail harder.

"Thanks," Nate said. "Now you're sure this isn't..."

"Just keep your door closed," she said, "because I'm an early riser."

"Oh right," he said. "Okay, then ... good night." He closed the bedroom door behind him, looked around the room. A kerosene lamp flickered on the table beside the futon. There was nothing else in the room except a small wooden chair, and he thought about fitting the back of it under the doorknob, the way detectives did in movies. Except for Sam Spade, because everybody knew Bogey didn't have a nerve in his body.

Instead, he just set the chair in front of the door. An alarm in case Mina Mallo turned into a ghoul at three a.m.

The futon was made up neatly, one corner thrown back for climbing into. He took off his shoes, left his clothes on, lay down, and realized as soon as his head hit the pillow that he was too exhausted to care much if she did come in at three a.m. and sucked his blood. He reached up and turned the knob on the lamp. The room went slowly black, then gradually grew silvery. He closed his eyes, felt Logan put a paw on the futon, wait, then softly add the other three. The dog lay down with his back against Nate's, sighed. Had they really just met less than twenty-four hours ago? Twenty-four hours between the world they'd always known and this? Or had time skipped forward into an entirely different dimension?

He thought about Mina Mallo. A dimension all her own. Then his thoughts drifted south. To Kimmy, distraught in her entirely lime green room that used to be entirely pink until she turned sixteen and declared it a nursery instead of a bedroom. Had it ever occurred to him while he was painting that putrid fluorescent color onto her walls that it would be the last chore he'd ever perform in that house? Had part of him suspected? Had part of him been wishing it all along? And was Kim lying in that bedroom this very second, staring at the moonlight touching those slime green walls the same as he was lying here and was she hating him? Would she be glad to be rid of him ... the weekend bowling, the fast food dinners, having to carve time for him out of her busy eighteen-year-old life. And if any of them could see him now ... K, Priscilla, Roberta, Esther ... would they even think it was all that strange? Daddy, Nate, Nathaniel sleeping in a crazy lady's house somewhere near Niagara Falls. On a futon. Beside a dog that didn't belong to him.

A sound slid through his lips that signified he might laugh if he had the energy, and for a few minutes, he was dimly aware of how quiet it was, and then he wasn't aware of anything at all for the next ten hours.

CHAPTER TEN

It was late, that's all he knew when he opened his eyes. Later than seven, later than eight. And the dog wasn't barking. Logan. Christ, what had he done.

It all came back. The dog. The flight. The damn car. The deserted neighborhood. The warm light through the window of one house. This house. The woman who could have been part of the Addams family.

He raised his head. Logan was still on the futon, snoring lightly, and Nate sank back against the pillow.

Maybe she was gone off to work, and he would be free to sneak away. Maybe the car would start. He looked at his watch. Ten-thirty. Maybe he could find a barrel and go over the Falls.

He got up, Logan on his heels, listened. He'd never heard such loud silence. He slid into his shoes, moved the chair from in front of the door, poked his head into the hallway and then into the bathroom. He did everything he'd done the night before, more or less in the same order, then walked into the living room. The party table was clear, no cake, no extra plates. One place was set with a coffee mug, a bowl, a dish with an orange and an apple. And two boxes of cereal, both of them high fiber.

That's when he noticed the books. Stacks and stacks lined up knee-high against the walls. He picked one up. Djuna Barnes, whoever that was. Dostoevsky, Celine, Faulkner, Graham Greene. Philip Roth. Shakespeare's sonnets ... something he'd always meant to read but hadn't. The last book he picked up was Jean Valjean. In French, for Christ's sake. Who was this woman?

Then he saw her through the dining room window out in the yard pouring water from a bottle into a bird bath. Spring water.

He went to the front door and opened it. "Go ahead," he said to the dog, "you must have to go pretty bad by now," and Logan trotted out and stood there with his nose up, sniffing in one direction, then the other.

"There's your breakfast on the table," Mina Malloy said behind him. She was expert at making him jump. "Guess you had some sleep to make up?" She eyed him. "Yup, you look better. Then she turned toward the kitchen. "I'll get some milk for your cereal."

"You really don't have to go to any troub…"

But the refrigerator door was already opening, closing. Logan trotted back in and stood by his leg. Mina reappeared and set a quart of milk next to the cereal. She was carrying a coffee pot.

"Right," he said. "yesterday was a long day." He went over to the table. "Sorry I overslept."

She held up the coffee, and when he nodded she poured him a cup. "For what?" she said.

He sat down. "Beg your pardon?"

"What did you oversleep for?"

He looked at her.

"I mean you can only oversleep if you have something you have to get up for at a certain time. What did you have to get up for?"

He took a sip of the black coffee. "Nothing," he said. "I just don't usually sleep so late."

She shrugged. "Then you didn't really oversleep, did you. You just slept as long as you needed to."

He nodded. "I guess so."

She didn't look so odd in daylight. The circles under her eyes were gone, and her eyes weren't black beads, they were brown. Her dark hair was in a braid, her skin had color, and a pair of denim overalls gave a slightly wholesome flavor. He shook some cereal into his bowl and she pushed the milk closer to him.

"Toast?"

He shook his head. "No. Thank you. This is fine. This is great. I hope you didn't change any plans over this. Waiting for me to wake up. Do you work nearby?"

"I don't work. I used to work, but I don't have to now."

"I used to work, too," he said. He poured milk into the bowl. Took a mouthful. Good cereal, fresh. He glanced up at her, nodding, saw the question on her face.

"I got downsized about six months ago. Sort of a lead handshake." He looked up from his cereal, saw puzzlement. "As opposed to ... well, you know, a golden one. Handshake, I mean."

"Is that why you came up here? A job?"

He shook his head. "No. This was a ... a get-away."

"How long have you had Logan?"

"Only about twenty-four ... months," he said. "Twenty-four months. Two years."

"So you didn't get him as a pup."

He shook his head. "No. He was two when I got him."

She nodded. "Such a good dog. Is he neutered?"

He took another spoonful of cereal, shook his head.

"Really? I would have guessed he was. He's so calm. Sometimes they're not as well-mannered when they're not neutered. Never runs away?"

He shook his head again, feeling crappy for lying even though he couldn't see where it made any difference. "Not once."

"You're lucky. McDuff wasn't neutered, Ben wouldn't hear of it, and he ran off all the time. Four days once. The kids cried themselves to sleep every night."

"How many kids do you have?"

"Two. Scotty and Lydia."

"Off to college?" he asked.

She looked at him for a second, then she shook her head. "They're both dead."

She said it while he was swallowing and he almost choked. "That's ... awful." He put his spoon down, took a sip from his mug, glanced at her, then away.

"Pretty awful all right," she said. "You have kids?"

He nodded. "One."

"Girl? Boy?"

"A girl. Kimberly."

"How old?"

He sipped more coffee, wishing she'd stop. "Just turned eighteen."

"High school senior?"

He nodded.

"College?"

He nodded again.

She smiled at him. "You're going to miss her."

He took one last spoonful of cereal, swallowed the last of the coffee, wiped his mouth on a napkin. "You've been more than kind." He stood up. "But I think it's time I tend to my car and let you get on with your day."

She narrowed her eyes at him. "You're a mechanic?"

"No, I'm an engineer," he said.

She smiled. "I mean — do you know what's wrong with your car and how to fix it?"

"Oh," he said. "No."

"Well..." She picked up the milk carton and carried it into the kitchen. "I am," she called back. "A mechanic, I mean. So tell me the symptoms."

"No no," he said. Whatever she was, he was sure she was no mechanic. And whatever feeling the morning sun had dispelled was starting to creep back. He stepped away from the table. "I can't let you do that. You've already..."

"Look," she said, coming back from the kitchen. "I could drive you to a station, but then they'd have to send a tow truck. And frankly, I don't want tow trucks coming here." Her eyes were on him like magnets. "Do you know where you are?"

A trick question. Geographically? Existentially? "I think so," he said.

She looked at him expectantly.

"Niagara Falls?"

"You ever hear of Love Canal?"

He nodded.

She kept looking at him.

"This," he pointed to the rug, "is Love Canal?"

"Abandoned since 1979. This was my house. They paid us for it, so technically it isn't mine anymore. But..." She shrugged. "I couldn't get out of here fast enough once." She gave him a slightly crooked smile. "And then look what I do. I come back." She glanced around. "Here. The place that took it all away. Everything I had." Then, like someone had changed her channel, the pain went out of her eyes, her whole body straightened. "So tell me," she said. Even her voice was different. "You were driving along and what happened?"

It took him a second to switch his own gears. "Uh, I don't know ... it started losing power, but I wasn't sure at first. I mean, at first I thought it was me, letting up on the gas. But then on hills it started slowing down — to twenty, then fifteen, even with the pedal to the floor — and then I stopped for gas and asked the guy there about it, but he was just a clerk, told me there was a service station a few miles from there, and when I started it up again, it ran fine. For about a half-hour. Then it started all over again. Every time I stopped, though, when I started it up again, it was fine. But then I got lost and it happened a couple more times and finally it stopped and wouldn't start, and I ... ended up here."

"Chances are," she said, "if you started it up right now, it might run just fine. It sounds like a bad coil. It overheats and then the car loses power. If you let it cool off for a while, car runs fine."

"So you mean that's all I have to do? Just keep letting it cool off when it gets bad?"

She nodded. "Til it quits altogether, sure. Which it may finally have done. But even if it hasn't, what's the good of that? And anyway, it's just a guess. Could be a gezillion other things. So let me get my tester and we'll just see what I can find."

She hustled off and he watched her go, wondering what was worse, dealing with a bad coil or dealing with Mina Mallo. Malloy. "You sure you want to do this?" he called after her. "I mean, you can drop me off at a pay phone and I can call a tow. Car's not real near your house, so there's no reason they'd ... well ...."

But either she didn't hear or simply didn't answer.

So he looked at Logan, who wagged his tail. Then he looked around the room, out the window. Love Canal. Jesus. The place was one big chemical dump, and he'd slept here, ate here.

He looked at a set of shelves hanging on the wall above more piles of books. There were framed pictures of babies and toddlers, first day of school pictures, back yard above-ground-pool pictures. Snow pictures and beach pictures. A cub scout picture. A ballerina picture. Christmas morning pictures. Two kids growing up from shelf to shelf. Both of them just getting into those awkward pre-teen years when noses and ears and chins and mouths didn't add up to cute anymore ... and then the pictures stopped. *They're both dead.* He could still hear the flat way she'd said it. Just like that. Dead. He went over and picked up what seemed to be the last picture of the boy. No hair, gaunt face, smiling.

He stared at the boy's young old face. He'd read somewhere that smiling was nothing more than a survival mechanism. Something that showed the cave dweller from the other borough that you had no immediate intention of laying your pointy club against his low forehead. A universal sign of brotherhood. Peace, brother. And then all the little mutations that had crept in over the millennia. So now it wasn't always so easy to read. The sly smile. The false smile. The tight smile. The smile that was no smile at all. Had they smiled in concentration camps? In the bowels of the coliseum? In slave trade ships? Had there been anything in any of those places to smile at or for? And this boy ... Scotty, she'd said. Scott's smile was a shadow of what it must have been. A tired smile. A teenager tired of smiling, tired of it all.

He set the picture back on the shelf when he heard her footsteps. She was carrying a dull red metal tool chest and a thick manual with a Volvo on the cover. "Lucky you got a Volvo," she said. "Me, too. An '86 and mine's a wagon. I've done just about everything you can do to it. Brakes, tune ups, oil changes, rebuilt the carburetor, even replaced the timing belt." She gave him a look. "Now, *that* was a job."

"It's just that I don't want you going to a lot of trouble. I've already taken up too much of your time."

"Oh, a coil's no trouble. You find it, you test it, you pull it out and you replace it. And as far as time goes ... well, I've got plenty of that."

"But what if it's something else? Something hard and dirty and complicated?"

She looked at him. "You're not going to help?"

"Well, of course. Of course I'm going to help."

"Then it'll probably be as dirty, but only half as long and half as complicated." And she smiled that crooked smile.

She hugged the Volvo manual to her as if it was a baby and handed him the tool box. He followed her out the front door and down the driveway, and when they were in the street, he glanced back. There was nothing to make Mina Malloy's house stand out. It was as blank and empty looking as all the others.

"Don't you worry?" he asked. "Living here again, I mean. Isn't it still...? And isn't it illegal?"

"Course it's illegal," she said. "I keep my head down. And supposedly they capped it. Like all those ethers and ground waters could be contained. But if it didn't get me then, when I cared, what difference does it make now?"

"How long," he asked, "how long have you been here?"

"Two years. First we lost Scott. That was 1983. He was fifteen and a half. Then Lydia went in '85. She almost made it to her sweet sixteen. Three years after that, Ben. He'd been through the chemo and the radiation twice." She stopped and turned around, shook her head. "Isn't it crazy that something we get from poison, we treat with poison?"

Yeah, it was probably crazy, though he wasn't sure. But her eyes were on him, frank and open, and she was waiting for an answer.

"I think," he said, "when it comes right down to it, most of us will do anything to put off dying."

She sighed. "We took Scotty to Mexico, for the Laetrile? It's ground up peach pits. That actor, Steve McQueen, he tried it, too, but it didn't work for him either."

"Apricots," he said. "I think it's ground up apricot pits."

"That's right," she said, "apricots."

They started moving again.

"Why did you come back?" he asked.

She didn't say anything, and at first he was going to repeat it thinking maybe she hadn't heard, but then he wondered if maybe she just didn't want to answer and he wished he hadn't asked it in the first place.

"I don't know," she said. "It was just something I had to do. Like visiting the cemetery, you know? Except it turned out coming here was easier. Better. I stand at those stones and I look at those names and all I think is, dead dead dead. But here, I end up thinking, alive. There's the swing I used to push them on for half the afternoon, and there's the tree we used to sit under in August when the house felt like an oven. And that's where the school bus picked them up and there's the window Lydia used to wave from when Ben went off to work. I came here hating it, hating the thought of it ... I think maybe I had it in my mind to burn it down. My house. All the houses. Just set a torch and try to burn it out of my head."

His car was parked well beyond a metal fence. Both sides of a gate that once must have spanned the road were hanging from broken hinges, pushed off the macadam now, weeds and saplings growing up through the rusted mesh. He hadn't seen any of that in the dark last night. Just the far-off glow of light in her window. They got to his car and he set the tool box down.

"Then it hit me." She took a deep breath. "That this was the last place we were all together, all happy. And for some stupid reason, it was nice, you know? Feeling a little bit of that again. So I hung around. Just one day, then a night, then another. And..." She looked at him. "You think I'm crazy." Then she laughed. "I can tell — the way you were looking around at my party last night. The way you keep edging away."

"I'm not edging away."

She shrugged.

"I just don't quite know what to make of it all."

"No," she said. "Half the time I don't either." Then she bent down and snapped open the tool box. "Open the hood and we'll try this voltage meter and see what we've got."

It turned out she was right. Mina Malloy was right about the coil. She drove him into town. Not the nearest town. She never went anywhere twice in a row, she said. She didn't want familiarity, even though all she was going to do was sit in the car. She wanted to be invisible. So they drove twenty miles farther than they had to, and he bought a new coil and helped her put it in, and his car started, and they test-drove it to make sure it didn't lose power after it warmed up, and it didn't.

CHAPTER ELELVEN

After they scrubbed the grease off, Nate Madigan insisted on buying her a late lunch, and she actually considered it, the appeal of it. Of sitting in a restaurant and picking something off a menu, being almost like anyone else and not being alone, and the tiny flash of desire for these things, at least before she caught herself, was a surprise.

"We passed a restaurant on the way to the parts' place," he said. "It looked nice. It's the least I can do."

The Grille. She knew the place he meant, but only from the outside. Years ago it had been a Chinese restaurant, and since it was good and it was cheap, and because Lydia loved the tiny paper umbrellas they floated in her root beer glass, and Scotty, who picked at just about everything, would devour a whole plate of chicken wings single-handedly, they ate there almost every Friday night.

"I know a drive-through," she said, "decent and cheap. Let's go there instead." And then hearing herself, thinking what a stranger she was now to give and take, she said, "I mean, unless you'd rather not."

"Oh no," he said, "I have a good working relationship with fast food places."

And fifteen minutes later, with their bagged food on the floor near her feet, she was giving him directions to a scenic outlook where they could eat and she could relax at the same time.

But before the directions, as they'd driven away from the pick-up window, Nate had pulled under some shade at the *Not Just Another Burger* parking lot, stopped near two plastic picnic tables with attached benches and a children's purple plastic climbing bridge.

"Not here," she'd said. "I know a better place." And he'd re-started the car, no questions except for, "Which way?" at the exit.

There was something about him, even though it was easy to see he thought she was strange, that kept him just this side of pointing off behind her and yelling, "Hey, look!" then running like hell in the opposite direction.

I didn't used to be like this, she wanted to tell him. I used to be fun. Funny. My phone used to ring. And my doorbell. I was good at charades. I sang and played the piano at parties. And my husband and kids loved my chicken soup with dumplings.

But she didn't say any of that. Instead, she decided, just for a little while, to take advantage of his tolerance and the fact she had someone real to talk to for a change.

Anyway, it was going to end in a few hours, and when it was over she knew she was going to feel more relief than regret. But for this moment she'd accept Nate Madigan's dispensation of grace. Why did it hardly ever occur to her she was lonely?

Looking out at the view of hills and valleys, she handed Nate his hamburger and took a bite of hers. It tasted wonderful. The drippy creamy sauce, the soft melted cheese. She lifted a fry from its white paperboard boat and bit it in half, the heat, the salt, the crunch a satisfaction on her tongue. She dripped ketchup on her shirt and dabbed at it with the corner of her napkin.

In the back seat, Logan sniffed gently at her shoulder.

"Were you in the military?" she asked.

He shook his head no.

"I just thought maybe ... you know ... you're about the right age. Ben, my husband, he was exempt because he had..." she tapped her right ear, "...a bad ear drum. He was half deaf." She smiled, "which the kids caught onto pretty quick and used to every advantage. They knew exactly when to speak up nice and loud and when to mumble. She raised her voice, *Hey Dad, Mrs. Howell says it's okay for me to sleep over* ... and then ... *"if it's okay with you,* with their lips barely moving." She laughed a little. "Tintitus, that's what he had." She tapped her ear again.

He nodded. "Yeah, kids get your number, don't they? I think they know us better than we ever know them." He took one bite of his burger and the thing was half gone. "Tinnitus," he said, "I think that's what it's called."

"Oh right," she said, tinnitus."

She held a fry up, cocked her head toward the back seat, and when Nate nodded okay, she offered it to Logan, who took it gently, without touching her fingers, swallowed it whole.

Nate finished off his burger in two more bites then crumpled the wrapper and sat there with it in his hand. She'd noticed the way he stared off into blankness every so often, a man with no anchor at the end of his tether.

"You'll have to leave soon, I guess," she said, "I mean, if you don't want to be on the road after midnight." Then she waited.

He nodded, tipped his waxed soda cup until the ice tumbled down, and sat there chewing on it slowly. The sound of his teeth biting into it made her cringe.

"You should call your wife while we're near a phone," she said. "Let her know."

He blinked. "We're divorced. Haven't lived together in over a year."

"Oh," she said. She passed another fry to Logan. "And you got the dog?"

"Well..." He looked over at her, seemed to come to some sort of decision. "Actually, I haven't had him very long. I got him just a couple of days ago."

"A couple of days?" She looked at Logan, whose eyes were glued on Nate. "He seems awfully attached for a forty-eight hour dog."

"Probably he's just grateful," he said. "I sort of ... liberated him."

"Oh. So you mean, *she* got him and you just stole him back?"

He shook his head. "He wasn't ours. He belongs to a neighbor. He was tied up morning, noon, and night." He marked off a square with his hands. "He lived in this ... rectangle. They never let him off the chain."

She popped a fry into her mouth, chewed it, swallowed. "Maybe for his own safety."

He cracked a piece of ice with his molars and she winced. "Maybe." He shrugged.

She looked into the back seat, offered Logan another fry. "So he's hot," she said.

A momentary silence hung between them. Then Nate half-turned to her, saw the look on her face and smiled. Which made her chuckle.

"Yeah," he said, "hot. He's a hot dog."

She popped another fry in her mouth. Cold now, the nice little crunch gone.

"Do you think," she said, holding up two fingers, "that there needs to be two people before either one of them can laugh? I mean, I never laugh. I probably haven't laughed in ... five years. But I'm always alone. Well..." she rolled her eyes, "most of the time." She looked at him. "Something would have to be very funny, you know? To make one person laugh out loud? Something would have to be very very funny. It's such an odd thing anyway, laughing. I mean, it's not always because we're happy."

She looked at an inchworm crawling up the windshield. "Liddy and I had this silly song we used to sing. *Oh, the monkeys have no tails in Zamboanga. They were bitten off by snails in Zamboanga. Oh the monkeys have no tails, they were bitten off by snails. Ohhhh, the monkeys have no tails in Zamboanga.* Except it wasn't really snails. I got that wrong. I do that, get words wrong sometimes. It's supposed to be *whales*. Ben's the one that pointed that out, his music background, you know, but I got it wrong from the start, and there was two-year-old Liddy singing snails, and what difference did it make anyway? Snails, whales. At the end, when she never woke up anymore, I sang it over and over to her. It always made the kid in the next bed laugh. And hearing him laugh, I'd laugh. And believe me, there was nothing funny about anything going on then. But I laughed anyway."

He didn't say anything, just sat there rolling a folded straw wrapper between his fingers, listening, and she had the image of a bolt creaking a few inches open inside her, though she knew she could slam it back into place again if she had to. "I guess it's not the kind of stuff a person likes to hear about, is it?"

He held the wrapper still. "It's okay," he said, "it's fine. Really."

So she told him little things that were small enough to slide past that old rusty bolt … about Lydia's make-believe friend Pogo who was always slow getting in the car and always made them wait, about Scott's mania for volcano models and the time one exploded right in his face so the only parts of him that weren't black were two rings around his eyes, and about the way Ben always got their anniversary wrong, always. And after a while she noticed Logan was curled up asleep in the back. So she stopped.

Nate rolled the window down a little more. "Truth is…" he said, then he sighed. "Truth is … I guess you could say I'm on the run." Then he put both hands up, palms open, a gesture that said, it's okay, you don't have to worry. Not that she would anyway.

"You know, losing my job, the divorce, Kim's tuition. Everything piling up, and all of a sudden the idea of the open road — of distance seemed pretty inviting." He glanced at her, shrugged. "A guy thing, huh?" Then he smiled. "Or just a stupid thing."

"So in other words," she said, "you don't have to be anywhere anytime soon."

He shook his head. "Nope."

"Plus you've got to keep this dog here under wraps." She took a deep breath. "Then since we both have the time, I'd like to show you something before you leave."

She registered his hesitation, and then something like acquiescence. Or was it tolerance? Of her. Of the way things might seem. Which made her want to offer some reassurance that, like him, she wasn't dangerous either.

"It's not far," she said, "and it won't take long. Plus it's right smack in the middle of downtown Niagara Falls."

He dropped his empty cup inside the white and blue Burger bag, then his crumpled napkin. "Sure," he said, "why not?"

Probably all he was doing was paying her back for the coil, and probably he'd rather be on his way sooner than later, but still, it was a kindness, and she felt a flood of feeling for this little thing, this habit he seemed to have of dispensing small graces. It made her think of her mum, who had lived through the Depression and never let any of them forget it, nagging at everyone for leaving food on their plates, for putting a half-eaten apple in the garbage, for letting the water run while they got a glass down from the cupboard. *Jeez, Mum, it's only a glass of water*, she'd say. *Only a glass of water to you, missy, but maybe all the difference in the world to some of God's creatures.*

All the difference in the world to her. This kindness.

He started the car. "You'll have to navigate," he said.

When they got to the downtown lot, she paid the parking fee, and he parked under the only tree for the shade. They left the windows down for air, and Mina placed three cold fries on the back seat. "Like I said," she whispered to Logan, "it won't take long."

They walked down the main street, busy as usual with tourists, couples holding hands, loud with music, bright in the spring sunshine, past the tee shirt shops and the postcards and the plastic miniature falls, past *Ripley's Believe It Or Not*, past the smells of corn dogs and pizza and sweet cotton candy. Honky-tonk. Still honky-tonk and strangely comforting for it.

"In here," she said, and led him out of the bright sunshine, in under the *Wax Museum* sign, past a line of Japanese tourists queuing up for tickets. She saw him staring through the glass front door at Marilyn Monroe with her skirt blowing up around her hips, those red red lips pursed in a perpetual kiss.

The Duke! Queen Elizabeth! Jack the Ripper! Arnold Schwarzenegger! Welcome to the House of Wax!! Still that awful recording, distorted, hurting her ears.

It was Owl Woman taking tickets. "When on earth are they going to replace that damn speaker," Mina said to her.

Owl Woman glanced at her, the usual impassive expression in place, black braids curved tight against her head. "Doesn't seem to bother anybody but you."

Owl Woman was practically the only person she saw who she actually spoke to. Brief exchanges that had early on pointed out their similarities. A staunch desire for privacy, a tendency toward one-sentence answers, a basic mistrust of everything and everyone. Owl Woman was the closest thing to an acquaintance Mina had, but she couldn't get over the feeling that Owl Woman knew more about her than she knew about Owl Woman.

"A guest," Mina said, glancing over her shoulder at Nate, and when Owl Woman looked at Nate, Mina felt a tiny flare of triumph for putting a hairline crack in Owl Woman's 'nothing can surprise me' manner.

Inside, it was dark and quiet and there was that little flutter of anticipation that always came over her. Different now, touched with an edge of nerves because for the first time she wasn't alone.

"Jeeze," Nate said, "they look so real."

He was standing in front of Jack and Bobby. Jack, who seemed to look straight at you while Bobby looked off into the distance, as though he was seeing something nobody else could. "I was walking down a street," Nate said, "in Manchester, New Hampshire and there was a crowd in front of a TV store. Five sets all tuned to Walter Cronkite. Nobody could believe it."

"People blamed Jackie for trying to crawl off the back of the car," she said, coming up beside him, "like she was trying to get away, save herself, as if that proved something awful about her. It made the secret service guy running behind the car almost crazy, because what she was really doing was trying to help her husband. *Help Jack, help Jack*, she was saying. With his brains on her suit. I mean, what do people *want*?"

They stopped in front of Charlie Chaplin. "I read something about him once," she said, "that he was supposed to visit a school in England, a school for orphans. He'd lived there himself as a kid, him and his brother. And the orphans were excited, you know? Waiting with the tea table all set for the great Hollywood star who'd started off just like them." She shrugged. "Then he went off to have lunch with Lady Astor instead and never showed up."

"So he was really a selfish bastard?"

Mina shrugged.

She waited while he lingered in front of Mae West, Princess Grace, Elvis, Franklin Roosevelt. She tapped her toe and almost said, "We didn't come for this. For all of *them*." But she reminded herself that just because she walked by them so often she didn't even notice them anymore didn't mean that Nate Madigan shouldn't look. Besides, shouldn't grace be mutually granted?

He stopped in front of Ben Franklin and said, "Don't the utility companies know you're there?" He turned to look at her when she didn't answer.

She glanced around. "The fridge is propane. And the stove. I carry in my water. I don't need electricity. There are the kerosene lamps for reading. I have a propane heater if it's cold. I wind my own clocks. The radio runs on batteries. And in the winter I go someplace warm."

He nodded.

"Besides," she said, as he moved on to Sophia Loren, "I'm not one of those people who gets noticed." Then she smiled. "Do you think *she* ever suffered from that?"

He gazed at Sophia, shook his head slightly.

"When you go home," she said, "will you return the dog?"

"*If* I go home." He shook his head. "No."

"Good," she said. "He's happy with you."

They moved along, and then he stopped again in front of the thirty-seventh president of the United States and shook his head. "Tricky Dick," he said, "wouldn't you know. Some people you just can't get away from."

She waited for him to explain, but all he did was point up. "A ceiling thing," he said. Then he leaned closer to the glass. "I wonder how they do it, get the likeness so perfect."

"It's sculpted," she said. "It's an art. Sometimes they do a direct mold, but usually it's from pictures and measurements. They know what they're doing. The hair..." she pointed at Nixon's head, "...sometimes it's a wig, like him maybe, because these are mostly cheaper, but for a high-class product they put it in one hair at a time. Real hair. And glass eyes, porcelain teeth. The heads are beeswax and the hands. The bodies are fiberglass."

He leaned a little closer. "It's so real, it's weird."

"Weird," she said, "is the guy who comes in here and stands in front of the Queen Mother, whistling *God Save The Queen* two hours every Friday."

He looked around. "Really? The queen mother?"

"And Marilyn Monroe disappearing twice. Most of her anyway. The first time, one of her legs broke off and they left it behind." She walked on ahead. "Each time it was a huge deal. All over the news. Everyone seeing her -— in passing cars, glimpses through windows. All kinds of rumors. Even in wax, she manages to be bigger than life. Except the insurance company wouldn't pay the last time they stole her."

"They're insured?" He came up behind her. "Like real people?"

"Of course. They're expensive, even the cheap ones. A huge investment. Thousands of dollars each."

He looked at her. "Do you, did you work here?"

"No."

"You seem to know a lot."

She shrugged. "I come here a lot, that's all."

She led him past Einstein, Madonna, Hitler, and then she heard his footsteps slow, and when she turned around, he was walking backwards looking at Key Largo. When he caught up to her in front of Mao, he was whistling it under his breath ... *we had it all, just like Bogey and Bacall, sailing away...* and it made her wonder if he'd left his wife or if it was the other way around.

She stopped in front of the door marked Staff Only and glanced to see who was nearby. An Indian family, the mother wearing a salmon-colored sari, a father in heavy-framed glasses, three teenage children who were pointing at things in the gory Jack The Ripper display and saying "ohmygod" over and over to each other. But they weren't paying any attention to her and Nate, so she pulled the key out of her pocket, noticing that her heart was beating a little fast, and unlocked the door. She pushed it open, motioned Nate inside, noticed his half-second of hesitation, then stepped in after him and pulled the door shut behind her before she found the wall switch and turned on the light. And for just a split second, when the room lit up and she saw them, she was home, they were all together, and she was completely happy.

CHAPTER TWELVE

"Do you hear it, Ben?" she asked, setting the potato salad on the picnic bench, cocking her head and listening to the shrill, high-pitched chirring that pierced the heavy August air.

"Yeah," he said, looking off across the yard before he went back to prodding the hamburgers on the grill, "a cicada."

Scotty glanced up. "What's that, Dad?" He was supposed to be setting the picnic table, but so far all he'd done was find an old hornet's nest attached to one of the wooden underpieces and cut it in half with a plastic knife.

"A grasshopper," Ben said. "But this one only hatches every seventeen years. When the male hatches, he sings ... like that ... so a female can find him."

Mina went back across the yard toward the kitchen to get the ice, thinking about Pa and the first time she'd heard that sound fishing for trout with him, and wondering if Gray was hearing it now, too. Always wondering about Gray. Where he was, what he was doing, if he was thinking about her, too. There had to be something humans gave off, some energy that was invisible but just as potent as that chhrrr filling the air. So unignorable it scrambled your brain, operating below the level of reasonable thought. She picked up Lydia's little pink trike by one handlebar and moved it off the walk. How else to explain it? How else to explain Gray?

It certainly wasn't because she was unhappy. She wasn't. She was content. And it wasn't because she was looking. She hadn't been. Which meant there was no reason at all. And no excuse.

And it wasn't because she was irresistible. She wasn't even pretty. She knew that. No one had ever made a pass at her. Not even Ben. She and Ben had just sort of ... aligned. Mostly a matter of proximity. Ben in accounting, her next door in personnel.

She closed the screen door tight behind her. The mosquitoes were a scourge this summer ... with the heat, the humidity. She opened the freezer and let the cold wash across her face, took out one ice tray and emptied it into the insulated wooden bucket.

Gamin. That was the most she could hope for. The pixie cut, the arching eyebrows. Eyes that weren't exactly brown, like it said on her license. Topaz her mother used to call them. But so what when it was blue she wished for. And blonde hair, straight and shiny. Or even curly. It was what she'd seen all her life — on the page, on the screen. And she was so far from the ideal, but at least it didn't bother her anymore.

She refilled the ice tray under the faucet, slid it back into the freezer, picked up the ice bucket and set it down again. And then there was Gray. Not particularly tall, not handsome. Solid, broad-chested. Hardly any upper lip at all. She tried so hard to restrict him to just after waking and just before sleeping, when the indulgence didn't eat at her. Although it was amazing how the mind had a mind of its own. So that she found herself thinking about him at red lights or waiting for the sink to fill or watching the school bus disappear around the corner. Sometimes she wondered how she could think about anything else. That's how big it was. And oh god, how *could* they? How could *she*?

She closed her eyes, but he was still there. He was always there. And she saw him for the first time all over again.

Had she been looking without knowing? But why? When she already had everything. More than everything. More than she'd ever hoped she'd have.

And still she'd known, been so damn sure. Sure as her feet were planted in front of that pyramid of oranges, with the soft whir of grocery carts passing and stopping, the fuss of a toddler near the Idaho potatoes, the soft ripping of a plastic bag close by, that this person on the other side of the fruit was sensing it, too. She could tell by the look in his eyes. Shock, fear, wonder.

She'd gotten out of there so fast, she'd come home with only half the things on her list. And then she'd laughed. Because it was just so ... asinine. Probably some high school prom song playing over the public address system ... *Tide on sale at 1.19, a special on sirloin tips, and don't forget, shoppers, to check our very own brand of heavy duty trash bags... 'Cuz I love yooou ... Yes, I love yooou ... Oh, how I love yooou ...*" Damn Moody Blues. Making you feel like you were fifteen and anything was possible. When you weren't and it wasn't. When you'd already dug your foxhole and it was way too late to un-enlist.

Not that she wanted to. No. God, no.

She picked up the bucket, some napkins, and headed back outdoors.

"Somebody new moving in," Ben had said. "The Gallo house. Guy works for Dow. A couple kids."

Ben was the first to stroll over one evening and offer a welcome, two cold beers, one in each hand. Ben was friendlier than she, more outgoing. Though she'd intended a visit eventually, with a coffee cake wrapped in a new plaid dishtowel. But there were already so many of them, endless husbands and wives and kids. On this street and the one over there, and the one behind. There were already too many neighbors to wave at, stop and chat with. Already too many three-year-olds to watch while someone ran to the pharmacy to pick up the latest prescription. Still, she had intended go. Eventually.

Then meeting him at the Benson's annual Memorial Day party.

Gray Stevenson. Mina Malloy. Mina ... and that's her husband Ben over there ... lives two houses down across the street from you. Is it Elaine? Oh, sorry ... Ilene ... Gray and Ilene just moved here from Wisconsin.

Hello, nice to meet you. And the hand that took hers, was it connected to some source of electricity, the way it warmed every cell in her body?

Kismet, Gray called it. Destiny. And yes, it did seem that way, at least when they were together. But when they weren't, when he was changing his Buick's oil, when she was vacuuming, when he was public relating at Dow Chemical, when she was milking a cow … then it felt less like kismet or destiny and more like a great big fat cheat.

So they broke it off. One week, the first time; nine days, the next, until one or the other of them caved in, and they came so quick at the New Dawn motel that sometimes all they ended up doing was rubbing against each other fully clothed. Stop it, she told herself. Stop it stop it NOW!

"Where's Liddy?" she said, setting the bucket on the picnic table. The hamburgers and hot dogs ready on the grill.

"Go get your sister," Ben said to Scotty, flipping the hamburgers one last time, lifting the hot dogs onto a plate with a set of overly long metal tongs.

And by the time the four of them were passing mustard, licking mayonnaise off their fingers, sipping the ice-cold lemonade … the sun had slid down the sky, and with it, the heat, at least a little.

The cicada song had stopped, and in back and side yards up and down the street, you could smell the smells and hear the neighbors in various stages of outdoor supper … sausage, ham steak, chicken, beef … kids squealing, mothers calling, dogs barking.

And was Gray cooking? Was that child crying one of his? Or were they indoors since mosquitoes loved him so? And was he thinking about her? Anxious because it was still four days away, their next meeting. Four days. An eternity.

And during all the minutes in between, life was going on. Her real life. What used to be her real life.

"Scotty, did you take a shower this afternoon after you went swimming?"

"But Mom, I went *swim*ming. Why do I need to take a shower when I just went *swim*ming??"

"Mrs. Nelson says I can sleep over tomorrow, okay, Mommy? Kitty's mommy already said okay and Mrs. Nelson says we can make pizza, but you have to call her. Okay Mommy? Don't forget to call her, okay? Right after we eat?"

"Yes, Lydia, I'll call her. Eat the rest of your potato salad. Want more lemonade? Ben, did you call about the insurance?"

"Mom..." Scotty looking at her with those wide green eyes. "Did you know that a wasp commits suicide when it stings an invader? Because the stinger stays in the invader, like the time I got stung picking strawberries? And when the wasp flies away after it stings, and the stinger stays in you, the bee's insides get ripped out with the stinger. Mr. Mahoney said."

"Yuk," Lydia's face wrinkling, tongue sticking out pink and smooth and pointed, "that's so gross Mommy tell him that's not true. Tell him."

"It is, too. Mr. Mahoney said. And he knows more than you. You don't know anything. You're nothing but a baby."

"Am not. Am not a baby," a tear bubbling up out of each eye.

"Okay, that's enough. Both of you." Ben looking from Scotty to Lydia. A lingering look that made them stop, made them look down at their plates.

Would it work, she wondered? *That's enough. Both of you.* Would she stop if Ben told her to? She couldn't believe he didn't know. *She'd* know. She was sure of it. Because how could you do it with two people and not slip up, it was so different. Different moves, different sounds, different things you'd do with one you'd never dream of doing with the other. She'd know Ben wasn't Ben anymore.

But he didn't seem to know she was a different Mina. Which made her wonder if he really knew her at all. All that time. All that time and he didn't seem to notice any difference in her. Nothing. Not one thing.

Scotty picked up a pickle spear and chomped the top off. "Is so," he said, wordlessly across the table at Lydia.

"Daddy..."

"Enough," Ben said, and this time they stayed quiet.

CHAPTER THIRTEEN

Nate stared at them, swallowed. Wax. That's what they were, just wax. Though that wasn't the thing that had shriveled his balls when the door shut behind them, when it was pitch dark and for a split second he was sure he'd just made the biggest misjudgment of his life.

What flashed before his eyes wasn't his entire life, but a page two write-up. *Man Found Murdered in Wax Museum Back Room by Cleaning Crew. Cause of Death, Violent Trauma to Head.* Or maybe it would be multiple knife wounds. That's what women chose, wasn't it, knives? Or was it poison....

Given an option, he'd have elected poison. But there was no time for a choice. Just pitch blackness when she shut the door.

He almost put his arms up to fend off whatever was coming. Which made him realize later, when he'd had time to think about it, that he would have made a piss-poor soldier. Someone who fended off. Or got shot in the ass. She was five inches shorter than he was, had no benefit of testosterone in her muscles, so he could have decked her. But the thought never even occurred to him.

And then the lights went on and a different kind of shock set in.

An hour earlier, in the car, he'd decided she was no crazier than some he knew, despite the fact her justification was greater. Besides, he was curious about the whole thing, and there was always the chance she wasn't crazy at all. That the only thing she'd done was turn her back on what was expected of her. Step outside the line. The way he had just forty-eight hours earlier.

But christ, they looked real. And happy. He and Mina had just walked in on a thoroughly enjoyable moment. They weren't on display the way the others were, stiffly posed, caught in moments of quiet contemplation or glory. They were sitting around a table, interacting, the man's head tipped back slightly in silent laughter, facing a blonde-haired boy about seven years old who was talking — arms raised, hands gesturing, face animated, a kind of glow coming off him. A girl, younger than the boy by a couple of years at least, leaning toward them both, elbows on the table, carroty hair framing her face, freckled cheeks, laughing, too. She was having fun. That's what you instantly knew. They all were.

"He was telling a joke," Mina said. She pointed to the boy. "Scottie loved to tell jokes. Why do people buy lots of toilet paper for a party?" She hesitated a second before the punch line. "Because so many people are party poopers." She smiled. "I took a picture. And that's what the wax artist used to create them."

"Scotty," he said, "and...?"

"Lydia. They were five and eight. And that's Ben. My husband."

His senses were still realigning, and it wouldn't have been all that strange if the guy had stood up and put out his hand. *Nice to meet you.*

He felt he should say something, but he didn't know what. Everything seemed an inadvertent reminder of how dead they really were. And then it came to him. "It would" he said, "be the way I'd like someone to remember me."

"Yes," she said, seeming to lose an inch of tension. "It was a fine moment."

***

On their way back to the car after the museum, he found a pay phone and called Priscilla. He looked at his watch, three-thirty, hoping it wasn't too late, that she'd answer the phone and be only fractionally sloshed. Which she was.

"So you've decided to take a vacation," she said. "How nice for you, Nate."

"I'm going to check in with you, Pris, every few days. Just to make sure things are okay. I don't have a phone. I left a message with Roberta to call you if anything comes up."

"And I'm supposed to take care of it?"

"No. You're the go-to person. All you have to do is take a message, give a message. Can you do that?" He didn't want to get into an argument. He just wanted her to do this one favor.

He heard her sigh. "Yes, Nate. I can handle that."

"Okay," he said, "thanks. And Pris..." But what was he supposed to tell her, that maybe she hadn't lost as much as she thought? And what good would it do ... would she suddenly see how good life could be if she gave it half a chance? "Talk to you soon," he said, and hung up.

Mina was waiting for him a polite distance away, somebody's unremarkable, normal-looking wife or mother, but in reality only a look-alike, and he walked toward her unsure if he'd come to believe that it wasn't such a strange thing after all — the return to Love Canal, the wax family — or if he'd simply slipped a cog into the same abnormal set of gears she was riding. And maybe it was the same old familiar blue sky overhead, the mild air against his skin, the ordinariness of the people moving past him, but he had the feeling that the day's experience should have been a significant blip on his radar screen. But it wasn't.

Instead, he couldn't shake the feeling that all he'd done was meet the folks.

He knew a little about them now, that Ben was an accountant, older than Mina, that he'd played the trumpet and the sax before she'd met him, traveled for a while with a band, spent a couple of years in Buenos Ares. "He used to tell me he sewed all his wild oats before he met me," she told him, "but sometimes I wished he'd saved a few. You know?"

He knew Scotty was a cut-up, that a semester never went by without a call from the principal. Stuff like setting the pet hamsters loose or sticking French fries up his nose and getting the whole elementary school cafeteria in an uproar. A popular kid who knew how to make everybody laugh, even in the hospital, so that when the jokes finally stopped, she knew it was close to over.

Then there was Lydia, who used to stand in the front yard waiting for her brother's school bus. It was how she learned to tell time, every hour radiating forward or backward from three-fifteen. She was shy, petite, had taught herself to read before she turned four, could play a passable piano at five.

And he knew they were both gone before they could graduate from high school.

"So," Mina said, as they headed back to rescue Logan from the car. "I know a park where we can take him to stretch his legs and pee. And then, maybe you'll be on your way?" She looked up at the sky, the sound of a plane overhead. "Or if you want, I'm thinking of quiche for dinner."

Quiche for dinner. He tried to think of something else he could be off to, somewhere else he could head. Somehow he felt he shouldn't land in one place too long, that he should keep moving or run the risk of losing what little energy he still had for this sort of thing, end up inhabiting some piece of the world where he never really lived but just permanently visited. And although he didn't really believe it anymore, there was still an outside chance that Mina Malloy was a spider and he was sitting just at the edge of her web. But he didn't think so.

Of course there was also the chance that what the tai chi lady by the lake had told him while she taught him proper breathing was true … that nothing ever happened by chance, and why reject something that was fated to happen on the possibility it might be something bad.

"If you'll let me buy dessert," he said.

She shook her head. "With my quiche, you don't need dessert."

***

They were drinking root beer by candlelight, the crust of his last piece of quiche still on his plate, but he was stuffed. Though he figured he could probably fork in the remains of the salad with the good sweet dressing.

She'd decided they'd eat in the living room on the big cushions. No chairs. No sofa. Nothing in the house she couldn't carry in herself. And all those books stacked unevenly against the walls like pathetic parapets against invaders.

The IBC empties stood like a set of candlepins with the four gutter pins gone. "I don't drink," she'd told him, "but I'd be glad to pick something up ... beer, vodka, gin, whatever you drink."

He'd told her root beer was fine. Besides, he didn't know what a buzz could add.

Logan was lying beside him, lightly snoring. There'd been a run-in with a big brown retriever in the park, twenty seconds of wild mock-violence that he and the retriever's owner vainly tried to stop and then finally gave up on.

"Maryann Healey, my neighbor directly across the street..." she aimed a thumb behind her and over her head, "three miscarriages in less than three years and then finally she had a little boy who was born with a cleft palate. There were five birth defects just on the four streets around here." She drained the last of her root beer. "I bought Lydia some patent leather Mary Janes, her first pair, and she wore them outside, came in all muddy, and when I wiped them ... the shoes..." She placed her glass in a circle of flickering light on the floor beside her cushion. "...they melted in my hands, the patent leather just — disintegrated. And I thought, what kind of shoes did they sell me? Cheap leather melted by a little water and mud? When actually it was probably the benzene, it's a solvent you know. Or maybe TCDD ... dioxin. Then there were the wild strawberries that grew around the canal, probably still do, and the kids and I would pick them. We'd say we were going to make a pie, but we always ended up eating them before we even got home." She shrugged. "People grew vegetables, and you know how there's always too much zucchini? So you'd find a bagful on your doorstep and there'd be zucchini bread for supper, eggs and zucchini omelets for breakfast." She sighed. "Lydia started having nose bleeds a month to the day after Scotty's first round of radiation therapy ended." She frowned. "It didn't seem possible."

She picked up her empty glass and set it down again. "Ben got sick a year and a half after Scott died. Lydia was responding okay then, and we had a good report from her doctor, but she was delicate. The chemo, you know, it kills everything — the things that are killing you," she shrugged, "plus the things that keep you alive. He blacked out one day just as he was starting to drive home from work. We were in Buffalo by then, they'd bought us out here, and his job was a hell of a commute, hour-and-a-half each way." She shook her head. "It didn't seem like such an odd thing. I mean, ten years, all that stress. He didn't even bother to tell the doctor."

She started to pour the last of the root beer from her bottle into her glass, then put the bottle to her lips and drained it, set it down. "Then it happened two more times, and they put him on valium. After that, the headaches started, headaches so bad he'd cry with the pain. They went on for days. Then all of a sudden they stopped. And just when we began to breathe again he started having these kind of spells ... like he was made of stone all of a sudden." Her hands fluttered, settled back in her lap. "Didn't hear, didn't see, didn't respond." She tapped her head. "Brain tumor. Inoperable. But they shrank it. We had some time. Then we lost Liddy and Ben gave up." She sat forward. "I hardly remember him sick. I mean, I know he was. And I know I was there through it all. But..." She sat back. "It bothers me, you know? I should remember. I should have taken better care of him."

The dog rolled over and sighed, farted softly, and Mina looked at Logan with a hint of the crooked smile. Then her eyes shifted back to his. "Do you believe in God?"

He would have understood if her tone allowed for only one possible answer. And he would have complied, would have said 'yes' earnestly and with conviction. But this was no plea. This was curiosity. So he shrugged. "Well ... there are times when it seems like there's *some*thing out to get us, but..." he shook his head, "maybe it's because I had so many to choose from that I picked 'none of the above.'"

Her eyebrows went up, a silent question, and by the time he'd sketched out the nuns, and the bar mitzvah Esther ruined because she threw a fit over the neighbors' lemon sponge cake, which she'd made, too, the priest who told him hell was waiting when he declined the old man's request to become an altar boy, and the rabbi whose teeth came out at the dinner table eating Esther's apricot rugalach. By the time her questions had elicited descriptions of Pris, Roberta, Kimberly, his job, in other words a pretty damn accurate picture of the mess he called his life, the candle was burned out and there was the diminishing moon again shining through the windows, painting shadows along the floor, and he'd been wondering for a good forty minutes if she was really all that interested or if it was just that she could sleep with her eyes open.

CHAPTER FOURTEEN

The sun was in her eyes when she woke up. Unusual. She'd never been able to break the habit of being the first one up, even though she was the only one now.

It used to give her time to get ahead of the day — start a wash, make a grocery list, a half-hour to herself. A morning person. A person who could rise at four and be helping with the milking by five, home for a shower, and breakfast on the table by seven. "I never knew you were a closet dairy farmer," Ben would say. What he never knew was that it had nothing to do with the production of milk or the stoic smelly solid bodies of the animals. It was lying beside him she needed to run from. Staying up late, too, a sudden stretch of insomnia that coincided with the milking job, not to mention Gray ... eleven months, fourteen days. Not even a year. And look how she'd paid.

She turned over on the futon and met Ben's gaze. Open, relaxed, satisfied. Clear all the way to his soul, and why not — with nothing to hide. He'd been on a fishing trip in that photo. Tarpon in Key West, caught nothing himself. But somehow someone had got him to pose on deck. Amazing considering how he hated having his picture taken. The sun setting into the Gulf behind him, happy, she guessed, just to be there. And she'd been happy, too. Eight days without having to think up an excuse, manufacture a hasty deception.

It had changed the tension of the affair, the ease of those eight days, loosened it enough to let some imagining in. Imagine if it were like this all the time. Imagine if you came home to me. Just imagine.

She'd thought, when the news came a month later, that it was the transfer that broke it off, but it came to her eventually, actually a long time after, that it was those eight days, the relief of that exquisite tension and the imagining of having it gone altogether, *that* was what broke the lust. It was important to call it what it was. Not love. She'd only imagined it was love. A pure convenience. She didn't know it then, but that ninth day was the beginning of the end of everything.

She turned away from Ben and stared at the too bright ceiling. Quiet in the house. So he'd slept in, too. Mr. Madigan and his hot dog.

Last night he'd shrugged, "that's it. You know the whole story." And she'd nodded, though she knew hardly anything. Just the facts.

Just the facts, ma'am. Who was that…? Friday. Joe Friday. But really his name was Jack Webberly, and was he actually like that? So stiff, a smile might break his face. Did he come home after a day's shoot and nod stiffly at his wife. *Good evening, Ma'am.* But he'd been married to someone beautiful … she closed her eyes … Julie London. And it wasn't Webberly, it was Webb. Jack Webb. She wondered, did they talk after they had sex?

Ben didn't. He went to sleep immediately, his arms still around her. Gray never fell asleep. He told her things. But how could she know for sure? There'd always been the clock ticking away their time. Talking may just have been a way of staying awake. A way of avoiding disaster.

"It's interesting," she'd said last night, shifting her position on the cushion. "People are endlessly interesting."

"At least the stories," Nate had said, "because you haven't heard them already. I used to think my wife was boring, but I think maybe it was the other way around. I think I bored her to death."

"Are you sorry?"

"That I bored her?"

"That you don't have her anymore."

He'd shrugged. "I'm not sure. It's complicated."

"You should find out."

"It wouldn't do any good. She's moved on. She's doing fine."

"Not for her. For you. You have to go over every little thing. Like you're looking for clues. Because it's too easy to make up what happened and why, go along with what makes you feel better or supports what you already think about yourself ... you know, justifying, rationalizing. And what good does that do anybody?"

They fell silent for a while, and she noticed that the rectangle of moonlight wasn't on her foot anymore but had moved a good five inches away. Or had she moved her foot? "You're a comfortable person to be with, Mr. Madigan," she said, because it was true. A person who didn't think his role in life was to fill every silence.

He looked up. "That's the nicest thing anyone's said to me in a long time." He said it with a slightly British accent, for some reason. Which made it a joke. Something he was good at, not letting things take too much of a serious turn. "Good food," he said, without the British accent, "a little history. Now I guess it's time to go to bed." Then he seemed to realize he'd said something he might not have meant. She heard him swallow.

"You don't have to worry," she said, "I've given it up."

He gave her a look that said, *huh?*

"Sex."

"Oh ... well, I wasn't ... I didn't ... not that I wouldn't ..."

"It's okay," she said, "I know that wasn't what you meant." She'd waited a while before she went on, wanting to be as sure as she could that she had his measure. "But I have my own proposition for you."

Except now, in the cold light of morning, she didn't understand why she'd gone and done it. She'd given up trust such a long time ago, and she'd known him for what ... forty-eight hours? Though when you thought about it, it had taken Logan less time than that to trust him. And she'd always figured dogs had ways of knowing. She turned onto her side and looked out the window up at the patches of blue sky between the top branches of the oak trees in the back yard.

He'd had a kind of quizzical look on his face, watching her, waiting, and she'd looked down at her hands, taken a slow breath. "There's something I need to do. But I can't do it alone. I'm going to need help. I'm not even sure yet what it is, but if you stayed a while, a couple of weeks, maybe..." She hesitated. It all seemed of a piece in her mind, but setting it out, actually putting words to it — then it all threatened to come tumbling down like a child's stack of blocks.

"What...?" he said.

She looked at him, clasped her hands together, leaned forward a little. "You'd think that after what happened here, after this place got raped the way it did — along with everyone in it — and all of it on TV and in every single headline ... you'd think it couldn't happen again, wouldn't you? That it could never never happen here again?"

"I don't know." He frowned. "I guess not. Why?"

She sat up straight. "Because it is. It's happening. There's chemical dumping. Near the reservation."

"How do you know?"

"I've watched it." She unclasped her hands. She'd been sitting too long and her knees were stiff. She rubbed them. "I've done more than watch it. I've studied it. I've logged it."

"And you need help to do something about it?"

She nodded. "If I can try and stop it, maybe then there'll be some raveling to everything that's happened ... the kids, Ben, all the others. And me still here. Some kind of *point*." She went silent for a second. "Besides, I can't get this thing out of my head that you found your way here for a reason."

He didn't say anything, but she decided the look in his eyes said he'd taken it in and he was at least willing to consider what she was telling him.

"But it's late now," she said, sensing she needed to let him off the hook she'd just hung him on. "And like you said, time to go to bed." She nodded.

He nodded back.

She stood up then, lifting herself off the cushion with more difficulty than she would have liked. She used to run up stairs, jump rope, dance. Been light on her feet. But not anymore. She leaned down and picked up four of the root beer empties, two necks between the knuckles of each hand. He got up, too. His knees creaked. He stacked their plates, grabbed the last two bottles, and even though they were both in stocking feet, their footfalls registered in the air, Logan's nails clicking across the linoleum behind them when they reached the kitchen.

They deposited everything on the counter.

"We can clean these things up in the morning," she said. She yawned.

He yawned back, started to turn toward the hall, then stopped. "Can I ask you a question?"

She nodded.

"Is that what you do?" he said. "Examine everything that's happened to you?"

She frowned, then she got it. "I try."

"Doesn't it bog you down? Keep you here," he pointed at the floor, "when you might be out there?" He swept his hand in a small, non-specific arc.

"Out there, in here," she shrugged. "I was doing nothing out there. I was paralyzed. Here, though ... I got something back. Maybe it doesn't look like it, but I've been doing something here. I've been trying to understand. Make some sense of it." She fell quiet. "I mean if I don't, if I don't make some sense of it, then I end up back where I was for so long. And there's only one thing to do when you're there." She went silent for a second. "But for whatever reason, I couldn't do *that*. Though god knows I thought about it. Then one day after I came back here, there was this spider building a web outside the kitchen window. In the rain. And I watched it. And when I stopped, I realized that for two whole minutes, I'd been interested in something outside of me. I was like this flat landscape, far as I could see. But watching that spider ... suddenly there was something vertical in me, a post to hold onto. And after a while, there were a few more, until they became a kind of direction." She shrugged. "It's been enough."

He reached out then, took her hand and shook it. "Thank you, Mina. It was a very nice evening. And thanks for the quiche. It was excellent."

That made her smile.

And it made her smile again now.

She tossed off the sheet.

She had to be careful, though. Because it was seductive. The talking. The company. She had to remind herself to be strict, to guard against it. Friendship, fun, intimacy, imagining ... it all lived on the space on the board that read START. And she was very far away from all that.

She pulled on her robe and headed down the hall toward the bathroom just as Logan appeared at the other end, tail wagging, a smile on his face. She opened the back door and let him out, stood there watching him sniff his way around the yard. Mrs. Dalloway hadn't shown her face since he'd arrived, but each morning the bowl of cat food she left just inside the cat door was empty. Not that it mattered. If she didn't leave the food, Mrs. Dalloway would survive. She was a born killer. Mice, baby rabbits, birds who were a tad too slow. Mrs. Dalloway had adopted *her*, not the other way around, so there was no need on the cat's part, just a decision.

Logan came running back and she left the inner door open after he was in because the cold spring morning air smelled too good to keep it outside.

CHAPTER FIFTEEN

He never actually came out and said he'd do it. Hang around for the two weeks she'd asked for. He just kept staying and couldn't really say why. They fell into a routine of sorts. Up early, a breakfast of oatmeal or eggs or cereal. And he had his own little private routine, too. Deciding almost every night when he got in bed that when he got up in the morning, he would pack up and be on his way. Because what in hell was he doing here, anyway? But then when he woke up with the sun on his face, he'd wonder where to go. Home? To realize all over again he didn't have one anymore? Besides, putting together a new one was beyond him, and then there was always the chance that time would work its magic and he'd wake up a new man one day.

He paid for his food by fixing things he had a feeling she could probably fix better and faster herself. Though she said she couldn't do it on her own, keep up with the way the place was falling apart. So he spent two days replacing a rotten sill beneath the back door, half a week gluing down the edges of the floor tiles in the kitchen, an entire morning up on the roof feeling exposed and scanning the horizon every five minutes for the cavalry while he tarred over the patches that looked the most worn.

On Saturdays he went to a Laundromat, one of the three she gave him directions to. He went on Saturdays because they were the busiest, and sometimes he could find some other solo guy to strike up a conversation with while they waited for the clothes to stop sloshing and for the dryer to buzz. One Saturday it was a guy chomping on a cold pipe whose wife had died three years ago, who climbed a Class 4 mountain twice a year, raised bees, and predicted the Giants wouldn't win another Super Bowl for a decade now that Parcells was gone. Another, was a guy with a scar down the left side of his face who taught high school chemistry and said if Clinton got elected it would be the beginning of the end for America because he was the product of a generation with no moral compass and would end up burying whatever morality was left. He said he could already see it in the kids he taught.

Nate just listened. He'd been paying no attention at all to whatever was going on out in the world.

In addition to the Laundromat, he took himself away for at least a couple of hours every day, he and Logan just driving around, partly because he figured she deserved the time alone and partly because he needed to reassure himself on a daily basis that he *could* leave.

He'd never gone to camp, but he'd always spent a significant amount of every summer imagining what it was like. And now he'd decided it was like this. Like being someplace that felt like an island, but wasn't. On a piece of land that seemed to have ripped itself away from the continuum, folded its edges and kept itself so still that even if someone came along and looked right at it, it would only seem to be a trick of the light or the feel of an odd breeze. When he was a kid, he would imagine himself hiding away when everyone was packing up to go home, only coming out after he was sure they'd all left. That way, he could stay on his little land island forever. And then there was the invisibility. He'd achieve that by eating a special berry that no one had ever eaten before. So even if his parents came looking for him, they'd move right past him without so much as a second thought. Invisibility. Had he finally found it?

He read. He'd never had such close access to so many books. *Story of an African Farm. The End of The Affair, As I Lay Dying, Lolita.* P.D. James, Evan Connell, Gabriel Garcia Marquez, Cormac McCarthy, and his favorite, *Memoirs of a Mangy Lover* by Groucho Marx. "Have you read them all?" he asked her, and she nodded, with a look on her face he didn't understand until he thought about it and realized that reading a thousand books in '90's America said you had way too much time on your hands.

He missed Kimberly like crazy, so he wrote to her every few days. And because he couldn't address the obvious, he avoided it by riffing on what they used to do when she was still young enough to want a story every night. It had been something Roberta could never understand, K's preference for a daddy story with no pictures, over a mommy story illustrated by Maurice Sendak. *Here I am,* he wrote in his first letter, *sitting on a stony outcropping on Pisco. That's part of the Cordillera Blanca, K — remember where we had lunch that Thursday we had to set the balloon down in Northern Peru? From all the pterodactyl-like shapes in the sky, I'd say Peru is full of condors, and the rock ledge I'm sitting on seems to belong to one of them. For a good fifteen minutes, one has been gliding back and forth above the ledge, looking down and around as if it may have gotten its ledges mixed up, but now it seems to have decided I'm the one who's gotten things wrong here, and it's getting close enough for me to see a look in its eye that's not exactly welcoming. Since it has a beak the size of a tool box and its wingspan is longer than the Pontiac station wagon we had when I was a kid, I'm going to get the heck out of here. Then I'm going to give this letter to a passing llama to mail, so please pardon the teeth marks on the envelope. I miss you. Love, your dad.*

He checked in with Pris, called from a pay phone in town every Friday. Short conversations. She seemed to have relegated him to some low phylum like Nematoda, though she did check in with Kimberly a couple of times a week. And Kimberly was fine. Just *fine.* Well, thanks a bunch, sis, he wanted to say, and did I tell you that just the thought of dialing your number is beginning to give me stomach spasms? Although he had to admit Mina's cooking was fixing his stomach problems.

When he wasn't fixing or reading or writing or working up his courage to call his sister, he took Logan for walks, and after a couple of weeks, Mina started to accompany them. She insisted

that her cat liked walks, too, and she'd stand in the yard and call —
"Mrs. Dalloway, c'mon Mrs. Dalloway, want to go for a walk?"— the
three of them standing there to a count of ten before they gave up
and went without her.

There was never even a hair to be seen of the cat, though Mina
set out a bowl of cat food every evening that was licked clean every
morning. Still, anything could be eating it, so the cat remained a
conjecture. Was she real or wasn't she?

One day they walked along an abandoned road that led to an
abandoned cement block building, Logan with his nose to the dirt
following zig-zag trails into and out of the perimeter of trees
around the decaying parking lot that was returning to the wild.
Giant weeds grew along the foundation, right-angled cracks traced
the joints of the cement block walls, the windows were semi-
boarded up. Graffitists had been there. FUCK THIS TOWN. BREAK
RULES. ZIGGY. FREDDY LOVES LUCY FOREVER.

"Do you think he still loves her?" he asked, pointing.

Mina looked at the drippy faded blue letters and shrugged.

The place had the feel of having been abandoned more than
once. As if when the real business of what went on there stopped,
other business had started. But even those were long in the past ...
the beer cans rusted, the candy wrappers faded.

There were a couple of slightly rusty spray paint cans lying in
the weeds, and he picked one up, shook it, still half-full. He looked
over at Mina, who was watching him with her arms folded, a kind of
bemused look in her eye.

He found a clear section of wall, and a peculiar sense of delight
caught him by surprise. It was the kind of thing people like him
didn't do, against all the rules he'd been taught to follow by his
parents and the nuns, and by friendly Officer Maloney who visited
each classroom once a year and summoned them to virtuous deeds
and respectable behavior. And silly as it seemed, a phantom weight

pressed down against his arm as he raised the paint can — Sister Anne? Sister Immaculata? But he fought it and won, spelled out

D O W N S I Z I N G S U C K S in small neat letters on the wall.

"Here," he held the can out to her. "Your turn."

She shook her head, her lips planted firmly together.

"Oh c'mon," Mina," he said. "What difference can it make? Think of it as an art project ... an opportunity to express yourself. A little therapy?"

She held her posture for a second, then unfolded her arms, took a few steps toward him and took the can. She stood there for a while staring at the wall. Finally she shook her head. "I don't know what to say to the world."

"What if it's the only chance you'll ever get?"

She moved one step closer to the wall, came up a little onto her toes, as though the wall was too high for her to reach and wrote quickly, compactly, D O S O M E T H I N G.

They stood back and looked at what they'd done. Then Logan came trotting around the corner of the building with a shoe in his mouth.

He came up to Nate and stood there holding it with a kind of questioning look on his face, as though he wasn't sure he'd done something right or something wrong. Then he dropped the shoe in the grass near Nate's foot.

It was a woman's shoe, open-toed, white once, with a narrow high heel. A fancy shoe. So what the hell was it doing out here?

Mina seemed to be thinking the same thing, because she made a little worried noise, and Nate started reluctantly in the direction Logan had come and Mina fell in beside him.

Mid-way along the building, some boards had been torn away from what once had been a door, and Logan trotted past them and disappeared inside.

Nate bent his head and looked through the hole, but it was too dark inside to see much.

If he'd been alone, he would have considered his options, with number one being leaving immediately, but he felt like he had something to lose here, and it surprised him to discover it mattered if he slipped in Mina's estimation.

So he gave himself no more time to think, just stumbled on through the hole, feeling like a big clumsy bug.

There was no smell, aside from dust and disuse. No movement, and he made space for Mina as she joined him.

Then Logan came running.

Mina's eyes must have adjusted quicker than his, because he heard her gasp softly. "Look," she said, pointing.

At first, what he saw didn't make sense, and he realized he'd had some grisly image in his mind right from the time he'd seen the shoe in the dog's mouth.

It was a woman, half-lying against a wall in the opposite corner, as though she'd been standing, and then fallen backwards still in her standing position.

Mina went closer. "My god," she said, stopping, "it's Marilyn."

And it was. As soon as Mina said it, he saw that pose in his mind, the stiff legs slightly spread, the hands down by the thighs holding the skirt, the chin off to one side. The platinum hair.

They walked over to it, the sound of debris crunching under their feet. Logan was standing near Marilyn wagging his tail, his whole body saying, *Look what I found!*

She seemed bigger than life, all that white white skin. No dress. And as he got closer, he could see that whoever had made her had done a pretty damn precise job.

They stopped about a foot away.

"Are they all like this?" he whispered.

She shook her head. "I don't know."

He had a sudden urge to take off his shirt and cover her up. He looked at Mina, then around the building, back at Marilyn. What must have gone on here? What might still be going on?

Mina reached out and touched Marilyn's arm. "She's dusty." She held up her fingers. "Whoever brought her here hasn't been back in a while." She sighed. "But she looks like she was well used."

He cleared his throat. He thought about kids sitting in classrooms, their minds and their pricks counting each tick of the minute hand, waiting for release. Did they have real girls now? Didn't need this one anymore?

"Here," Mina said, "help me set her straight."

They stood her upright in the corner. She was looking away from them, her eyes half-closed, as though she was ashamed.

Mina started hunting around. "Here's her dress," she said, picking up a dirty, gauzy white rag in two fingers. "Let's put it on her, okay?" She gave it three or four shakes.

He held Marilyn up off the floor, puzzled at first where exactly to grab her, while Mina slipped the dress up over her feet. Even he could see the dress had been carefully made. The material had heft, the skirt still held its pleats. Even the zipper still worked.

Mina adjusted the halter top. "Poor thing," she said. And he realized she was probably right. That the real Marilyn probably *had* been a poor thing.

They only had the one shoe, and decided it wasn't worth looking for the other.

"Should we do something about it?" he said, blinking in the sunlight after they'd stepped back outside. He propped the torn-away boards back in place.

She shook her head. "This one had two legs, so It's not the first one that was stolen. And there's no way I'm reporting it."

On the way back through the trees to the path, they didn't talk, but Mina began to hum softly, and then to sing, almost to herself, as though she didn't even know she was doing it. But he recognized the tune, could see Marilyn making love to the microphone, making Jack Lemmon and every other guy in the world fall in love with her.

"I'm through with love," Mina sang. *"I'll never fall again, said adieu to love, don't ever call again…"*

CHAPTER SIXTEEN

He'd participated in other pauses that could be described as pregnant ... the morning, for instance, Roberta asked him, over waffles, if he knew someone named Maryann, with a certainty in her voice that told him saying no wasn't going to do any good.

The pause he was participating in now, with Mina, on this beautiful blue-sky, light-breeze, warm-air morning, felt close to term. Full with whatever she was about to tell him. And whatever response he was going to make to it. Made fuller by the smallness of everything they'd done since they'd come together in the kitchen. She, as usual, a little before seven. He, as usual, a little after.

At six, he'd heard her close the bathroom door, stay in there longer than usual, then he'd listened to her slip-ons flap the soles of her feet, the sound almost undetectable by the time she was at the end of the hall. He'd been dressed for half an hour by then, but he'd sat there on the bed trying to read *The Plague* and massaging Logan's ears. It never felt right to be up before Mina, inhabiting her space before she had a chance to claim it herself.

"It's been three weeks," he'd said the night before, washing the dinner dishes while she dried. "Are we ready to talk about how to handle this problem you've discovered on the reservation?"

She'd said she needed about a couple of weeks, and more had gone by, and so he was asking. But he'd known it was a mistake even before the question mark had placed itself at the end of his sentence.

A pause. A tensing. And then she'd said, "Okay. We'll talk tomorrow at breakfast."

Then she'd gone quiet, into some private place, not hostile the way Esther used to be, but withdrawn from any sense of the ease they'd gradually fallen into. She'd said an early goodnight, taken a book to her room, making him wonder what this whole thing was about really. Bringing back the feeling of his first night here, so that in the Love Canal nighttime silence, with the image of the wax family behind his eyes, Mina Malloy's balance shifted. From eccentric to insane. From oddball to fully loaded psychopath. And even though, as usual, the sun rising outside his window this morning had tempered those feelings, he'd decided, before he got out of bed, that no matter what she told him this morning it was time for it to be over, this time of hiding out.

He sat on the edge of the bed and re-read an entire page of Camus for the third time, though reading wasn't really what he was doing. Wrestling was more like it. Him trying to grab the thing by the neck. The damn book always getting the edge.

As far as he could see, suffering, intense physical pain that set your eyes to bleeding and made throwing yourself into a gigantic set of lawn mower blades seem like a preferable option, wasn't meaningless. Suffering had great meaning and was something to be avoided at all costs. And while he sat there trying to develop his argument, it occurred to him that Mina might have interpreted his question as something else. She'd asked for two weeks and he'd given her that, yes, but had she seen the question as a push? To keep her end of the bargain so he could be on his way? Was that what she thought he wanted? And didn't he?

"Would you like jam with your toast or peanut butter?" she asked, after he appeared in the kitchen and sat down at the table. The sun was slanting through the window above the sink, hitting him in the eyes and making him slightly blind. But even that wasn't enough to hide the fact that Mina wasn't looking like Mina anymore.

"Jam, thank you," he answered, dodging the sun, trying to get into a patch where he could clearly see what she'd done.

"Like to try some sour cream with your oatmeal?" she asked.

"I'm happy with milk," he said. "You cut your hair."

"Yes," she said, pulling at a piece curling across her ear. "It's the way I used to wear it. Easier to deal with."

He moved his chair. "I like it short."

She smiled.

He thought pixie. Audrey Hepburn. Girlish. "Yeah. I really like it."

So they sat there. The table arranged. The coffee and oatmeal steaming, butter melted into the toast, two small glasses of orange juice dripping moisture down their yellow polka dot sides. And Mina with points of hair coming down along her forehead and curving up onto her cheeks, beside her on the table, a small hard-bound notebook with that free-form black and white design on the cover, the kind he used to fill with lines of cursive practice, connected ovals and connected slanted lines that had to fill one lined space exactly, only touching the lines at top and bottom, never dipping below or rising above. Or else a ruler came down on his hand.

The notebook took him all the way back to Sister Mary Benjamin's third grade classroom, to that faint smell of bologna, tuna fish sandwiches, and sour milk leaking from the swinging cloak room door directly behind him, to the heavy rustle of Sister's long black skirt, the swing of the black wooden rosary beads that hung at her waist, the constant sniff of Tommy Gill's snot-filled nose beside him.

Mina sighed, took a sip of her coffee. "You remember Owl Woman at the wax museum? She was the one taking tickets?"

He took a sip of his orange juice, nodded, placed it back on the table exactly within the moist ring it had left on the green plastic cloth.

"Well, really she's Sally DeSoto. I mean that's her given name, the name everybody called her until she had her conversion." She tipped her head to one side. "Or maybe it's not a conversion … a, a, reclamation or a transformation or well, she just went native, you know? She rediscovered her heritage. She became Owl Woman."

He ate some of his cereal, sprinkled it with more sugar, tasted it again. "Renewal?" he said.

"No. It's not that, an epiphany a … oh, it doesn't matter what it is, you get the idea."

He took several more spoonfuls of oatmeal, which was really very good, exactly the way he liked it. Thick enough to leave an edge when he removed his spoon, sweet enough now, and nothing like the runny porridge Esther used to put in front of them every other morning.

"You see," Mina said, "the reason for this whatever-you-want-to-call-it was that the river started to glow."

He glanced at her, a spoonful of oatmeal half-way to his mouth.

"I saw it myself. Well maybe it wasn't *glowing* exactly, sort of an iridescence or a shimmer or maybe a kind of mist." She shrugged. "But that was a lot later that I saw it. After she thought it was the *wakan* talking to her and after she changed her name and after she got religion. Well…" she made a face, "not religion really, it's not a religion, what she's got now, it's an Indian thing, a Native American thing."

He swallowed the oatmeal. "You saw it glowing?"

She nodded. "Well, it had this *tinge*. But soon as I saw it I knew what it was. Nothing mystical about it. Cadmium. Paint thinner, enamel, lacquer, mixing with organic compounds."

"You mean it still glows, still *tinges* after all these years? The pollution's still *that* toxic?"

"Oh this is new toxic. This is the stuff that's being dumped right now."

He looked at the oatmeal still in the bowl, put his spoon down. Was this a *theme* with her? She studied it, *logged* it. That's what she'd said that night, *I've logged it.*

"Who's doing it?" he asked.

"A small contractor. One guy. He has a couple of small customers and they pay him a dumping fee. Once a month, the last Thursday of every month, he doesn't go to the hazardous waste disposal plant. Instead, he pockets the dumping fee and dumps his load in the river. Then he takes the money he's saved and blows it in twelve straight hours at the casino."

She took a bite of toast, chewed and swallowed. "There's a thousand acres of reservation up here," she said. " And I spent a lot of nights the last few summers camping out in it. Creeks, ponds, swamps. Any place that seemed likely. Until one night I caught him doing it." She looked at Nate. "Do you know you can keep mosquitoes away by rubbing yourself all over with Bounce?"

He shook his head. "The dryer stuff? Really?"

She picked up the notebook and held it to him across the table.

It was all entered in purple ink. Dates, once a month; times, around two a.m.; place, River Road, a highway route number followed by pole numbers; and then a description of a truck followed by the word 'Piggy.'

"But this is exactly what you need," he said. "It's all here. All you have to do is turn it over to someone — the EPA or the cops."

She shook her head. "It wouldn't do any good."

"What do you mean it wouldn't do any good? It's their job."

"If it's their job, then why aren't they doing it? Sally DeSoto may think it's spirits, but her Uncle Roy doesn't. He brings the fish he finds with tumors and melted fins and drops them on the sheriff's desk. He's gone to the game warden. He's even gone to see his congressman. And no one does a thing."

"Then *you* should go," he said. "With this." He waved the notebook. "You've got proof."

"So does Uncle Roy. Uncle Roy had the *water* tested. And like I said, cadmium. Interacting with organic compounds."

"And?"

"And nothing. He got a letter saying his complaint is 'under consideration.'"

"So that's good, isn't it?"

"That was a year-and-a-half ago."

He looked at the notebook again, closed it, looked at Mina, at the set of her jaw, the expression in her eyes, both of which were more pronounced now with the points of her hair curving toward them, and it began to dawn on him.

"So *you're* going to do something about it."

She nodded.

"And you want me to help."

She nodded again.

"Help you do something the entire EPA can't or won't do."

"I've been trying to come up with a way to stop it for more than a year," she said. "But I can't. Not by myself. And then, with the chance of help, your help, I thought, *finally. A chance to do something.*" But I can't figure it out. What that *something* should be. It's all I've thought about for three weeks and I'm no closer to a plan now than I've ever been."

"Maybe," he said, "because there is nothing you — or you and I — *could* do." Maybe because there *is* no plan that's going to let two people fix this."

For a second, she just looked at him. Then she reached across the table and took the notebook out of his hands. "Point taken," she said. "It's a ridiculous idea."

"Well what exactly do you think you can do?"

She sipped her coffee, not answering, making he feel like he was seven years old again, Esther looking right through him, sipping *her* coffee, while he sat there miserable and scared, wondering what he'd done now. "Look..." he said, because he wasn't seven years old and this woman wasn't his mother, wasn't anyone to him, and he owed her nothing, except maybe a glimpse of the real world. "...I'll ask you again, what exactly do you think you can do? Conk some guy over the head with a two-by-four and tie him up with vines? This guy knows what he's doing is illegal, and he knows if he gets caught he could go to jail, or pay a fine that will permanently bankrupt him. Has it occurred to you that anyone who attempts to cause either of those things could end up as part of the *tinge* floating past Sally DeSoto's wigwam? How's *that* going to hit Sally? What's *that* going to do to her reclamation or her reconciliation or whatever the hell it is?"

They stared at each other.

"It could be argued," she said, "that the things I do don't exactly make sense. But what have *you* done lately that does?" She set her cup down hard enough to splash coffee onto the green tablecloth.

He thought about it for a second. "Probably nothing," he said. "And I get it. You're serious. This is important to you. But you can't go doing something that could get you hurt. Or worse."

"Nate," she said, "do you know what's going to happen? One of these days, Sally DeSoto's grandson's liver is going to be twice as big as it should be and his immune system is going to go all to hell. It'll get his brothers and sisters, too. They eat *fish* out of that river. They *swim* in it." She leaned toward him across the table. "It took ten years for the authorities to rescue us, and as far as I'm concerned, that was nine years and eleven months too long. And while they diddled and screwed around, refusing to believe we were being poisoned, my kids got sick enough to die. And my husband — who didn't believe it either, by the way, who didn't want me making a fuss, *marching around and yelling and making a general fool of yourself* is what he called it. But I marched and yelled and acted the fool anyway, and if I hadn't, if those of us who were desperate enough hadn't, do you think anything would have been admitted by those fucking companies at all? Ever?"

He watched the color rise in her face until her cheeks were so red they looked burned. "You did the right thing," he said.

She sat back in her chair, closed her eyes and then opened them again. The burn of her skin notched down a shade. "I just want to stop him," she said. "So far, I can't figure out how. But I'm going to do that eventually."

She meant it, and nothing he could say was going to make a difference, but he decided to try anyway. "It's different now," he said. "Because of this," he motioned around them, "because of what happened here. Now they know. Now everyone knows."

She nodded, but it was hardly agreement.

"Mina, this has nothing to do with making sense or not making sense. It's about taking a risk that isn't worth it. I'm not going to help you figure out how to do something dangerous and I'm not going to help you do it, either." He looked at her for a second. "Tell me you'll give it up."

She looked at him long enough and hard enough to make him wish she'd stop.

"Hasn't there ever been anything important to you?" she said. "Isn't there anything you'd risk everything for?"

Her eyes were too bright in that still-pink face. They glittered hard enough to make it impossible to not tell the truth.

He shook his head. "No."

It was one thing to admit to himself that his life had been something less than a hardening process, that he'd always taken the easy way out, always given in and given up, hadn't ever fought for anything. But admitting it out loud to someone else....

She put her hands together on the edge of the table, cocked her head at him, her look gentled, the hard glitter faded. "Once upon a time," she said, her voice conversational, "you had an idea of who you were going to be. I'm wondering, is this it?" She nodded her head at him. "The person you are now, is this the person you pictured you'd become? Because I'm not who I wanted to be. I wanted to be a singer. I sang all the time. I know the words to any song you can name. Go ahead, name a song and I bet I know the words." She nodded at him. "Go ahead."

"I can't think of any songs."

"One song," she said, "just one song."

He looked around the kitchen. Two minutes ago they'd been yelling at each other about risking everything to save the world, and now she wanted to sing him a song.

"C'mon," she said. "You have to know at least one song."

"Happy Birthday," he said.

"Oh for heaven's sakes." She shook her head. "I'll sing you a medley. I'll start with my favorite." And she began to sing...

A cigarette that bears a lipsticks' traces ... An airline ticket to romantic places ... And still my heart has wings ... These foolish things remind me of you...

He sat there stock still, listening to a voice that wasn't half-bad. A little dusky, smoky, sexy. She leaned toward him a little.

The way you hold your knife ... the way we danced 'til three ... the way you changed my life ... no no they can't take that away from me...

He had to smile. And then she started to bounce a little.

Gotta get my old tuxedo pressed, gotta sew a button on my vest ... 'cause tonight I've got to look my best ... Lulu's back in town...

When she stopped bouncing, except for Logan's breathing, it got very quiet.

"Also," she said, "I wanted to be happy. I wanted someone to love me. I wanted to be a bride. I wanted to be a mother. And once I had those things, then I knew I'd be happy every day of my life. It was guaranteed."

"And were you?" he said.

She looked past him. "Maybe. Every once in a while." Then her eyes came back to his and her face softened. "Yes. A few times I was very very happy. Maybe you could even call it joy. But in a million million years I never imagined I'd end up as me. Never imagined losing everyone I cared about. Never imagined being left alone with ... nothing."

It was hard to look at what he was seeing in her face. But looking away would have been even worse. And then suddenly the pain in her eyes disappeared.

She crossed her arms. "So what about you, Mr. Madigan. What did *you* want. What was the thing you wanted most of all when you were seventeen?"

He looked past her, out the back door at the bird feeder and the birds that flitted back and forth across the yard, trying to remember being seventeen and what it was he wanted that he didn't have then. He smiled and shook his head.

"What?" she said, "what are you thinking?"

He thought of all the seventeen-year-old Miss Americas who wanted world peace and an end to all hunger and suffering, as they spun their batons and tap-danced across the stage.

"One thing," he said. "I wanted one thing."

She uncrossed her arms and sat forward. "What?"

"Sex," he said. "Every night. Someone there to have sex with whenever I wanted it."

She laughed. A short expulsion of sound. "And you got it?"

"After Roberta and I got married. For a while, I guess." He looked at her and smiled. "Two months. Or maybe it was six. But after that ... not even close." And having answered her, having remembered how simple his idea of heaven once was, he realized how the failure of that plan had truly staggered him. How simple it seemed, how easy and sure, such a small thing to ask, to expect, and then to get it and have things turn out so absolutely unlike he thought they'd be. Complicated. Unfulfilling. Completely miscalculated. Was *that* his undoing? Had he been living in a state of total shock and disbelief ever since? Had he never grown up? Who was he, for Christ's sake, Peter fucking Pan?

She took a breath and looked at him as though she'd just figured out the right answer to everything. "You know what I think?" she said. "I think it's time for you to go home. You miss your daughter. Your sister needs you. Maybe you even miss your ex-wife."

He raised his eyebrows.

"Well," she said, "if nothing else, they at least remind you who you are." Her face seemed to lose energy, sag. "Which is easier to forget than we think. Besides..." She patted her new hair. "You know what I've gone and done?"

He shook his head no.

"I got myself ever so slightly sucked in. I mean, here I've lived all this time, so careful to stay away from anything that might tangle me up and make me doubt that I can do what I have to and do it all by myself. And then all that fine independence of mine gets derailed in four short weeks?" She shook her head. "You and your dog." But she said it with a soft voice. She sighed. "It's not your fault, Nate, but, really, I think it's time for you to go home. You're not good at this."

Then she pushed her chair back and stood up, walked over to Logan, bent down, and patted him. "Still, I'm glad your car broke down and I'm glad I answered the door. If the truth were told, I think I was actually getting a little more derailed than anyone should. And you got me back on track. Well, on *my* track." She straightened up.

"Look," he said, "let *me* do it. I'll take your proof and the uncle's proof and I'll deliver it to someone who'll really do something about it. You're not the only one who needs to get back on track, Mina. It'll give me a focus. I need that."

She patted his hand, much the same way she'd patted the dog.

"It'll be fine. Don't worry, okay? I mean it. We'll both be fine."

***

An hour later, he was showered, his plastic grocery bag full of more stuff than he'd arrived with … three sandwiches, a bag of potato chips, six bottles of spring water, the half-full bag of dog food along with Logan's dish and water bowl.

She walked him out back to his car, Logan following with a little sideways hop to his gait that Nate had come to recognize as wariness.

"You have a safe trip back," she said. She shook her finger at him, "and no more break-downs. God knows who you'll run into next." And she laughed.

"Thanks for everything," he said.

She looked up at him, squinting against the sun. "You did more than your share. And I thank you." She squatted down in front of Logan. "And you…" She put her arms around his neck.

"So," he said, looking around as she straightened up and Logan nosed her hand. "Maybe Mrs. Dalloway will come home now."

"Yes," she said, "I suspect she will."

Then he put his arms out and she stepped into them, his chin just higher than the top of her head. He had no idea why it should surprise him that she knew how to hug back.

CHAPTER SEVENTEEN

Logan's bobbing head kept getting in the way as he watched the place recede in his rear view mirror.

He was pretty sure, as he negotiated the craters in the macadam and slid between the strewn parts of the broken gate, that after heading south for a while it would all start to seem unreal. Love Canal, the wax family, the woman who'd lost everything. Eventually, he'd find himself on Route 93, familiar things rushing by on either side, familiar voices and jingles on the radio. He wondered if Logan's ears would perk up, familiar smells reminding him of home. And what would home mean to Logan? And to him? Was it possible to welcome the rope you'd hated? The new rented room? The new Mrs. Cready? The new job hunt, the new lonely lady in the unemployment line, the old Priscilla, the old Esther? All of it reminding him, like Mina had said, of who he was. The old Nate.

But it was really the other thing she'd said that wouldn't leave him alone. Self-examination. Was she right? Was it something you needed to do. *Should* do. Another addition to the list — right after flossing, exercise, staying adequately hydrated — all those things you'd one day wish you'd done. Except by then it would be too late.

As he entered the animate neighborhoods, made his way through the semi-busy downtown, the car sliding bumpless across the unpocked road, he began to feel a certain neatening of his edges. As though order were being restored.

He saluted the *Thank You For Visiting Niagara Falls Come Back Again* sign, and thought that someone famous had said something famous about self-examination. Ben Franklin. Yes, Ben Franklin. Who must have written down every damn thing he ever said or thought. Much of which people seemed happy to consider, if not live by. Poor Richard. *The Almanac.* But why Richard? Why not Poor Ben? Except it wasn't the guy with the kite. It was the guy with the pond. Walden. Thoreau. Henry David. Or was Henry simply quoting Franklin? Or were both Henry and Franklin quoting one of the Greeks ... Plato? Socrates? Diogenes? More likely Socrates, who put his time to good use before the hemlock and figured out lots of things. An examined life. Worth living. Which must have made it all that much harder to give up.

He settled more comfortably against the back of the seat. So was his own lack of self-examination the reason he was where he was?

And where, exactly, are you? he asked himself out loud.

Nowhere essentially, he answered.

And where was Mina Malloy? Wasn't she nowhere, too? Though at least Mina was after a plan. A crazy, round-the-bend plan.

He looked at Logan in the rear view mirror. "Nuts. Totally nuts," he said.

He wondered if there was a particular age to go back to and start this ... thing. Seven, perhaps, when reason was supposed to suddenly engulf you.

Or maybe a particular situation, something you'd never really been able to understand, though even thinking about examining anything to do with Esther made his gut tight. And Roberta — examining all that might be helpful if he ever got married again, but it was a lot of trouble for something that might never happen.

His work life had been pretty straightforward. Always good with numbers, concepts, able to visualize a project from start to finish. He'd never been competitive enough to be seen as a rival, got along with everyone, made no enemies. Better engineers had passed on to better jobs. But his purpose for being there, first and foremost, had always been the two checks the firm direct-deposited every month.

Still, he'd done his job competently. Always got the raise due him. Satisfactory reviews. Though he had to take into consideration the fact he'd become disposable. Not to mention that he'd never seen it coming.

He shifted in his seat. This self-examination thing stunk.

A big red Caddy blew by him, doing ninety easy, an old peeling *Reagan/Bush* sticker waving goodbye on its bumper.

Ronnie Reagan. A decent enough chap. And to think he'd voted for the guy first time around, too. Not something he admitted anymore since it had turned out to be a little like taking out a contract on his own life.

But how could you not vote for the Gipper? For the guy in the cowboy hat and the jaunty neckerchief, the guy who took you weekly to the old West — the place America was all about. Plus he had it all — height, strength, ease, charm. Ronnie gave you a sense of solid, yes. At least before trickle-down economics. Before eleven thousand air traffic controllers got fired. As though the employees, the people who really did all the work, were lucky to be doing it. Easily replaced and, when you thought about it, largely expendable. August 5, 1981. The day all the young men who would be middle-aged in ten years started marching toward their doom. Golden handshakes for the lucky few. Pink slips for the unlucky majority. This notion that the worker didn't count anymore. That it was the CEOs who deserved the glory.

All thanks to Ronald Fucking Reagan.

It was more of the TV fantasy, all those macho men and their pretty little gals. The perfect families they played on the screen and made you believe in, even though, or was it *because*, your own was hell on wheels.

Down the street, Tommy's folks threw dishes at each other on a regular basis, Janet's mother hid Vodka in the toilet tank, Harold's father liked to hug little boys. But it was so easy to ignore it all and wish that Ron Reagan on horseback was your father and Mrs. Cleaver, who always understood, your mother. So easy.

Was it only in America? Did little kids who squatted in dumps popping maggots into their mouths have the comfort of fantasy? Though it didn't seem logical that you could imagine something that was outside your realm of experience. Which meant what … that fantasy was something imposed on you? A pleasant term for propaganda?

Ten miles down the highway Logan got tired of the view, made a few tiny circles in the back seat and curled up. Nate heard him sigh.

Going seventy, he passed a Polar Beverages truck. Mass license plates. Heading home, too. It made him think about the polar bear at Franklin Park, back when zoos were places with animals on display in small metal cages. There'd been no ecological conversion then, no idea of animal habitat or research or conservation or open range.

The polar bear was huge. In a cage that was so small the thing couldn't even turn around. No ice. No water. Ten hours a day of metal bars and cement. Yellowed fur, head down, drooling, locked in a kind of truncated dance … sideways, back, sideways, forward … over and over and over. Doing its daily hundred miles inside a ten by four crate.

He glanced at Logan in the rearview mirror. Like you, he thought.

The bear and the dog coping with the life they'd been handed. The bear pacing, Logan barking. And what was that endless dance, the continuous barking … was it complaint? Or just the expression of whatever possibility existed. Was that what most of us got locked into? Expression within the confines of our own personal cage? Real or imagined, but still a cage. Looking pathetic or ridiculous or both to those on the outside.

Of late, it seemed his own personal choice of expression had morphed into hiding. Not that he was alone in that. Not with Mina *in extremis* Malloy.

But no, that wasn't right. Because there she was, living on her chemical island, shunning the world yet counseling intense relations with the self. Consideration. Assessment. Evaluation. Mina Malloy was a *seeker*. And anyone who'd ever been a kid, knew you couldn't hide and seek at the same time.

So on one hand there was his own life — fuzzy, out-of-focus — but under a seeming normalcy — the degree, the marriage, the career, the basement workshop, the fatherhood, the brotherhood. Though he'd never looked one bit of it in the eye. Just banging off of everything like a pinball — random hits, lights going off, boings, points chalking up — and all of it as haphazard, arbitrary and accidental as hell. Nate Madigan, human ricochet.

Mina, on the other hand, wasn't a bouncer. She was the antithesis of making all the proper sounds and trajectories, didn't give a damn about racking up the points. She was setting out to become the paddle. The lever. The master of her own peculiar fate. She might not get wherever it was she wanted to go, but damn, at least she was trying. She, of all people — the real thing.

A circling hawk caught his eye and he watched it until it disappeared above the roof of the car. So if Mina was the genuine article, then that made him the fake. An expert in pretense, illusion, deception, trickery, a hoaxer, a cheat, a master of bullshit. Was it so obvious that everyone saw it ... Pris, Roberta, Kimberly? And now Mina. Though it was only Mina who saw it for exactly what it was. Cowardice.

Pris disdained him because she was convinced that while *she* was trapped, *he* had escaped. Roberta had ignored his shortcomings as long as he appeared to be keeping up his side of their bargain. And in K's eyes he was only now starting to slip. Though not because of what he *was*, but because of what he no *longer* was. Superdad, existing only to grant her every wish.

Esther, who cared not one whit who or what he was, who saw him only as an extension of herself, a third hand at the end of some twisted piece of cartilage, useless to her when it pulled free and crawled off to its own fractured destiny.

And Mina, with all her frustration, all her suffering and isolation. The least self-focused of any of them. In less than a month, she'd taken his measure, seen through him as clearly as she saw herself. Was that what it took to kill the ego? Did one have to be stripped of everything else first?

The image of a Phoenix came to mind. Something tough inside her that wouldn't give up and die, kept whispering inside her head — like she'd written on the wall of that abandoned building — *Do something. Do something. Do something.*

A station wagon passed and he thought, *turtle*. Turtle Bug Turtle Bug. The game he and Kimmy used to play on long trips. But now there were hardly any Beetles left on the road. Another good idea that had run its course.

He rubbed the back of his neck, stiff, cocked his head to one side, then the other. Logan's tail tapped the back seat twice.

So here he'd been asked to join someone in a first step back to life — maybe the purest request he'd ever been offered — and he'd refused it. Schlemiel. Nincompoop. Twerp. Schmuck.

Something Mina had considered for a thousand days and he'd dismissed it in an instant. And then, on top of everything else, he'd lectured her. About risk and danger. *He'd* lectured *her*. As though she knew nothing about them. No wonder she'd dismissed him. Sent him packing.

Shame spun through him like a logjam breaking, but instead of wriggling away as usual, this time he suffered it, suffered it for three long miles of highway, and then a half-mile further. Mina was right, he did need to go home. He had a sister and a daughter and an ex-wife and a mother and something to say to each one of them.

But first, he decided, he had something else to take care of.

He eased off the gas at the next one-mile-to-exit sign, slid the car across the lanes, made the loop back onto the highway heading north, thinking the whole time that it was possible the crazy blood his father had muttered about that day was finally claiming him, too. But ... what the hell.

CHAPTER EIGHTEEN

Long before he pulled up behind the house, Logan was bouncing from one side of the car to the other making excited whimpering noises, and when he'd turned off the ignition, Mina was standing in the kitchen doorway, her face full of genuine surprise.

Then a movement caught his eye. Something disappearing into the tall grass behind the shed. A cat. Maybe. Though it could have been anything.

"So," she said, both of them standing in the kitchen, "you're sure?"

"Well," he said, "yeah. I'm sure."

She looked at him. "That doesn't sound all that sure to me."

He shrugged. "It's something you should know. I'm never all that sure about anything. I'm an uncertain kind of person."

"You mean you lack confidence," she said, "what's the word for that?"

"Unconfident?"

"No," she shook her head, "when you're unsure of yourself."

"I don't know."

"You're a doubting Thomas."

"That's something totally different. I don't doubt you or what you say, I doubt myself."

She smiled. "A self-doubting Thomas."

He walked over to the kitchen cupboard where the calendar hung, and straightened it so May was no longer cockeyed. "When I was ten years old," he said, "me and my best friend Harold All were two angry young men. I had Esther, and Harold had a tic. He cocked his head constantly. No one could stand it except me. There was this other kid, Billy Baldini, who probably grew up to be a mob boss and had done nothing but bully us since the first day of fifth grade. And now it was June and we'd had about as much of him as we could take." He leaned back against the counter and folded his arms. "It was also youth baseball season, and Billy Baldini, who lived in a more unfortunate neighborhood than Harold and I and had a long hike across town to the playing field, always rode his bike down the same path through the woods to get to the games."

"I can see this is going to take some time," Mina said, "so if you don't mind I'm going to sit down." She went over to the table and pulled out a chair. Logan touched her hand with the tip of his tongue and lay down at her feet.

Nate stayed where he was, arms folded, comfortable. "We'd just finished a week of lessons on the martyrs at school," he said, "you know, Catholic school, nuns big on martyrs. And I'd been telling Harold, who was Unitarian and had never heard of martyrdom, all about it ... how they were roasted, boiled, flayed, garroted, you name it. And it gave us an idea. About Billy Baldini."

"Please tell me you didn't cook him," she said.

"We opted for garroting. One day we cut down Mrs. All's clothesline and strung it across the path, just about where we figured Billy's overly thick neck would be biking by."

She got a worried look on her face. "What happened?"

"Nothing. It occurred to us almost right after we strung it up that if it did what it was supposed to, our fingerprints were all over the rope. So we took it down."

He smiled a little. "So what I'm trying to say is ... glory's hard to come by and that's the closest I've ever been. Maybe it's time I gave it another shot." He went over to the table and sat down across from her. "Besides, there was something I wanted to tell you."

Her eyebrows went up.

"I took your advice," he said, "about self-examination. And like you said, you and ... who was it? Socrates? Franklin? Thoreau?"

"Socrates," she said.

"Well, I tried his advice, and it's going to take a little more practice, but I think I got the idea."

"You were only gone a couple of hours," she said. "That's not a lot of practice."

He looked at her. He hadn't expected criticism. "There are rules?" he said, "specific allotments of time?"

"No." She shook her head. "Of course not. I'm impressed. Really."

They sat there looking at each other. There were birds singing in the yard. Logan stretched and yawned.

"So," he said.

"So," she said.

He drummed his fingers once on the tablecloth. "Right. So go ahead and tell me exactly what you have in mind."

She made a face. "That's the problem. I don't have anything in mind. I think and think and it always comes to nothing." She glanced away, then back at him. "I'd hoped you'd help me figure it out."

"You have no ideas about how you want to do it?"

"Well yes, a few. But they've all turned out to be like most three o'clock-in-the-morning ideas." She shook her head, stood up. "C'mon, I'll show you."

He and Logan followed her out the kitchen door, across the yard toward the small wooden shed that was almost completely ringed with trees.

"One thing," he said, "we don't kill, maim, or inflict physical pain, right?"

"What do I look like," she said, "Madame Defarge?" and when he didn't say anything right away, she turned back and glanced at him.

"Madame who?"

"Defarge," she said, continuing toward the shed. "In *A Tale of Two Cities*." She turned half-way, showing that she was making motions with her fists. "She knit vengeance toward all. The book's in the stack under the middle window in the living room. You should read it."

He made a mental note, and at the same time noticed the Mina Malloy walking ahead of him. She didn't remind him of Mrs. Munster anymore. The new short hair, the brisk walk. The overalls were gone, replaced by pants and a bright purple oxford shirt. She made him think of a blurred picture suddenly brought into focus.

She unlocked the door and walked over to a table covered with a blue plastic tarp, picked up one corner of the tarp and folded it back. She rested the tips of her fingers on a multi-colored box with the black menacing silhouette of a man and a spray of purple rays advancing in his direction.

"This is a day/night camera," she said. "It's supposed to take pictures in pitch black with ultra-violet light. I tried it, but it doesn't work. All you get is black pictures with a hint of purple."

He went to pick up a good-sized flashlight beside the camera, but it was so much heavier than he expected, he almost dropped it.

"Careful," she said, "don't press the buttons. That's not a flashlight."

He set it down. "What the hell is it, a bazooka? It's heavy as hell."

It's a shooting net," she said. "You aim it, press those two buttons, and a net flies out and catches whoever you're aiming it at."

"You're kidding."

"It cost almost a thousand dollars. That's nothing to kid about."

He picked it up again in both hands, hefted it. "Does it work?"

"It did in the movie they showed me. But it only has one cartridge, and what if you miss? And how would you ever get the net back inside if you did?"

He set it down. "What's this?" He pointed to something about six inches long that looked vaguely like an inflated hard rubber condom.

"It's an exploding paint cartridge," she said. "And that," she pointed to something that looked like a battery charger, "is supposed to disable any engine that runs on an electric charge within a hundred feet of it."

"That's impossible," he said.

"I know." But I'd already bought it before I found that out."

He looked at the other things on the table. A coil of nylon rope, a book on tying knots, cans of pepper spray, an ice pick, a sack of sprouted potatoes, two walkie-talkies, a megaphone, and something that looked like a .22 but was really a starting pistol.

He picked up the pistol. "This is not a good idea," he said. "No one who carries a gun is going to get close enough to see it has no bore. And everyone else is going to see it as assault."

"Like I said," she shrugged, "three a.m."

He smiled, shook his head. "You know what you are? A really bad Q."

"Q?"

"James Bond. Q. The guy who invents all the gadgets."

"Oh," she said, "him."

"Except with you in the lab, Bond would never have made it out of *Dr. No* alive."

She put her hands on her hips. "You have suggestions then I hope?"

"Well," he said, deciding that the whole thing needed some perspective, "the exploding cigarettes from *You Only Live Twice* would be a nice touch. Or maybe the key chain from *The Living Daylights*," and when her face said she had absolutely no idea what he was talking about, "it emits a gas that renders your enemy helpless. The key chain. Course it can render you helpless, too, unless you happen to be wearing a gas mask. Which might tip off your target that something's up."

She frowned.

"I used to be a kind of James Bond aficionado," he said. He looked at the starter pistol he was still holding. "It was never quite the same after Connery left." He set the pistol down. "The cigarettes were easy to toss, lots of noise and good damage containment. And unless you put the key chain on 'explode', it was effective but non-lethal." He looked at her and laughed.

She crossed her arms. "Are you done?"

"Yes," he said, trying to look serious, but then he shook his head. "No, as a matter of fact, I'm not."

Her face didn't change and she kept her arms folded, but she took the tiniest step away. As if she needed just a little more distance between her and whatever it was he was about to say. And he didn't blame her. Because he'd heard it, too — a kind of alien sobriety in his voice that even *he* didn't recognize.

"I didn't mean to make fun of this," he said, gesturing at the table, "and I certainly wasn't making fun of you."

She put a hand up. "I didn't take it that way, Nate. Not really. Don't you think I know how it seems, how *I* seem?"

"But that's just it," he said, "I don't think you do. And I only said that stuff because ... because that's all I know how to do ... I mean, when I don't know what else to do." He cleared his throat. "I think it's a leftover from growing up with Esther. If I could make Pris laugh after Esther had done a number on us, then maybe we could both pretend it hadn't happened, that everything was better than it really was."

He stopped, frowned, because he'd never looked at it that way before.

"But that's not what I really wanted to say. What I *wanted* to say was that what you're trying to do is..." he struck around for the right word, "...commendable." Then he shook his head. "No, it's more than that. It's brave. And even if none of it works, it's more real, the thing behind it is more real, than anything a lot of people ever do — than anything I've ever done. And I just wanted you to know that." He stopped for a second. "It's not what you *seem*, Mina, it's what you *are*. And that's why I came back. Because of what you are. Who you are." He hesitated a second, then he nodded. "You're fine. You're absolutely fine."

And as soon as the word was out of his mouth, he wanted to take it back. He'd meant *fine* as in superior, first-rate, exceptional. But instead it had come out meaning flat and unremarkable, as in, *How was the movie? Oh, it was fine. And how about the spam sandwich, how was that? Fine, too?*

Her eyes had descended from his face to his waist to his knees to his shoes. And then to his horror, a drop, a tear? fell onto the floor near her feet and she took in a ragged breath. It was just the way Kim used to sound, as though her whole world had disintegrated and no effort would ever be enough to put it back together.

"Mina ... oh christ ... I'm sorry..." He took two steps toward her and took hold of her wrists while she shook her head and more tears began to drip. He stepped closer, put his arms around her, held her while she sobbed, for so long he wondered if she was ever going to stop.

"I'm sorry I'm sorry..." He kept saying it, because he was. Sorrier than she'd ever know. All he'd wanted was to make her feel better, and instead, he'd done the exact opposite.

"Look," he said, "we can do this. We'll come up with something. I mean, if you still want my help."

"Want your help?" she said into his shoulder, "why wouldn't I want your help?" She sniffed. She took a step away. Her eyes were red. And her nose. She wiped at her face with her purple sleeve.

"I didn't mean it, Mina — the way it came out. You're not fine. You're much more than...."

"You didn't mean it?" she said. "I'm not fine?"

"Well of course you're fine, but what I was trying to say was you're more than that. More than just *fine*."

"But don't you see that's all I want," she said, wiping her nose on her sleeve. I *want* fine. Fine isn't crazy. Fine isn't pain. Fine isn't grief. Fine is ... just *fine*. And no one has said *you're just fine* to me in a very very long time."

She wiped her nose one more time. And then he put his arms out to her, and she stepped right back into them, smiling her slightly crooked smile, and because her lips were only about an inch-and-an-eighth away, he went ahead and kissed them. And like the hug, it surprised him, the way she kissed right back.

CHAPTER NINETEEN

All he could think when he woke up the next morning was how much stranger could life get?

She was there next to him, looking, asleep, almost like a girl. Like someone who couldn't possibly have had even one of the things she'd told him about actually happen to her.

He watched her, the sheet rising and falling with her breathing, her hair mussed. And wouldn't you know ... Mina Malloy knew how to make love.

He came up on his elbow so he was looking down at her.

And christ, he'd been good, too. Helped, he supposed, by the long dry spell. But twice? When was the last time *that* had happened? And damn if he hadn't been good the second time, too.

Even Mina had said it. Not sounding surprised as much as awed by it all. Him, too. Awed.

He wanted to touch her but he didn't want to wake her. Wanted to touch her because she touched well. Sort of melted to him, against him. Soft. There was a word for that. He thought for a second. Cleave. She'd *cleaved* to him. So there was something to say for flesh that camouflaged bone and muscle.

And then there'd been that hunger. In both of them. Not just for the satisfaction or the arousal. More than that. For the closeness. Which made him realize exactly how lonely he'd been. Always.

A hint of a dream came back — Marilyn in that filmy white dress — the wax museum — the Charlotte's Web exhibit — the pig — Walter ... Willie ... Wilbur.

Mina made a little noise and turned her face toward him, seemed to sense him and opened her eyes.

"Oh," she said, and pulled the sheet up over her chin. "Good lord, not in full daylight."

"You have curly eyelashes," he said.

"Well, yes, I suppose I do." She brushed at her hair with one hand. "They used to be my best feature. Actually, my only good one."

He bent down and kissed her on the nose. "I think you have several."

She giggled, squeezed her eyes shut, opened them again. "You're still here! How did this ever happen?"

"Well," he said, "first, I kissed you, and then you kissed back. With your mouth open, by the way. And then I led you to your futon and unbuttoned your blouse..."

She put a finger against his lips. "I remember," she said, "believe me, I remember all of it. And you know what I meant. How did you come here and why did I let you in and why did I want you to stay and why did you stay. That last one, that's what I wonder most. Why on earth did you stay?"

He shook his head. "I think I was spelled."

She looked at him. "You think I put a spell on you?"

"Not you," he said, "something. I think we've both been spelled." He leaned down and kissed her. She tasted good. She sighed, reached up and put her arms around him. Good god. That cleaving again.

***

Was it his imagination, or had sex intensified his taste buds? The milk on his cereal looked like it always did, but man, how rich and sweet it tasted. He rolled it over his tongue. Astounding. And to think it came from a cow. And the oatmeal — some of it soft, some of it chewy, and all of it nattily delicious.

He picked up his glass of orange juice, able to smell it before it was anywhere near his nose. He took a sip and it exploded in his mouth, sweet and acid, tangy, the way it must have been the first time he ever tasted it.

"You know what I think?" he said.

She leaned toward him a little across the table, her robe opening so he could see the brown edge of one nipple. "No. What do you think?"

"I think you've turned my clock back." He pulled his eyes away from the nipple and looked around the kitchen. "Everything's so..." He struck around for the right word. "Fresh."

"I'm glad," she said.

"It's not that way for you?"

She sat back, poured some milk into her tea and stirred it. "I feel light," she said. "Not so much fresh. But if I jumped into a pool right now I think I'd float like a feather." She spread her arms and smiled at him, and another fragment of his Marilyn dream appeared and disappeared.

"Tell me about Piggy," he said, the outline of a plan suddenly in his head.

"Piggy?"

"Our chemical friend?"

"Oh." She put her arms down. "Piggy." She took a sip of her tea. "Well, he lives a town over. His real name is Peter, but no one ever calls him that. And I already told you that after he dumps his poison in the river, he heads straight to the Casino and gambles all night. Mainly Blackjack."

He took another spoonful of oatmeal. "Does he really look like a pig?"

She shrugged. "Maybe. A little. But it's not his looks that got him the name, it's his habits."

"Guy's a slob."

"Complete and utter." She picked up her tea and held the mug in both hands just beneath her lips. "His place is a sty. You know, everything he's ever owned and used spread around the yard — cars, washing machines, thing-a-ma-bobs." She took a sip. "He ran a tire dump in his back field for years. Had a mountain of them as tall as his barn until just a while ago. They caught fire I don't know how many times, and the town finally told him to get rid of them." She shrugged. "I guess he made an attempt, but half of them are still there. About the only thing he has going for him is keeping cats. Strays." She shook her head. "But he doesn't spay or neuter, so they're constantly multiplying. It's a cat zoo."

"Anything else?"

She thought for a second. "He lives alone. Was married once, a long time ago. The story is she was a mail-order bride and after a couple of months she ran off."

"The glow didn't last?"

She laughed. He liked to hear her laugh.

Logan came out from under the table and sat with his eyes on Mina, the easy touch. Sure enough, she tore a corner off her toast and held it out to him.

"Is he mean?"

"Supposedly that's why the mail order bride disappeared."

"Does he ever go to the Wax Museum?"

"Piggy?" She shrugged. "I don't know. I've never seen him there."

"The dumping, is it noisy, loud?"

"The pumping out is, yeah."

"Would you have to yell to make him hear you? *That* loud?"

She nodded. "Maybe."

"What does he do while he's pumping?"

"He leaves. I mean, he walks away a fair distance. Who'd want to stand there and breathe *that* in? He walks off and smokes a couple of cigarettes. Not cigarettes. Those foul-smelling cigars is what he smokes. Stogies."

"How far off?"

"Nate ... for Pete's sake what's all this about? Why do you want to know how far away he walks?"

"Because if I'm going near his truck, I want to be sure I can do it without him seeing or hearing me."

"Going near his truck? While he's dumping? While he's right there?" She put one hand to her forehead. "You can't do that!" She looked at him for a second. "My god, it's rubbed off on you. I've gone and made *you* crazy, too." She shook her head. "No. Whatever it is, Nate, whatever you're thinking, you can't do it. We can't do it."

For a second, he wasn't sure he'd heard right. He sat back in his chair. "Can't do it? What do you mean, 'can't do it'?"

He counted off six seconds of silence, felt his fledgling sense of purpose swaying beneath him. "I thought this was important to you, Mina. Important enough to risk everything for — isn't that what you said?"

After a while she nodded. "But..." She massaged one temple like she was getting a headache. "So far it's only been this *thing* floating in my imagination, and here you're making it..." her eyes moved off his, then back again, "real." She said the last word so softly he almost didn't catch it.

"Real," he repeated.

Another silence. Then she laced her fingers together on the edge of the table. "You said you did some thinking after you left yesterday. That it made you decide to come back. Well, some time after you arrived on my doorstep, I made a decision, too. To try and get a grip on what's real and what's not. Because it hit me that I wasn't sure anymore. So I began *defining* everything." She held up two fingers. "Real, not real." She laced her fingers back together.

"And I think I'm going to have keep doing it for a long time before I'm absolutely sure I know the difference."

She stopped and he waited.

"The birthday party the night you arrived? Not real. You knocking on the door. Real. Though for days there was always the chance it wasn't. That you weren't real at all. Logan..." She glanced down at him. "Real." She looked back at Nate. "Having a conversation with Ben. Not real. Buying a present for Lydia's birthday." She sighed. "Not real. And this notion about stopping Piggy." She moved her head to one side, shrugged. "It wasn't real, Nate. Not anymore than the birthday party. It's just been something..." she shrugged, "...for me to live on I guess. But I need to see that. I need to know that I know the *difference*. Or else..."

She left the sentence unfinished, and a look he hadn't seen in a while was in her eyes again. Lost. Scared. And christ, it would almost be funny, if it wasn't so damn sad. Because just yesterday, there was Mina pressing on, and him putting on the brakes, and now it was him pushing forward and Mina yelling *stop!*

He nodded. "Okay," he said. "I get it. Though I don't think you're alone about not being sure what's real and what isn't. Sure, there are things that aren't real. Or at least never will be again, much as we want them. But on the other hand, where do the real things start? Last night, for instance, us, was that real?"

"Of course," she said.

"Well, it wasn't when I first got it in my head a whole lot earlier than yesterday. All there was before yesterday was the unlikely *chance* of it."

The corners of her mouth turned up.

"What Piggy's doing," he said, "that's real, isn't it?"

She nodded.

"So if what he's doing is real, then making him quit, that would have to be real, too. And even if it didn't work, the trying would be real. Agree?"

She seemed to consider it, then she said, "agree."

"So I say that's what we do. We try. I know it's a cockamamie idea. That there's more of a chance it won't work than it will. But there's a chance it just might. So doesn't that make it worth trying?"

Again he counted the seconds of her silence, and then she nodded.

"Good," he said, "so we'll try." He sat forward. "And where were we…? Oh yeah, Piggy seeing me. Well, you've been spying on him, and I guess that was for real?"

"That was for real."

"Well, he never saw *you,* and all I need is access to his truck for five minutes. Just five minutes. And one more thing, too. Directions to his sty."

Her eyes got wide. "His *sty*? Why for heaven's sake? Why would you need to go *there*?"

"Because," he said, "we can try to get him on the dumping. But if, as you say, nobody cares or the people who should care will do nothing, then there has to be some other way. Remember how they got Capone?"

"Al?" She narrowed her eyes. "Bootlegging? Murder? Extortion?"

"Tax evasion."

She nodded slowly. "Oh right. It *was* tax evasion. So your plan is to break into his sty and find his sloppy tax returns."

He grinned. "Sort of."

She leaned toward him. "What are you thinking, Mr. Madigan? Exactly."

"I'm thinking that in addition to providing some simple but emphatic proof of Piggy's illegal dumping — on the chance that somebody will do something about it — there needs to be something else. Piggy needs to commit some *other* crime. Something so sensational it can't be ignored. And since we can't count on Piggy doing that all by himself, then we're going to have to frame the bastard."

"Frame the bastard," she repeated.

He sat back and folded his arms. "I think most of it came to me in a dream, and I still haven't figured out how to connect him to the site. But the frame — I know exactly how we're going to do that."

Logan's head appeared and Mina gave him another piece of her toast without taking her eyes off Nate's face.

"There's going to be a theft. Actually, a repeat of a theft. We're going to steal Marilyn."

Her brows contracted toward each other and her eyes widened at the same time. "Monroe? From the Wax Museum? Are you kidding?"

He shook his head. "No. I mean — how hard can it be if it's already been done twice?"

"Why on earth would we do that?"

"Because *she's* the frame. You said her disappearance was a big deal. Bigger each time it happened. Think how big it'll be when it happens again. Except *this* time they're going to catch the thief."

She leaned forward a little. "We're going to steal Marilyn and let them catch us?"

"Not us, Mina. Piggy. They're going to catch Piggy."

"You think *he* stole Marilyn?"

"I have no idea who stole Marilyn, but *this* time there's going to be no question that it was Piggy."

She sat back with a little moan. "And you laughed at my shooting net."

"What's the security like?" he said. "I mean, it must stink if they already walked off with her twice."

"Well maybe it *did* stink," she said, "but since the thefts they had to tighten it up or lose their insurance. There are cameras, alarms, I don't know what else."

"But you come and go whenever you want."

"When it's open I do. Or nights when Owl Woman is working late. I'm sort of a benefactor. But I don't have keys. I don't own the place."

"Oh," he said.

They sat there looking at each other.

"Then we're going to need more information," he said, "and probably some help." He drank the last of his orange juice. "A kind of inside operative." He drummed his fingers on the table. "Owl Woman. She's got a stake in making this thing work. You have to talk to her, Mina, get her to help."

She was staring at him as though she'd never seen him before. "Owl Woman?" She wrapped her arms across her chest. "Oh no. I can't do that. Not in a million years." She shook her head. "No. No. Definitely no."

He slid one hand, palm up, across the table and waited until she reluctantly unwrapped one arm and put her hand palm down on top of his. "Here's what I know," he said. "You're not crazy. I'm not crazy. And this thing ... *it's* not crazy. We can do this. We *need* to do this."

"Nate..." An actual look of pain crossed her face. "I don't even *know* Owl Woman. We've never said more than a dozen words to each other. I can't talk to her. I can't talk to anyone. I've ... I'm pretty sure I've forgotten how."

"You talk to me."

"I know." She shook her head. "And it makes no sense."

"But you know all about her. Her real name — the native thing — the glowing water — all the stuff about Piggy."

"But *she* didn't tell me any of that. It was her uncle. Roy. *He* told me. Roy and I worked together on a farm back when Ben and I and the kids used to live here. And last summer, when I was tracking Piggy, Roy was out there. Nearly scared me to death. Though Roy didn't even seem surprised, like it was entirely normal running into each other in the middle of the night in the middle of nowhere after a dozen years."

She stopped for a second.

"You know, he was one of the few people who didn't actually live here who supported us. Came to the protests, every single one. Quiet. Never called attention to himself. I remember at the farm one of the cows kicked him and he just shook it off and kept on working. 'A scratch,' I think he said. And then the next morning he showed up with a cast. A broken wrist." She shook her head. "Some scratch."

Logan's head appeared again and she took the last corner of her toast and gave it to him. "Last bite," she said.

"Anyway," she looked back at Nate, put her hand palm down on his again, "he appears all of a sudden, near the river, stands there for a second and then just sits down beside me — like it was a meeting we'd both arranged." She shook her head. "I'll never forget the first thing he said — *a long time has gone by but I'm still sorry to this day for what happened to your family.* Then he asked if I knew it was still going on, the polluting, and I said yes, and he told me about Sally — Owl Woman — about everything he'd tried to do. About Piggy."

She pressed her finger against a crumb on the table, brushed it off onto her plate. "Then he just got up and left. I don't even think he said goodbye. Made me wonder in the morning if it had been a dream." She shook her head, smiled a little. "Real or not real? I'm pretty sure it was real. Later on I remembered someone at the farm saying he'd done time, been in jail. But there's not a thing about him that would scare you. In fact, the exact opposite."

She went silent for a second, then got a funny look on her face. She lifted her hand off his and slapped his palm. "Nate, we don't need the Marilyn at the museum. We already have one. The one we found that day in the building."

"Yeah," he said, "we're going to need her, too. But the one at the museum has to disappear because we know it'll cause a stir. And that's what we need. A really big stir."

She slid her hand off his.

"Mina."

She looked at him.

"Will you trust me? It would be good to have someone trust me for a change."

Slowly, she put her hand back on his, and he covered it with his other hand, and then she put her other hand on top of his and they both laughed.

"A pact," she said.

And he nodded.

CHAPTER TWENTY

On Mondays and Thursdays Owl Woman cleaned and waxed the floors and spritzed the thick viewing glass on each display inside and out. Not just the quick sweep and swipe she did before she left other evenings. A good four or five-hour stint.

It meant Mina could count on Monday and Thursday wax-family visits with no tourist footsteps outside the door, no laughter drifting through, no conversation. Just her and Ben and the kids two nights a week. Owl Woman would let her in with a nod and she'd let herself out when she was done, the rear door to the building clicking shut behind her, Owl Woman's nod and her own 'thank you' the only interactions. Easy.

But as she approached the door this Thursday, with a chill in the air and the sun newly sunk below the hills, she was feeling butterflies, had been the whole drive over, struggling with it, this thing she didn't know how to do anymore. Talk. Conspire. Relate. Why on earth had Nate asked her and why on earth had she said yes.

"Because, you fool," she muttered to herself, "he thinks it's what you want. Isn't it what you want?"

Beside her, Logan glanced up. "It's okay," she whispered, "just me yelling at myself."

It was something her mother would have said ... *Careful what you wish for, missy, cuz you just might get it.*

She pictured a see-saw. Mina up, Nate down. Nate up, Mina down.

Okay, it *was* what she wanted, what had kept her going for the last couple of years. Except the wanting was one thing, and the doing ... well, that's the thing that had her stymied.

Logan shook his head beside her knee and the metal leash clinked. It was the only way she'd been able to get herself out the door and into the car, holding on to Logan's leash. Her very own four-legged talisman.

With Nate it was different, had been from her first look at him. She'd been way out of touch then; almost, she supposed now, lost. But there'd been that acceptance in Nate's eyes, something she understood better now, knowing something of his past. And of course there'd been Logan.

But Owl Woman, she was another story.

Mina saw the museum sign, dark now, and slowed her steps. Logan looked up, those brown eyes saying he was willing to slow down, too ... willing to do anything she asked.

She stopped in front of the shuttered glass door and Logan sat, his body turned toward her, his mouth open, panting slightly, waiting.

Just keeping herself there took effort, and knocking twice — well, that was going to be nearly impossible. Besides, there was the other thing, too. She was going to have to face *them*. And she couldn't shake the feeling they'd know. Know she'd betrayed Ben yet again. And the kids, too. Because didn't it mean they weren't enough anymore? Grabbing a little life? What right did she have?

She was standing there with her head down, staring at the gum-marked concrete when the museum door swung open. It surprised her enough that she almost lost her balance, made Logan jump up.

"Have to knock louder," Owl Woman said. "Didn't hear you."

Mina looked at her, cocked her head sideways toward the dog. "Is it okay?"

First, Nate in tow. Now, a dog. Too much for even this unflappable Mohawk.

Owl Woman opened her mouth, but nothing came out. She extended a hand toward Logan, who stuck out his tongue and delicately touched the knuckle of her thumb, then looked up at her with a 'pleased to meet you, too' look on his face.

"Course," Owl Woman said.

Mina put her hand in her jacket pocket and gripped her key, walked past Owl Woman, Logan's nails clicking toward the Employees Only door. She knew she should turn around and say something now — *When will you be done? I need to talk to you about something.* A simple thing to say.

But just like Owl Woman, she couldn't get the words out. Then came an unignorable sliver of relief at the chance Owl Woman would be gone before she emerged from the family room. And then came a swelling of guilt.

She gripped the Employees Only doorknob, inserted the key, let Logan go in first and closed the door behind her. She stood there with her back against the door for a second in the dark, then reached for the switch and felt everything melt away under the rush of pleasure when she saw their faces.

"I've brought a surprise," she said.

She walked a circle, touching a face, an arm. "This is Logan. Isn't he just like our McDuff?"

Logan sniffed at each figure, at the floor, at the chairs they sat in. Not even the hint of a tail wag. So ... they didn't seem to conjure 'people' in his mind.

She let the leash go and sat down across from Ben.

How she'd ached to join them — for days months years. But something always stopping her. *Coward,* she'd hiss at herself in the mirror.

For a time, she decided it was her fate, her purgatory. But now...

Logan came and stood beside her and she put one hand on his back.

"I'm so sorry, Ben," she said. "It's just that these last few weeks, waking up and not thinking, *oh god, another day to get through*. I feel guilty as hell if that helps." She looked at him. The pose had caught him laughing, but that wasn't really Ben. Oh, he'd had things that made him happy — his music, the kids — but mainly, he'd been a serious man.

"Remember the time you told me I sparkled?" she said. "That was something I've always remembered." She smiled. "Me, sparkling." She hesitated. "There's something else ... I can't figure out if it's important or just plain nuts. You know, one of those things that's so much better in the planning than the doing? It probably won't work, so is it even worth trying? Is it worth the risk?"

She knew what his answer would be. "No way." Always the pragmatist. "Give it up, babe," he'd say. "The odds aren't in your favor. They hardly ever are. Just try to control the things you can. Believe me, doing that's hard enough."

She looked over at Scotty, that rascally sparkle in his eyes, thinking how he used to make her half-crazy — the calls from the teachers — *He's taken the class away from me, Mrs. Malloy. And he's absolutely unrepentant about it.* The time he and Alex Howe put the smoke bomb in the school piano because it was the first day of spring and wasn't it better that the whole school spent it standing out in the parking lot instead of in some dark smelly classrooms?

Always pushing a little too far, a little too fast. As though he knew he had to cram it all into a too-short time.

"Oh, honey," she said, "I know *you'd* do it." With bells. The crazier, the better. She leaned toward him and wrapped her hand around his wrist. Impatient, eager. Her boy. God, how she missed him.

"And you, Sweetie," she said, turning toward Lydia.

Her little shadow. The same inflections in their voices, the same lift of one eyebrow when things weren't going their way. "You and your Ma," Ben would say, "two peas in a pod."

She cringed thinking what kind of role model she'd been these last few years. Hiding, forgetting who she was, disappearing little by little.

Is that what she would have wanted for Liddy? If things had been different, if Liddy had been the survivor would she have come and whispered 'give up' in her daughter's ear?

She ran her hand along Logan's soft back, patted him twice, and sat there for a long time until finally she stood up and walked the circle again, touching, giving three kisses. She was just about to turn off the light when she remembered something, pivoted back toward Ben. "I heard a wonderful trumpet," she said, "on the radio. I memorized his name. Wynton Marsalis. Marsalis, Ben. Ellis's boy. I'll get a tape and bring it next time."

She turned back to the door, took hold of the knob, then looked over her shoulder at them one more time. Real. Oh god yes, they were so real. Then, *had* been, she corrected. *Had* been so real. Once.

After a second she turned the knob, clicked off the light, clucked her tongue to Logan and walked him out into the museum.

Owl Woman was a dozen feet away spritzing the queen's glass cage.

Mina took a breath. "When will you be finished?" she said.

Owl Woman stopped in mid-spritz, droplets falling through the air.

"The thing is," Mina said, "I need to talk to you … maybe we could get a cup of coffee?"

For a long second, Owl Woman stood as frozen as the queen, then turned her head. Logan's tail wagged.

"It's important," Mina said, "else I wouldn't ask. I know you want to get home."

Owl Woman nodded. "About fifteen minutes."

"I'll put the dog in the car and meet you across the street."

She went down the back hall, past the door to the storage room, and out the back door into the alley, heard the lock click behind her.

Not easy, no. But not as hard as she'd imagined.

***

"My Uncle Roy," Owl Woman said, "has a big mouth."

"He's discouraged," Mina said. "Frustrated. After everything that happened here, and still it goes on."

Owl Woman set her coffee down on the green formica table.

There was only one other customer in the donut shop. He was sitting near the door with his head in a newspaper. *Space Shuttle Discovery places Hubble Telescope into Orbit* the front page announced. There was awful music coming out of the speakers, Madonna or that Jackson girl, Michael's sister. God, how Ben would hate it.

"He's an old fool," Owl Woman said. "He has no right carrying our stories outside our circle."

"What do you think would have happened if we hadn't carried *our* stories outside *our* circle," Mina said. "Back then. Would there be healthy children playing in every Love Canal yard today? Edible flowers sprouting in the streets?"

Owl Woman lowered her eyes to the table.

Mina sighed. Such a wonderful way to enlist someone's help. With bitterness, sarcasm. "I didn't mean that," she said. "But don't you think I know how you feel? We were disrespected, too. Completely disregarded. No one paying a lick of attention to us for years. *Years.* If there hadn't been hundreds of us. If it hadn't become overwhelmingly unignorable..." she shrugged.

"Then why would he go to them expecting anything?" Owl Woman said. "One old man. Why would he go to them at all? And why would he talk to you."

Mina leaned forward. "Because we're on the same side. We want to see it stopped. Roy. You. Me. My friend."

"With tests and complaints."

"And your floating pots of burning sage? Have they worked?"

Owl Woman tensed and again Mina wanted to give herself a kick in the ass. If Owl Woman got up and walked out, what exactly was *that* going to accomplish? Mina rubbed the spot between her eyebrows where a headache was gathering. Ever since Owl Woman had slid into the red naugahide booth across from her, she'd listened to herself feeling her way through the conversation like a blind person. Missing all the right turns.

"Look," she said, "that was a stupid thing to say. I've been alone so long, I'm not good at this talking thing anymore. Besides, there was a time I was willing to try anything, too."

She looked into her coffee mug, still three-quarters full, too much half and half, tasteless.

"Back then," she said, "it was the women who did it. We were fighting for our children. Their survival." She hesitated. "It didn't work for all of us. But even if I'd known what was going to happen to me, I still would have fought along with them. I'm trying to do it again and it may not work. But my friend and I are going to try. And we need your help."

Owl Woman said nothing, but her eyes had lifted from the table so Mina kept going. "We have a plan. We need to — borrow something — from the museum. We need your help to do it. You don't have to do anything that will risk your job. But we need to know some things about the museum. And I guess I don't have to ask that you'll keep it inside *our* circle."

The man with the newspaper pushed back his chair, stood up and left with his paper tucked under his arm. Owl Woman finished her coffee, probably cold now, then she nodded at Mina. "Okay," she said. She sat back, pulled the two edges of her sweater together and buttoned the top button. "And from now on," she said, "call me Sally."

CHAPTER TWENTY-ONE

Mina took her coffee out onto the back steps. The top step was a capstone, warm from the sun, and that's where she sat. The sky was azure, just enough of a breeze to rustle the new leaves. She felt … well, she wasn't sure how she felt. Strange. Different. She'd gotten so used to the hours feeling like lead that she couldn't fit into this new — this sense that time had acquired a vitality. Purpose. Anticipation. Such foreign words. She blew on the coffee and took a sip. Still too hot. She set it down beside her on the step.

Nate had left a note. Up early so he could go into town for some things. She looked at her watch. Almost eleven-thirty. She'd slept late. The coffee klatch with Owl — with Sally— thank God that was over. She looked at her watch again.

Logan came trotting from the bushes and plomped himself down on the grass. She leaned over and patted him between the shoulders. "What would I have done without you last night, huh boy?" His tail brushed back and forth.

She closed her eyes, concentrated on the sun touching her face. Was she always going to feel like this? Did she dare trust it?

Logan made a noise and she opened her eyes. He was looking toward the bushes, ears up, body tensed. "That you, Mrs. D?" she called out. But there was no answering mew and after a few seconds, Logan lowered his head onto his paws. If Mrs. D did come home, sashaying across the yard, tail high, yellow eyes narrowed, would the cat even recognize her? Was that what was keeping her away? This stranger who only looked like Mina Malloy?

Or was it nothing more than Logan's presence. She looked at him, his eyes half-shut, resting but alert. "Well, Mrs. Dalloway," she said, "you're going to have to adjust to this beast or never see your rocking chair again. Because he's here for as long as he cares to stay."

She picked up the mug and took another sip. It was just right now.

Last night, after she and Sally had headed in opposite directions, she'd gone to the car and leashed Logan, waited while he stretched and then jumped carefully out from the back seat.

Even though it had been close to midnight, sitting behind the wheel and driving home felt impossible. She'd felt edgy, prickly, all her neurons firing.

So she'd headed for the little tourist park off the town center, walked it three times around. Chilly, deserted at that hour, but she'd needed the motion, the time to let things settle.

The evening felt like it had lasted a week. With much much more having happened than any minute-by-minute reenactment could ever show. By the odometer, she'd traveled about twelve miles to get into town. But, god, it felt more like she'd been gone a lightyear.

And then there was that eerie sense that when she *did* get back in the car to drive home, she'd never really get there. At least not to the same place she'd left. Or maybe it wasn't the place. Maybe it was her. *She* was different. And she was pretty sure she'd never go back to who she was just three hours before. A good thing.

The heat from the mug warmed her hands, she took a sip, breathed in the comfort of the smell. Nearby a jay screeched and Logan's head came off his paws.

"A ceremony's what we need," she said, and Logan looked at her. "You know, to acknowledge the new me."

Then his ears perked, he let out a little cry, and he was standing, his tail wagging when Nate's car came around the side of the house.

"Paint," Nate said, setting the gallon can on the kitchen counter. "Crossing Guard Yellow." He reached into one of the bags and took out two pieces of metal pipe, which he stood on end, then four metal end caps, then a plastic baggie with six metal blocks inside that sounded denser than they looked when he set them on the counter, a roll of clear plastic tubing, and a smaller baggie with white plastic thingies inside.

"Should be something else in here," he said, upending the bag over the counter.

A can of shoe polish fell out onto its edge and started to roll. She picked it up. "I haven't seen a can of shoe polish in so long." She twisted the opener and the top popped off. She took a sniff. "My father used to polish his good shoes every Saturday night for church on Sunday." She smiled. "I used to beg him to let me do it, and sometimes he'd let me put the polish on, but he always had to shine them himself." She snapped the lid back on.

"I called Pris," Nate said.

There was a smile in his eyes that usually wasn't there after those Friday phone calls.

"And before I even asked her how she was, she said there was someone there waiting to talk to me."

"Ah. Kimberly," Mina said.

He nodded. "So she says, 'Hi Daddy, it's me,' like I wouldn't know. And then she says, 'Thanks for all the letters. They're funny. I'm saving them. Oh, and I'm all set with UMass. Mimi Sarantopolis and I are rooming together. We went shopping yesterday and bought a whole bunch of stuff for our room.'"

His relief might as well have been written across his forehead in Crossing Guard Yellow.

"Then she said her mother sold her cookbook and if it hits the best seller list maybe she can transfer to Wellesley next year, except she doesn't really care about Wellesley all that much anymore. And then she wanted to know when was I coming home."

Mina didn't say anything, just looked at him.

"I told her I'd see her soon. A few days before her graduation."

"I'm glad." She said it like she meant it. Which she did. Though not completely. Because if he went home, would he come back?

She looked at the things on the counter, picked up one of the metal pipes and fit an end piece onto it. Nate took a propane torch out of the second bag, a roll of duct tape, a roll of solder, and then an opened package of shortbread cookies. The sudden buttery smell made her think of the Christmas cookies she and the kids used to make, staying up late, Scottie and Lydia pressing out tiny Christmas trees and snowmen and angels and Santas, dousing them with too much red and green sugar crystals while she manned the oven. That one was real. Just not anymore.

"Shortbread cookies," she said, "I love shortbread cookies." She put the pipe down and slid a cookie out of the package. It snapped just right when she bit it, slightly crumbly, slightly crisp.

"I think I thought of everything," he said. "Solder the ends on, drill a bunch of holes, fill them with paint." He took one of the metal blocks out of its bag. "With the magnets, they should snap right up into the front wheel wells." He mimed with the magnet. "Boomp Boomp. One above each front tire."

"Piggy's tires."

"Piggy's tires." He hefted the magnet on his open palm. "I just hope the pull strength is adequate." He took it between two fingers and lowered it slowly until it sucked one of the pipes right up off the counter.

"That works," she said.

He had to strain to pull the pipe and magnet apart. "Yeah, but you have to take the weight of the paint into consideration. And the condition of the metal above the wheel well." He shrugged. Then he looked at her and smiled. "Guess we'll find out, huh?"

She brushed the cookie crumbs off her hand. "And this is going to do what exactly?"

"Turn Piggy's tires an arresting shade of..." He glanced at the paint can.

"Crossing Guard Yellow," they both said at the same time.

"Plus," he said, "leave a compelling tread mark leading from the dump site. Or at least that's the idea."

"So you really intend to go right up to his truck while he's twenty feet away."

He picked up the shoe polish. "Thought you said fifty to a hundred? Besides, this will help. Black face, black neck, black hands. And of course black clothes. With the noise, he'll never know I was there. Then, I was thinking maybe a letter, with photos, to the *Niagara Times*."

"There *is* no *Niagara Times*."

"Well, whatever passes here for the *Niagara Times*. By then, the story will have broken about Marilyn, who will be found in Piggy's sty along with her sister, Marilyn 2."

"And the two Marilyns will get there...?"

"While Piggy's gambling away his profits, of course. Quick in, quick out." He took a cookie out of the package. "Then somebody has to *discover* them ... haven't quite figured that one out yet. But we'll get there."

She didn't know what to say. She picked up the small baggie with the little thingies inside.

"Plugs for the holes," he said. "They get pulled out just before the cylinders go in place."

She knew if she half-tried she could come up with ninety-nine 'what ifs'. But in her strange new state of mind, the whole thing sounded strangely doable. So she reached for another cookie and chewed in silence while Nate read the propane canister.

"So tell me again," he said, "what Owl Woman told you. You were a little sketchy last night."

"Sally," Mina said, "she wants to be called Sally, and I was a little more than sketchy. I was almost totally incoherent." She drew circles with the cookie beside her head. "But I'm better now."

"Yeah," he said. "You looked a little beside yourself." He bent down and gave her a kiss. "But you did it."

They smiled at each other and then his smile faded. "It's the back door that's the problem, isn't it," he said.

She took a last bite, brushed the crumbs off her fingers. "It's keyless. Opens only from the inside. Since that's how they got in the last two times, that's where they spent the money. This new door is pry proof."

"Or it's supposed to be."

"She said the cameras are a joke. The ones inside are dummies and the ones outside the front and rear doors don't work and haven't for months. Roy does repairs there from time to time and he'd been changing the film cassettes, but then they ran out and none have been ordered."

They each reached for another cookie.

"She said as far as the owners are concerned the new back door is enough."

He leaned against the counter, frowning, took a bite, crossed his arms.

Logan had been sitting at attention watching the cookies disappear and now he put one paw on Mina's leg. "You can't have one," Mina told him, "they're not good for your teeth."

Logan blinked at her then lay down between them, sighed.

"I want you to come," he said.

"Of course I'll come. You can't do this all by yourself."

"No. I mean Boston. The graduation's on the tenth, so I thought we could leave around the fourth. Take our time. See things on the way."

She found that she really didn't want the third cookie she was holding and slid it back inside the package. "Nate..."

"Uh-oh ... I don't like hearing my name said that way. It usually means I'm going to hear something I don't want to."

"I appreciate," she said, "very very *very* much that you want me to come. But it's not the right time. Not yet. For one thing your daughter wants *you* there, not you and some strange woman. But mostly — you have to understand I'm not ready. Not nearly. You have no idea how hard last night was, just talking to Sally, initiating that. The hardest thing I've done in a long long time. It actually..." she laughed a little, patted her chest, "...it gave me palpitations. Not that I shouldn't have done it or that you shouldn't have expected me to — I *needed* to do it. I did. It was hard, but it was important. Not just for this, but for me." She picked up the bag of plugs, tilted the bag so they all slid from one corner to the other. "But it was *just* a step, Nate. Going to Boston — well, that's a lot more than a step." She tilted the bag in the other direction so all the plugs rolled back again. "I need time, Nate. That's just the way it's going to be. You go and enjoy the graduation. Enjoy being with your daughter."

"You wouldn't have to come with me that day. You and Logan could do something else. See the city, take a walk on the beach." He bent down a little so she had to look him in the eye. "Think about it? Promise me that?"

She nodded. And when his attention went back to the propane directions, she watched him for a while, knowing that thinking about it wasn't going to make a difference. She wasn't ready for that particular kind of test. Plus, as much as she didn't want to think about it, it was going to be a test for Nate, too. So he could discover where he really wanted to be, needed to be. And when he discovered that answer, he needed to be on his own.

"You can't use the shoe polish," she said. "There's naphtha, carbon black, ethylene glycol — that's the stuff they put in antifreeze — turpentine, and you can't be absorbing that stuff through your pores. I'll get you something else."

He mumbled an okay, and she put the bag of plugs on the counter and went back outside, sat down on the step. The sun had moved, but the air was warmer. She picked up her coffee cup, still mostly full, gone cold now, and was bending over, pouring it into the grass when the cat was suddenly brushing against her leg.

"Mrs. Dalloway!" she said, "where have you been?" The cat jumped up into her lap, arching its back, pushing its head against her chest, humming, and behind her, on the other side of the screen door she could hear Logan's nails tapping the floor, his breath coming in pants.

"So this is Mrs. Dalloway," Nate said, behind her. "Don't worry, I've got hold of his collar."

"Yes," Mina said. "This is Mrs. Dalloway."

"Mina..." Nate said her name low and in a tone she'd never heard him use before, a kind of warning, which made her glance up from the cat, and there, only a few feet away, was Roy — with his gray pony tail, his standard moccasins, his beat-up Tilley hat.

He nodded at her.

"It's okay," she said over her shoulder to Nate. "It's Sally's uncle. Roy." She waved a hand toward Nate. "Roy, this is my friend. Nate Madigan."

Behind her, the door flew open and hit her in the back. She jumped up, stumbling sideways off the step, Mrs. Dalloway leaped away from her, and Logan pulled Nate out the door and down the steps before breaking loose. The dog flew across the yard after the cat, who by then was nothing more than a blur, Nate after them, shouting. But just before Mrs. Dalloway hit the bushes, she stopped dead, turned, her back arched, her tail sticking straight up, her teeth bared, looking for all the world like a Halloween caricature, and Logan hit the brakes, swerved to one side, and turned into a statue about four feet away from her.

Nate stopped yelling. He and Mina and Roy watched as the cat took one step toward the dog and the dog took one step back.

In an instant, all the energy in the back yard changed. Mrs. D's back went flat, though her tail stayed high, the tip of it twitching back and forth, and she walked back the way she'd just fled, passing Logan as though he'd suddenly ceased to exist. Logan shook his head as if he'd been sprayed in the face with a hose, and Mrs. Dalloway came back to Mina, purring, rubbing against her legs.

"That's one impressive cat," Nate said.

Mina laughed. "I think she's just nuts."

"It's always a good thing to be reminded that David slew Goliath," Roy said.

Mina and Nate swung around to look at him and for a second no one said anything.

Roy cleared his throat. "I'm sorry to come this way. To this place. Unannounced. Though it seemed necessary..." He looked from Mina to Nate and back again. "I came to offer my help."

CHAPTER TWENTY-TWO

"This door," Nate said, "is impregnable. No edges to pry against, no key hole, no knob, no nothing. Plus it looks like six solid inches of titanium."

They stood there in the moonlit back alley behind the museum and stared at the door.

"It could be left ajar," Roy said.

Nate shook his head. "Absolutely not. There can't be any question of guilt on Owl Woman — I mean, Sally. Or anyone else who works here. There has to be an obvious break-in from the outside or the whole thing's no good."

They continued staring, as if the door itself might deliver up a solution. Was this, Nate wondered, where it all came to a screeching halt?

Roy had picked Nate up down the street from Mina's house just outside the broken gate, had been waiting with his headlights out when Nate got there. Though with the full moon so bright, who needed headlights. He'd walked behind his shadow all the way from Mina's back door to where Roy was parked.

In town, Roy had pulled up beside *Jake's 24*, an all-night convenience store, gone inside to buy something, and then they'd walked the six blocks to the museum in total silence. Mostly silence on the drive, too, not that Nate hadn't tried. There'd been some nodding, and a few short answers—

Boy, some moon, huh?

Corn planting moon.

Oh, right. That time of year. Right. So, did you grow up here?

Nod.

Mina tells me you're an elder of the Mohawk nation.

A small nation. Not a hard job.

He thought he'd struck pay-dirt with *How about those Yankees?* But even that went nowhere after a headshake and *Their spirit has worn out.*

He'd had to toss that one around. Did Roy mean the Yankees' spirit was broken — because of Billy Martin, maybe, or because they'd been on top so long? Or was he making a reference to the Great Spirit — meaning the Great Spirit had deserted them.

But by then the moment for follow-up had passed, so all he'd said was, *hmmm.*

Not that the nearly silent ride or the completely silent walk were particularly uncomfortable. It was like Mina had said, Roy didn't emote. But what he did have was a kind of benign solidity, a not unkind air that tolerated chatter but said it wasn't necessary.

Besides, as they'd marched off the blocks, Nate hadn't felt much like making small talk, anyway. He couldn't help glancing around, wondering what somebody might make of two men walking along a deserted center a little after two in the morning. He kept trying to affect Roy's ease, but it didn't quite take. He couldn't get it out of his head that they were on a reconnaissance mission and hadn't bothered to make up a story in case they were challenged.

A dozen hours earlier, in Mina's back yard, Roy had agreed that the museum's rear door was a problem. "Too bad," Roy said. "A ten-year-old would have been able to defeat the old door."

So now he and Roy stood here, the too bright moonlight reflecting across the door's impervious silvery surface.

Roy crossed his arms. "It might be easier to go through the wall."

Nate eyed the cement block exterior on both sides of the door. It was hard to tell — was Roy serious or was he making a joke? He didn't seem to be the sly type, though it occurred to Nate that it was a perfect situation for testing the guy from the big city to see if he was really stupid enough to consider such a thing.

"Or a window," Roy said.

Nate moved his eyes a few feet up the wall. He hadn't even noticed there *was* a window. "Yeah," he agreed, eyeing it, "if it wasn't covered with iron bars, huh?"

Roy unfolded his arms, adjusted his Tilley hat, walked over to the window and reached up. He grabbed the very bottom of one bar and shook it a little. The whole unit rocked back and forth, pieces of broken mortar skittering down the wall.

"Aluminum painted black," Roy said. "And a bad cement job."

Nate looked at him. "You mean it would come right out? The whole thing?"

"If you pull." Roy let go of the bar and came back to stand with Nate. "The window will be unlocked. When you leave, shut it, then toss a rock through it. That way you don't have to deal with broken glass." He pointed to some trash cans stacked against the rear wall. "Or a ladder."

Nate uttered a noise, half-laugh, half-revelation. "Sometimes," he said, more to himself than to Roy, "you can really get stuck on seeing things one way."

"There is a police patrol," Roy said, "but only before two and not again until after four. Never on foot and never back here."

"Mina will be waiting with the car. It shouldn't take me more than what ... a half hour?"

Roy crossed his arms. "I would say twelve to minutes."

Nate smiled.

"If you change your mind," Roy said, "and want me...."

"Thanks, Roy. But no. You've already done a lot, and it's best if you and Owl — if you and Sally — are nowhere near here."

Off in the distance a siren whooped and went silent.

"After he dumps and heads to the casino," Nate said, "he's never home before noon, right?"

Roy nodded.

"After that..." Nate rubbed the back of his neck, stared at the window, at the door, back at the window. "Is the part we haven't quite figured out yet. Not that we won't. It's just that we keep going around and around about it. How to get the right person out there at the right time. Before Piggy gets back. Someone upright enough to see Marilyn and report it. I mean, I don't know ... Mina thinks all my ideas are..."

Roy cleared his throat. "I'll handle it."

Nate looked at him. "You'll handle it?"

Roy nodded.

"Um ... any idea how?"

Roy shrugged. "An idea, yes."

Nate waited, but that was it. He felt half-relieved, half-doubtful. Roy had already solved one big problem, so it didn't seem right to push. Still... "The thing is," Nate said, "everything we come up with seems too chancy, and..."

Roy shook his head. "It won't be chancy."

"Okay." Nate said, "okay. Good. Thanks."

Roy rocked back and forth on his heels.

"So..." Nate started to rock back on his own heels, made himself stop. "I guess that's it then. I guess we have ourselves a go."

Roy pulled at the front of his Tilley hat, turned and headed for the street. Nate followed.

They walked back in silence the way they'd come, the moon no longer in their eyes, their shadows stretching sideways in front of them across the sidewalk and up the store fronts. Nate realized he was feeling almost easy. Not worried about seeming suspicious or being stopped or needing a story. The plan was set. And Roy, well

Roy didn't seem to have a nerve in his body, and even if nobody would ever say that about *him*, for the time it took to walk to the truck and drive back to Mina's he'd wear a little of Roy's composure.

When they got back to the parking lot, he hesitated, looked around. There was only one pick-up, but it wasn't Roy's. Except that Roy was heading straight for it and it took a second.... All Nate could do was gawk. Good god, how had he not noticed it before....

He started toward the truck, walked a slow circle around it, registering it all — the swooping fenders wrapping from the rear to the front tire. The round stand-alone headlights flanking an impossibly tall grille. The spare tire mounted behind the passenger door. And Jesus ... a perfect smooth paint job. He walked around it one more time, from the silver slanted wipers mounted above the windshield, past the narrow metal back bumper, to its twin on the front.

"What the heck is this?" he asked. "What year?"

"Ford," Roy said. "Thirty-seven."

Nate whistled. "Where in hell did you find it?"

"In the woods," Roy said.

Nate looked at him. "You restored this?"

Roy nodded, and after a while they climbed inside.

In the wash from the parking lot light, Nate studied the interior— the long, curved, wooden floor shift lever with its small black grip knob, the top-hung metal pedals, the round silver-trimmed dash gauges, the elegant three-pronged silver steering structure that joined the narrow wooden steering wheel to the circular center wooden horn. He pushed against the stiff leather seat back. "This is amazing." Roy turned the key and the engine came alive, humming. "Absolutely amazing."

"Engine's a sixty-seven Chevy two eighty-three," Roy said. "Original brakes, front and back."

"I can't believe I didn't notice it on the way here." He glanced at Roy. "Guess I was preoccupied."

Roy nodded. He might even have grinned, but they were backing out of the light and the smile was too quick to be sure.

They rode in silence, Nate concentrating on the way the truck felt. He rolled down his window, rolled it up again.

The only other car that had ever impressed him was a '50s English Roadster his college roommate's father owned. Bright red. He'd let them drive it once around campus and he'd never experienced the feeling of being one with the road before. Or since.

"This is great," he said. "Like my daughter would say, awesome."

It brought back that excitement he used to feel when cars were more than just four wheels that got you from one place to another. Made him remember him and Pris waiting at the top of the driveway, too wound-up to stand still. Pris spinning circles, arms out straight, skirt twirling from her legs until she got too dizzy and staggered against the garage door. Him throwing acorns over the garage roof, then at the neighbor's garage roof, then at the neighbor's house, Miss Teed's face appearing at her kitchen window, that sour downturn of a mouth, and then Pris twirling into him, their legs getting tangled so they both went down on the macadam just as their father pulled into the driveway in the brand new aqua blue Pontiac Star Chief wagon. The first ride in the brand new car always remaking the world.

"So," he said, "do you think it's crazy this thing we're doing? I mean, it's worth a try, right?"

Roy didn't say anything right away, which made Nate think he did and it wasn't. But then Roy said, "Taking Alcatraz, *that* was crazy."

For a second, Nate had to scramble — *taking Alcatraz, taking Alcatraz* — and then he realized what Roy was saying and turned and looked at him, thinking how you never really knew about people and what they were capable of. "You were there?"

The Tilley hat nodded slowly. "569 days. Each one worth it."

Nate sat back and folded his arms, trying to imagine the kind of guts it must have taken. Someone had died, he was sure of that, and still they hadn't given in. 569 days. A year and a half. The whole occupation was that long, for christ's sake. And he knew the last guys off the island didn't go voluntarily. He remembered what Mina had said — Roy did time. And here was this dumb little tchotchke of a prank, and Roy treating it as solemnly as....

"Even if they cover this up," Roy said, "they will know someone knows what they are doing. They will know someone is watching. And the final thing they'll know — is that someone is not afraid to do whatever it takes."

Like the night outside, it was cool inside the truck, not cold, but hearing Roy say those words, Nate felt a chill shoot right straight up his spine.

CHAPTER TWENTY-THREE

The next to the last thing Roy said when he dropped him off around four a.m. was, "She will need to be in the attic window at the back of his house."

"Marilyn."

"Yes. And bring window cleaner."

The last thing he said was, "According to Mina's records, he will dump on Thursday. From Monday to Thursday will be overcast. The lack of moonlight will give you cover."

Nate fell asleep as soon as he hit the futon and dreamed he was walking through a dusty brown field carrying his own head under his arm. He felt pleased that he'd thought of it, carrying his head, because he was keeping the sun off it and the sun was brutal. Huge and yellow and blazing hot, the kind of sun you might encounter on Mercury or Venus. Then a dog appeared, not Logan, a hairless dog with a short curly tail, and jumped up on him, knocking his head out from under his arm. He and the dog stood there watching his head roll away, and although all he had to do was go after it and pick it up again, suddenly he couldn't move. His legs wouldn't lift off the ground, his arms were glued to his side. Then he woke up.

In the kitchen, the table was set with one place, a bowl, a box of Raisin Bran, a mug. He turned the gas on under the coffee and got the milk out of the fridge. There was no Mina, no Logan. Her car was gone. She'd been sound asleep when he came in, and then, for an instant, he remembered being dimly aware of her moving quietly around the room, but he'd gone deeply back into sleep. Maybe that's when he'd conjured up the dream about his head.

He was finishing his coffee when Mina pulled in. The car door slammed and Logan was on the top step on the other side of the screen door, tongue hanging out, squeaking. Nate got up, and as soon as he pushed the door open Logan exploded into the kitchen doing his greeting dance all around Nate's legs. "So where have you been, huh?" Nate said, play-pushing him away, and when the dance finally came to a stop, he gave Logan a hard rub along his spine.

"You're up," Mina said, stopping the screen door from slapping behind her by letting it hit her heel. She was carrying a large plastic bag and she set it down on the floor. "What time did Roy get you back here?"

"We beat sunrise," he said, "but not by much."

Logan walked over to the doorway to the living room and went dead still, ears up, tail frozen in mid-wag. Mrs. Dalloway, curled into the rocking chair's cushion, raised her head and stared back, then lowered her head back onto her paws, her eyes fixed, unblinking, on the dog. Logan turned and came back into the kitchen, looking back once over his shoulder. They'd been skirting each other for three days, eyeing one another. Logan a little confused and wary; Mrs. D. completely self-possessed.

"So is the door problem solved?" Mina asked, then she cocked her head. "I say yes, since you've lost your pinched look." She sat down at the table and Logan pranced over and put one paw on her arm. She tore a piece of crust from Nate's cold toast and gave it to him.

"He's going to get fat if we keep giving him leftovers," Nate said, sitting down across from her.

"We'll cut down on his kibble," she said.

"I've had a pinched look?"

She nodded. "It went with my compulsive list making."

"The door has no possibilities. So now the window's taken its place."

Her eyebrows rose, "You're going through the window? That one with all the bars?"

"Roy says they're in place on a wing and a prayer. One pull and they're gone."

"Hmmmh." She took the last piece of the crust and popped it in her own mouth. "I'll cut down on my kibble, too," she said. "Is it wide enough to fit Marilyn through? Without damaging her?"

"If I can get through undamaged, I guess she can."

"You bend," Mina said. "So now I'm glad I bought a sleeping bag. That's where I was. You can slide her inside, zip it closed. Maybe it'll help her come through unscathed."

He nodded. "Okay. Oh, and you'll be happy to hear Roy's taking care of Discovery."

They'd started talking about it in four phases. Procurement was phase one, getting Marilyn out of the museum. Identification was marking Piggy's tires while he was dumping. Evidence was planting the two Marilyns. Discovery was getting someone to see one of the Marilyns and report it.

Mina looked surprised again. "Really? How's he going to do it?"

"He didn't say. He has an idea. And whatever it is it won't be chancy." He looked at her. "Except he said it in fewer words."

They smiled at each other.

"But I did get orders about where to put her."

She sat there looking at him.

"Attic window at the rear of the house."

This time, her jaw registered her surprise. "What? We're going to have to climb all the way to the *attic*? Through that *house*? In the *dark*? And then all the way back *down* again?"

"I assume there are stairs."

She pretended a shiver. "Pen lights," she said. "I bought two new ones. With power beams. Remind me to bring extra batteries."

"You don't have to go, you know. You can handle lookout."

"It's just the idea of it, Nate." She did a pretend shiver. "That house in the middle of the night." Then she made a pushing motion with her hand. "It'll be fine."

"I know it will."

Logan's nails clicked across the floor and stopped at the living room doorway.

"They're staring at each other again," Mina said.

"He'll have to learn to ignore her the way she ignores him. If he can."

Logan's nails clicked back to the table.

"So," she said.

"So," he said.

"I'm nervous as a rabbit," she said.

"Yeah. Me, too."

"We should go get Marilyn 2."

"Good idea." He looked at the kitchen clock. "Three days, twelve hours and the die will be cast. We have to wait for the moon to wane. Did you get a sleeping bag for her, too?"

Mina shook her head no. "Just a bedspread to cover her in the car. I'm glad we've got Roy."

"Are you glad we have me?"

She smiled. "Gladder."

"Yeah," he said, "I'm gladder we have you, too."

***

Marilyn 2 was exactly where they'd left her. Nate kept glancing around as they made their way toward her through the rubble on the floor. The first time, he'd been too spooked by the prone female figure to really see the place. Or maybe it had been a sunny day, more light coming through the cracks. But Jesus there was something in the air here. Gloom and doom. Murky shadows. Looming corners. The dirty crunch of glass and plaster under their feet. Anything that had been left after the place was cleared out had been smashed. Windows, walls. Why did people do that? Why did people smash things?

He tried to remember if he'd ever done it. No. Well, yes. Sort of. But he'd only been eleven years old, maybe twelve — Old Man Carter's fishing shack on the pond. He and Harold All trying the door they expected to be locked. Except it wasn't. And inside, the perfectly stacked cans of beans and soups and tomatoes. They hadn't broken anything, but god they'd made a mess. Tipped all the cans onto the floor, pulled the sleeping bags off the shelves, emptied the salt and pepper, thrown pop corn kernels at each other. Like the devil had pissed in their ears. And then, almost at the same instant, they'd both snapped out of it. Looked at what they'd done. Fled.

But why they'd done it? He had no idea. Maybe because they could. Because there wasn't anyone there to tell them not to. Because they'd unexpectedly found themselves out of the bounds they'd always known. It certainly hadn't been planned. They hadn't even said a word to each other while they were doing it. It had come over them the same way the craziness came over Auntie May. They'd gone momentarily berserk.

But he also remembered the afterwards. The guilt he wore waiting for someone to notice, the surprise when no one did. And then the gradual realization that they were going to get away with it. But not really. Because God knew. That's what the Sisters said. God saw everything you did. In fact, He got it on film. And when you died, God would sit you down and make you watch what you'd done. Every single nasty miserable second of it. After which, he'd quietly point the way to hell.

He stepped across a piece of a porcelain toilet, a purple branch from an artificial Christmas tree, the bright red handle of a mug, the flattened outline of a desiccated rat. The place needed purification. Fire. It was too depressing and degrading leaving it this way. The antithesis of inspiration.

"Ready?" Mina said.

He nodded. "To get the hell out of here? Definitely."

Mina took the legs while he followed with his hands under Marilyn's arms and they carried her across the broken glass, the debris, the dirt. "I hope our animals aren't tearing the place up this very minute," Mina said. She hadn't wanted to leave Logan and the cat alone together, but Mina's wagon was low on gas and Logan took up most of the back seat of Nate's sedan, and the back seat was where Marilyn was going because the trunk was too small.

"I think they've reached a kind of cold war standoff," Nate said.

"I hope." Mina went first through the doorway. "Tomorrow we should do a dry run to Piggy's. That way we'll know exactly how long it takes to get there and where the best place to park is."

"May I suggest," Nate said, glad to be back out into the fresh air even if the afternoon was gloomy, "that when this is all over and done, you consider a career with the FBI."

Mina shifted Marilyn's legs. "Is that what *you're* considering?"

"Not me. I'm thinking about computers. The next great *plastics*."

She glanced back at him over her shoulder.

"What? You don't think that's a good idea?"

"I don't know," she said, "maybe. Though I see you more as a migrator than a resident."

"Huh?"

"You know, a polar bear as opposed to a steer. A mover, not a muncher. I can't see you staring at a screen and a bunch of ones and zeroes hour after hour."

"Mina, I've been an engineer for twenty-five years. You don't do that swimming from ice floe to ice floe."

"True," she said. "Then maybe I only see you that way because you appeared out of nowhere one night and now we're doing this. But then I don't know who you were before this, do I. So I'm probably not a very good judge."

They got to the car and Mina spent five minutes brushing little bits of debris from Marilyn's wax face and hands, and when she was finally satisfied, they fit her across the back seat and covered her with the bedspread.

Actually, when he thought about it, he wasn't sure *he* knew who he was before this, either. Had he been misfiring career-wise, too, all those years? Is it why he never whistled on his way to work? Should he have been digging up femurs and jawbones in Africa? Guiding ships through the Panama Canal? Staring at a deep sea Fangtooth from the inside of the Alvin? He started the car and waited for Mina to fasten her seatbelt. A little late now for all that.

***

The next day they waited until there were a couple of hours to go until sunset. They found a road that brought them up onto the backside of Piggy's ten acres, walked through the woods until they could see the outline of his bow-roofed barn. The long south side of the barn faced them, or was it the north? The sun was setting to their left, on the west side of the barn. That made sense, the barn door open to the east, to the early morning sun.

Beyond the barn, a quarter-hidden by it, was the house, its back to the barn, its front to the road, looking like a misplaced stack of blocks, a peaked roof with mangy-looking shingles, clapboard siding devoid of paint in huge gray swaths, saggy windows, and there at the rear, just beneath the vee of the roof, Roy's attic window.

Looking at it, a bit of the chill that had already hit Mina, hit him. The place felt like a cemetery. What was it going to feel like at four in the morning?

The pumper truck was parked behind the barn alongside an ancient tractor that was alongside at least half a dozen rusted snow plows and what looked like an upside down snowmobile.

"He drives a red and white pick-up," Mina said. "A Ford. I don't see it, do you?"

Nate shook his head. He stepped out of the woods into the winter-bent grassy field. "C'mon."

"Nate," she hissed. But he kept going and then he could hear her steps on the dry grass behind him.

"If he's around, we'll say we just saw a purple fly-catcher swoop into his barn. He doesn't know us from Adam. We're birders. Everyone knows birders are a little crazy."

"What if he just shoots us."

"With what we're about to do," Nate said, "that's not something we can afford to even consider."

As they got closer, he noted the two caved holes in the barn roof, the pitch of the wall that sloped more than a foot from one end to the other.

They had to skirt what looked like a multiple-decade can and bottle dump, and Nate counted eleven cats lying on a rotting brown rug next to the snowmobile. The cats eyed and then ignored them.

He checked out the pumper truck. Oldish. With nice high fenders above each front tire.

A spring wind was blowing in fits and starts, and the barn was groaning with each gust. Most of the siding boards were rotted or chewed a good two-feet up, but above that they were weathered to a black and gold someone would pay a lot of money for. Except when they got right up against them, he saw it was too late. The boards had passed their antique prime decades ago. Now they were too dried out, too brittle to be good for anything.

He glanced up toward the roof, saw the wide outward bow of the wall, the places where boards had snapped or were about to from the downward pressure of the heavy roof timbers. The whole place looked like one good blow could take it down.

Some of the spaces between the siding boards were three or four inches wide, and they each picked a space to peer through. By now, the sun was close to setting and the low clouds had gone from purple to dark gray. Mina took out her pen light and aimed it at the interior.

"Look at that car," she said, "it's ancient." She moved the light slowly along the length of it.

"Looks like a Caddy," Nate said. "Maybe a '59 or '60. Jesus, look at the fins. Thing must be twenty feet long." He made a mental note to tell Roy, though he had the feeling Roy already knew.

Mina's light scanned the interior of the barn. Barrels, crates, rusted pitchforks on walls, half a truck chassis, piles of windows, lumber, three toilets, a brass headboard, a cigar-store Indian without a head. Then there was the muffled sound of an exhaust, which grew louder and louder, and Mina switched off the pen light just as headlights slashed across the barn. For no reason that made sense, they both shrank away from the wall, and then the exhaust went silent and the headlights disappeared.

"It's him," Mina whispered.

"We'll wait until he's in the house," Nate whispered back, "and then get the hell out of here."

Mina stepped back toward the wall and peered through the boards, though what she could see he had no idea. Still, he did it, too, and it turned out there were no doors on the front of the barn, so they could see clear through to the house and to Piggy sitting in his truck with the overhead cab light on.

They watched. The interior light went out. The truck door slammed. And then, like a small rocket, a red cinder flew through the air and lay glowing on the ground. Almost immediately, a smell blew in on a breeze. Stogie. Piggy had been sitting there smoking it down.

Silently, Nate counted to five and then another door slammed, a wooden door this time. "Okay, let's go," Nate said. "He's inside."

He turned around to face the open field. "Shit," he said, "I can't see a damn thing."

"Don't go yet anyway," she said. "Stay here. I want to get something."

And then she started walking along the wall toward the front of the barn.

"Mina!" His turn to hiss now. "Where the hell..."

The arm of her white sweater waved backwards at him, saying *shush*.

He watched her sweater moving through the ink. Where the hell was she going — into the fucking house? He heard a grunt, a thud, lost her in the dark and started moving after her, but then her sweater was there again, farther away now, still moving.

He stopped, started after her again, stopped, waited, had to bite his tongue to not call out, and then caught the sweater again, but not getting smaller, getting bigger now.

"You can't just go and do things like that," he hissed, when she was ten feet away. "Just take off like that and not tell me what you're doing."

"Here." She held something out to him. "Stick this in your pocket."

He reached for it. Something wrapped in a napkin? He stuffed it in his jacket pocket. All he wanted was to get the hell out of there.

Coming from the car, it had taken them twenty minutes to get through the woods, to the edge of the field behind the barn. Going back, it took them twenty minutes just to cross the field. He tripped over uneven mounds of grass, junk, stepped into holes, yowling cats flashing off in all directions.

"Thank God," Mina said, when they reached the trees and could finally turn on their flashlights. "Now it's just straight ahead."

Except it wasn't.

And after twenty minutes of wading through thorny brush and climbing stone walls, Mina stopped. "I don't remember any of this," she said.

Nate aimed his flashlight in every direction, but they all looked the same. "I think we zigged when we should have zagged. Though what he was thinking was what they taught you in Boy Scouts. That walking a straight line was impossible, unless you had one to follow.

"Do you smell something?" Nate said.

Mina sniffed. "Yeah, I do."

And then it hit him. Stogie. And for one irrational second, he was certain Piggy was right behind them. He even ducked. But then he felt the heat at his hip and looked down, saw that his fucking pocket was on fire!

He slapped at it. Yanked down his zipper, ripped the jacket off and flung it on the ground. He was just about to jump up and down on it when Mina stopped him.

"It's the stogie," she said, "don't. You'll smash it."

With two sticks, she pulled a mass of blackened napkin and cigar out of his pocket. "Sorry," she said, "I didn't think it was still burning."

"You gave me a *lit* stogie to put in my pocket? A lit stogie wrapped in a *napkin*?"

She put his jacket on the ground, aimed her light at the blackened pocket and ground it under her foot. Then she picked up the jacket, gave it a couple of hard shakes and handed it to him. "I said I was sorry."

"But why?" he said. "I don't get it."

She crouched down over the smoldering napkin and scraped it away, gingerly picked up the stogie. "Because now we have some evidence to plant behind the museum. A stogie. *Piggy's* stogie."

He didn't trust himself to talk, so he didn't. He just bunched the jacket under his arm and aimed his light ahead.

Not that it helped. There were yards of wild blackberry canes to walk through that hadn't been there an hour ago. There was a bog. There were branches slapping them in the face. And it was cold. Even after he put his charred jacket back on it was cold.

It was well over an hour before they stumbled out onto the road. And if it hadn't been for a barking dog giving them any sense of direction at all, they might have kept stumbling around in circles until the sun came up. Then they had to walk twenty minutes in one direction and forty in the opposite before they finally found the car.

Ten minutes and several miles down the road, he finally trusted himself to speak. "Well that was an auspicious beginning."

"I think we accomplished a lot," Mina said, rubbing her leg.

"Why are you rubbing your leg?"

"Because I fell down three times tripping over things in that damn mine field of his."

It was almost nine o'clock. He'd planned to have a good dinner and get a good night's sleep, spend tomorrow going over everything they had to do step by step. But now he seemed to have lost his sense of control over it all. Or his imagined sense of control. His stomach growled.

Suddenly, Mina guffawed. It was the only word to describe it.

"What?" he said.

"It's just that I can see you standing there with your pocket glowing. I've never seen anyone move so fast." And then she guffawed again.

His feet were soaked, his hands were numb, his right knee hurt where he'd cracked it into a stump.

"I'll need some space on this," he said.

"Oh," she said, "okay. Sorry."

Although actually he was pretty sure he wouldn't see anything funny about it ever. And he couldn't stop himself from chewing on it, either. How she could have fallen in some sinkhole in Piggy's back yard and broken a leg. How he could have burst into flames. And the thing was, they hadn't even started Phase One yet.

Another two or three miles went by and his hands warmed up. He shook off that feeling he'd gotten when he first smelled the stogie burning — that his head was about to be macheted from behind. He thought about Roy, who wouldn't have acted like a dick. Who would have stayed calm. Managed a slip of a smile when Mina laughed instead of getting his feelings hurt. But then Roy wouldn't have got lost in the first place.

He took one hand off the steering wheel and set it on top of Mina's. "Sorry," he said.

She squeezed his hand. "No reason to be. None of it was exactly fun."

"Yeah, but I didn't have to go and make a bad situation worse."

"I shouldn't have laughed. I think it was nerves."

"It was a good idea. The stogie."

"It wasn't worth it."

"It was."

"It wasn't."

All the way home he kept trying to think of a way to get her back there, to those few moments when she'd laughed. He'd never heard her laugh, not like that. But it was the kind of thing you couldn't manufacture. It was of the moment. A rarity. And now it was lost and it was his fault.

CHAPTER TWENTY-FOUR

"Uh-oh," Mina said.

As they drew closer, the emergency lights morphed from an indistinct glow into pulsing arcs against the dull black sky.

Two blocks ahead, the only other car on the road hit its brakes, hesitated a second, then made a quick left turn.

"Looks like the road's blocked off," Nate said. "Think they know we're coming?"

Mina stopped the car, put it in reverse and backed up all the way to *Jake's 24*. "I'll try to find out," she said.

When she came back to the car, she had two candy bars, a Twix and a Mounds.

"Here's some energy." She handed him the Twix. "It's a burst water pipe. We can take a left on Tyrone and a right on Pride. Pride parallels Main for a little ways, then heads off toward the interstate, which is where I told him I wanted to go. He said be sure not to get onto Cooper or I'd end up back downtown. But that should be well up beyond the museum, if we're lucky."

Nate nodded. He unwrapped the Twix and tipped one of the chocolate-covered bars into his hand. "Did they say how far the road's blocked off?"

"No," she said, biting into her Mounds bar. "I didn't want to ask any questions someone might remember later." She turned the key. "But I guess we better go find out."

The road block on the other end was exactly one block up from the museum. Close enough so Nate could feel the vibration of the pneumatic drill they were using right up through the floor of the car, close enough so the emergency lights cast a glow on the street as bright as Tuesday night's moon. So much for Roy's cover.

Mina pulled into the alley beside the donut shop, drove a circle around a dumpster behind the store and parked at the top of the alley facing Main Street. She turned off the headlights.

"This is ridiculous," she said. "There's a policeman standing five hundred feet away, all kinds of emergency vehicles going back and forth." She shook her head. "It's not worth it, Nate. Piggy will be dumping again next month. All we have to do is put it off until then."

But Nate wasn't thinking about leaving.

"I have a story for you," he said.

"A story? Now?"

"Yeah, now. You see, there was this little kid who lived across the street when I was growing up. Maybe two years old. Rusty, they called him. Mop of red hair. He almost drowned during a party in his backyard. I mean, he was fine, it all ended fine, but it was a big party, you know? Cars parked up and down the street. All the neighbors except us." He shook his head. "Don't ask. So there's hamburgers on the grill, people laughing, music, kids playing games. Lots of fun. Until somebody noticed Rusty floating face down in a tiny little kids' pool. I heard it from across the street, the way the sound of the party fractured into screams and yells."

"Awful," Mina said, "just awful."

"The ambulance was coming by the time I ran across the street. And after they got him breathing and his father took off after the ambulance, everyone stood around wringing their hands. They couldn't understand how nobody had seen him until it was almost too late. All those people and nobody noticed him in the pool."

She stared at him for a second. "Did you just make this up?"

"No," he said, "no, I didn't make it up. It happened. But it bears with the current situation, right? I mean, no one's going to be paying any attention to what's going on over *here*, because there's too much going on over *there*." He rolled down his window. "Listen.

There's so damn much noise, I could sing the *Star Spangled Banner* at the top of my lungs and no one would hear a thing."

He'd been worrying about that, the noise. Moving the trash can, yanking the bars, tossing the rock, breaking the glass — all of it loud as hell at two a.m. in that deserted alley.

"This is good," he said, "trust me. This is very good."

A service vehicle went by, its yellow lights revolving, and instinctively they both sank down in their seats.

Mina made a noise like a moan. "There are people all *over* the place."

He snapped his fingers. "Shazam. I'm invisible."

She gave him a look. It made him think about the ride home from Piggy's a few hours ago. Made him wonder why it was that two people physically only a foot apart were so seldom in the same place at the same time.

He opened his door, slid the backpack with the sleeping bag over his shoulders. "It'll be okay," he said. And then in his best James Cagney, "Keep the engine runnin', doll."

She didn't seem to appreciate that either.

CHAPTER TWENTY-FIVE

He kept to the shadows outside the perimeter of the blue-hued metal halide lights, the noise of the jackhammer vibrating the ground, the air, his teeth. The workers, when he could see them, were silhouetted against the brightness, most of them standing around doing nothing.

"Owl Woman knows it's tonight, right?" he asked Mina more than once on the way.

"She *knows* she *knows*," she said.

"I'm just asking. I mean … all this and then the window's locked. Which means I have to break it and deal with the glass."

"Sally won't let us down," she said. "Neither will Roy."

The first thirty feet after he got out of the car, he kept stopping every few minutes to look behind him, listen. But what he'd said to Mina, to mostly make her not worry, was so. If *he* couldn't hear his own footsteps in the din of the road work, no one else would either.

When he got to the museum's back alley, the noise from the digging became slightly muffled by a long tall row of hedge shrubs he hadn't noticed when he was there with Roy. The glow from the work lights lit the air to just before dawn, when it's no longer dark and not yet light. Just gray enough so he could see without having to turn on the mini headlamp Mina had insisted he wear.

"I'd rather not have to use it," he told her. "I'd like to be as invisible as possible."

"Well, just in case you need it," she said, holding it out until he took it and put it on.

He dropped the sleeping bag on the ground near the impenetrable door, walked over to the metal trash cans and carried one to the window, then another, and kicked a plastic crate into place beside them. He set the sleeping bag on top of one can and took a long look around before he stepped up onto the other. It put him at just about eye level with the lower half of the window, and he grabbed onto the bars with both hands, jiggled them just enough to get a feel for how loose they were. Pieces of concrete fell away, just like it had when Roy grabbed them and the bars felt wobbly as hell. Okay. He applied just a little more muscle, and this time the bars moved a couple of inches. He'd work them out slow. A little at a time. It would take longer, but his footing on the can was shitty, and what difference did an extra few minutes make?

He jiggled again. More concrete hit the ground. But this time, the bars twisted, went crooked, and seemed to get stuck. He shook them. Pulled up, down, sideways. Did it again. They wouldn't budge. He whacked them with the flat of his hand, shook them hard. Stood there on the trash can and hung his head. And this was supposed to be the easy part.

He took another look up and down the alley, tightened his grip on the bars. Twelve minutes in and out, huh Roy? My ass. He was already pushing six or seven and he didn't even know if the fucking window was unlocked yet. He gave the bars a shake, another yank. Nothing. He imagined going back to the car with failure stamped all over him.

He set his feet as wide as the top of the trash can would let him front to back, grabbed hold of the bars, pulled once, twice, then felt an urge to kill whoever had installed the goddamn things in the first place and pulled a lot harder than he should have.

The bars broke loose, and he went airborne. Flew backwards and hit the ground hard enough to see stars.

He lay there in the dirt, staring up into the gray air, the breath knocked out of him, thinking for a split second he might not ever breathe again, and then he threw himself forward into a sitting position and his lungs filled. The overturned can rolled twice before it came to a stop, and he scrambled backwards into the hedge, squatting, waiting for whatever it was that was going to happen — lights, yells, guns drawn or at the ready.

He stared at a small ray of light piercing the hedge and glinting off the metal side of the horizontal can. Its lid lay a couple of feet away. Was this really something he'd thought was even marginally possible?

He listened to the continued pumping of the jackhammer, waited. But nothing happened. Was it actually possible the crashing trashcan and the slam of the bars and his body into the ground had been heard by no one?

He blew out a long breath, stepped out of the hedge, rubbed the back of his head, his elbow. He tipped the trash can upright, retrieved the lid, looked around one last time, and climbed back on top of it. He pushed at one half of the metal casement window, which swung inward with a small creak. "Thank you, Sally Owl Woman," he whispered, then he pushed open the other half.

He stood there for a second, trying to figure it out. This was something that always looked easy. The cat burglar springing from the low ledge to the window sill and then slithering inside, looking like he could have done it with a martini in his hand, never spilling a drop. But the window sill was well above his waist and he couldn't remember the last time he'd had to lift his weight entirely with his arms. But he had to get on that sill. Because diving head-first through the window, that was just plain stupid.

He remembered the sleeping bag, leaned down, grabbed it, and threw it through the opening, and just then the jack hammer stopped. The air went perfectly still. He could hear voices. Christ.

He needed to get inside and he needed to do it fast, and the other thing he needed to do was to stop thinking and just do it. Just do it, he told himself, just fucking do it.

He put both hands on the bottom sill, bent his knees, and jumped the way he remembered jumping onto the horse in gym class. The top of his thighs caught the sill, and for an awful second, he was like a seesaw on a pivot, capable of falling either way. But then he stopped teetering, found a point of balance, steadied himself, got himself half-sitting on the sill. It wasn't enough of a perch to do anything from, and by the time he finally inched himself into a better position, he was sweating like a horse.

Inside, about ten feet away, there was the dull red glow of an exit sign, but the area immediately inside the window was pitch black, and although he didn't want to do it, he lowered his head as far as he dared and switched on the head lamp. The floor was a good eight feet down, no easy landing there. But then he saw the table. It was beneath the window, a big wide table, and the drop to it wasn't more than four feet. Bless Sally Owl Woman. Or whoever had thought of it. He switched off the light, swung one leg through the window, then the other and slipped off the sill just as the jackhammer started up again. It wasn't a graceful landing, but it was mostly right side up.

He slid off the table to the floor, got his feet tangled in the sleeping bag, kicked it away then picked it up and set it on the table, started silently reciting the floor plan. Down the hall, six feet. Through the inside exit door.

By the time he was in among the displays, his eyes had adjusted and he could see well enough by the eerie red glow of the exit signs to discover that they were all staring at him, the wax figures. Looking for all the world like they were watching him as he passed each display, if not exactly turning their heads, then at least following him with their eyes. All of it creepy as hell.

He turned left at Key Largo, right at Bela Lugosi, keeping his eyes off the vampire. And then, three down on the left, past the Marx Brothers, ET, and Albert Einstein, there she was, all glowing white skin, hair, and filmy gauze.

She was only protected from the public on three sides and, behind her, he stepped up onto the display. A stand bolted to the floor held her upright with a metal band bolted to the back of her waist, and he reached into his pocket, took out the wrench handle and the four sockets, one of which, he'd been told, was sure to fit. Except not one of them did; two of them a little too big, the others a little too small. He tried the larger sockets again and chose the closest in size to the bolt heads, pushed it onto the top bolt cockeyed, turned it slightly until it caught. He hit the handle with the side of his hand, short, easy hits until the bolt broke free and came out with a few quick turns. He did the same with the other, went around to the front and pulled Marilyn off the stand.

How long had all this taken him? Twenty minutes? Thirty? Mina was probably half-crazy by now.

He lay Marilyn near the edge of the display, jumped down, picked her up and started to retrace his steps. Then he remembered the tools, still on the floor back there where he'd left them, leaned her against a display window, and ran back.

Was it too much to ask that any of this go easy? That he not make a hash of even one fucking thing?

He re-hefted Marilyn and glanced up into the face of Jack the Ripper, who stared down at him, a maniacal gleam in his crazy eye, a bloody dripping knife at shoulder height.

Nate half-ducked and ran for the back of the museum, set Marilyn on the table below the window, grabbed the sleeping bag, and tugged at the zipper, which snagged six inches down.

He pulled hard enough to rip it right out of the material, but the zipper wouldn't budge, wouldn't go up, wouldn't go down. He climbed up on the table and tossed it out the window. If he was lucky, she'd land on it. And if he wasn't, well ... fuck it.

He got up on the table, stepped up on a box to get a little higher, picked her up and fit her through the open window, head first. He leaned out and lowered her as far as he could, hanging on to her ankles above the white silk high heels. And then, just before he let her go, she went, for a split-second, completely weightless, and something pulled her right out of his hands.

CHAPTER TWENTY-SIX

It was the same dream all over again. The sun, his head, the jumping dog that was really a pig, the inability to move. What in hell...

He opened his eyes.

Next to him, Mina was snoring softly. They'd come home feeling like each of them had got the basket that won the game, miraculous shots from outside the line that swished and got that collective intake of breath from the bleachers.

They'd recapped it all — what Nate had done, what Mina had been thinking — step by step for two solid hours, until the sun was coming up and Nate realized that he was too exhausted to move his lips anymore. He hoped he hadn't fallen asleep while she was still talking, but he didn't think so. He was pretty sure they'd both expired at the same second.

He closed his eyes and let his mind play the scenes in random order. The two of them lurching out of sync across the road with Marilyn 3 see-sawing back and forth between them, almost pulling out of Mina's arms on one step, his on the other. Trying to get Marilyn unhitched from the stand and every other complication every step of the way. Each second had felt like an hour. And then that instant that blew his stomach right down into the soles of his shoes when Mina grabbed Marilyn just before he let her go out the window.

"I couldn't just sit there," Mina kept saying, "how could I just sit there? And it seemed to be taking so long. Too long. Why didn't you use the sleeping bag? You were supposed to put her inside the sleeping bag. What if you'd dumped her smack on her face?"

Not that anything else had gone the way it was supposed to. The window bars yanking off. His header off the trashcan. The goddamn zipper. And maybe his finest moment — tripping over the sleeping bag he was holding under one arm as they ran across the street to the car and slamming his knee into the macadam. The same knee he'd slammed into the stump the night before.

All night long, the knee had brought him awake every time he moved in his sleep. Which was why he was avoiding movement right now.

Not to mention forgetting to leave the stogie and break the glass. But by then, getting out of there was the only thing on his mind.

"Don't go back," Mina had hissed after him. "It doesn't matter, Nate ... Nate. Don't!"

But it *was* important. Worth stiff-hopping back for. Worth giving Mina palpitations for.

He stuck his hand down under the sheet and made light contact with his knee. It felt like a huge piece of hot wood.

If he'd fucking *tried*, he couldn't have screwed it up more.

Still, they'd done it. They'd fucking done it!

Logan's head appeared and the dog clipped Nate's nose with his tongue.

"Hey, Boy," Nate murmured, stuck one hand out and gave him a pat.

"How's your knee?" Mina whispered.

"Swollen," he said, "a little sore. It's fine."

"Thank god Phase One is over," she said. "Weren't we thinking Phase One was going to be the easy part?"

"We're pros now," he said, "it's all downhill from here."

"Just think," she said, "Marilyn Monroe in our living room."

"Think she's pissed?"

Mina stretched. "I think she's the kind of person who'd be game for a little adventure."

"Like you," he said, slowly shifting onto his side so he could face her, keeping the effort of it to himself.

"Yeah," she said, "just like me. Me and Marilyn. Twins. It's killing you, isn't it, your knee."

"Think it's too late for ice?"

She'd insisted on stopping to buy a bag before they got home. But he'd been high on adrenaline. "Just a scratch," he'd told her.

"Well, it's just a bag of water now." She sat up. "I'll go get more."

He was going to say no, but just her movement on the futon made him change his mind.

"We'll get Roy to help tonight."

"No," he said, "I'll be fine by tonight."

"Let me look at it."

She started to pull back the sheet, but he grabbed it and held it tight. "I'm modest, remember? As for the ice ... maybe you could get three bags?"

He didn't try to get out of bed until he heard her car backing away. The knee looked even worse than it felt, reddish, yellowish, a nice contusion right in its center. But when he got himself standing, he found he could put his weight on it. It only really hurt when he touched it. "Bruised patella," he told Logan. "It'll be fine. But probably not by tonight. Don't tell her that, though, okay?"

When Mina came back, she looked at the knee and didn't say a word, just followed him from the bedroom down the hall into the living room. He sat down gingerly, stiff-legged, Logan beside him. "Not my usual nimble self, huh?"

Mina wrapped a towel around his knee, slid a larger one underneath and emptied a bag of ice into it until his knee was buried. Then she brought the ends of the big towel together loosely. "How does that feel?" she said.

"Cold," he said. "Good."

"I'll do it," she said.

"Do what?"

"Tonight. It's only fair I get a share of the glory, too."

"I'll be fine by tonight," he said.

"Okay. But just in case, show me exactly what you're going to do."

So he showed her how the paint cans would slip right up over the tires and stick to the wheel wells with the magnets. "But they'll be heavy when they're full of paint. Remember that. And you also have to remember to take out the plastic plugs just before you set them in place. Which means the paint's going to start dripping out right away. Which is okay, but you'll ruin whatever you're wearing."

"I'll look in the closet and try to find something old," she said.

He sat there with his knee in ice for three hours. Occasionally, he studied Marilyn. Even in wax she had star power. He couldn't imagine what she must have been like in person. He tried to read, but his concentration was shot, and after a while, he fell asleep. He didn't dream about his head rolling away. Instead, he dreamed that he and Mina were sitting in the living room and she was asking him if he wanted a scotch. "Dry or on the rocks?" she kept saying. But he couldn't decide. And when he opened his eyes, she was tying the ends of the towel back together.

"I added more ice," she said. "How do you feel?"

"On the rocks," he said.

"Want me to bring you some food?"

"I think I should get up and move around."

So she untied the towel and unwrapped the one around his leg. The knee didn't look nearly as red and the swelling had gone down. But when he stood up, it still felt like one jointless piece of wood.

He made his way to the table, had to sit with the leg straight out to the side.

"We should scrap Phase two," he said, "and skip directly to Phase three." He scooped a forkful of mac and cheese into his mouth, chewed, swallowed.

She shook her head. "All phases are go. There's no reason I can't do this. And just because you came up with all the ideas doesn't change the fact that the *premise* was mine. Remember that? Me, asking you to help? Besides, it'll give us a chance to see how good *you* are at waiting."

He hated to admit she was right. That he was feeling a proprietary sense about it as though nobody could do it but him. Even with Roy the other night, when he appropriated Discovery. Even though Nate had no idea how to accomplish it himself, still didn't, a piece of him hadn't wanted to give it over.

He knew for sure Roy wouldn't have lost his balance and fallen off the trash can or jammed the zipper or had trouble disconnecting Marilyn from the stand. He wouldn't have tripped crossing the road or gotten lost in the woods behind Piggy's. Roy was like a silent arrow heading in an exact direction. Whereas, *he* was — well, he didn't know what he was. Plus he had to live with the fact that last night had taken him almost fifty minutes. No wonder Mina had got impatient. Roy would have been in and out in six.

He sighed. "Okay," he said. "You're right. You'll do it better than me."

"Nate..." Her tone of voice said *you don't have to pout.*

"Okay," he said, "okay. But you have a back-up plan in case he sees you, right?"

She looked at him. "No. Do you?"

"No." He took another forkful. She'd put peas in it and they must have been fresh because they made a nice little pop when he bit down on them. "I mean, with the way things have been going, why would we ever think we need a back-up plan?"

After they ate, they both fell asleep on the couch, and when they woke up, it was already getting dark. Mina went off to change and get ready, leaving him restless, stiff-legging it around the kitchen, finally washing the dishes and cleaning up because he had to do *some*thing. Logan lay in front of the doorway to the living room with his tail facing Mrs. Dalloway in her rocker, his eyes following Nate back and forth, back and forth.

At least the dog was learning, ignoring the cat almost as well as the cat ignored him.

He was wiping down the chairs when Mina came into the kitchen. "Well?" she said.

"You look like a cat burglar."

She was all in black — shoes, pants, jacket, gloves, a black winter hat pulled down over her hair.

"It's my stealth outfit," she said.

"It's a little sexy."

"Wait till I put this goop on my face." She held out a jar of dark brown gunk. "Then I'll be irresistible."

He had a hard time getting his leg into the car. Even with the seat all the way back he had to sit at an angle.

Mina parked off River Road, on a side path that didn't go anywhere, that simply ended. He'd felt helpless watching her disappear into the blackness. "For god's sake be careful," he hissed after her, "and don't take any chances, understand? No chances. None!"

He checked his watch every two minutes at least thirty times until the pumper truck went by, or at least the pumper truck's headlights. Mina had been gone for forty-five minutes at that point. She'd been obsessed with the idea of being there well before Piggy arrived, ready and waiting. "It might take time to move to where he parks. It's always in the same general area, but not always the same spot. And trust me, I intend to be very very careful."

He kissed her on her lips before she went, both of them puckered up so they wouldn't smudge her goop. She smelled of licorice and dryer sheets.

He looked at his watch again, tried to shift his weight, but there was nowhere to shift it. He could always walk the road a ways. Meet her coming back. Piggy went only in one direction, so there was no danger of running into him.

He looked at his watch again.

They still had Evidence ahead of them tonight, the two Marilyns lying behind him in the back of Mina's wagon in a kind of weird embrace. He tried not to think about it — walking through Piggy's sty, climbing two sets of stairs. No way Mina was going to do that on her own. He could do stairs. He'd just be a little slow. She'd suggested getting Roy to help again, but he couldn't get his own sense of pride out of the way. He admired Roy. And he envied him. He wished he could be more like him — strong, silent, sure, nerveless. Roy would climb the stairs to the attic without a flinch.

He looked at his watch again. Seventeen minutes now since the truck had passed. He began adding up the minutes. Maybe five for her to get to the dumping site, three or four to get in position after Piggy set the pumper pumping. "Eight," he said out loud, "give it ten." They'd figured four minutes for placing each can. Maybe more if Piggy got close and she had to lie low and wait for him to saunter away. "Eighteen," he said. Because that's what Mina said Piggy did, saunter away from the truck, then saunter back, then away, back, away again. "So eighteen minutes," he said, "or twenty. Make it thirty at most." Christ, he couldn't stand it. Twenty minutes now since the truck had passed, and if she went past thirty, then what? Then what should he do?

He put his hand on the door handle and pulled up on it slowly, not that any noise he might make mattered. "Mina, Mina, where the hell..."

And then there was a movement in the dark and something was coming toward the car and the driver's door flew open.

"I did it," she said. "I did it, Nate. I did it. And it went like clockwork. Tick tock, just like a clock."

She sounded drunk. She was breathing hard. Her eyes were huge. Her black outfit was covered with yellow paint.

"Are you okay?" he said.

"Of course. I'm fine." Her breath came in pants. "Oh…" She took a breath, "…maybe I scratched up my knees a little. So it's a good thing you didn't do it. At first I crawled — but then the best way to move — the fastest, was to move hunched over. And to go from one side of the truck to the other? I crawled on my belly right straight under the thing. And then — he starts coming back, so I go totally quiet, totally still, but then he turns back around and walks off. You should have seen me Nate — creeping off, tiptoeing, and then when it was over — running like a crazy person. I couldn't help it — I just ran as fast as I could, faster than I've run in years! Till I thought my lungs were — going to explode. Like right now." She laughed. "I probably won't be able to move tomorrow!"

So now it was her turn for the adrenaline, the rush, and he felt it a little himself, just listening to her.

CHAPTER TWENTY-SEVEN

"I hate this place." As soon as he said it, he wished he hadn't. It was the kind of place that had ears. That could retaliate for being insulted.

"I know," Mina said, "I've tried not to let myself think about it, but it has a *feel*, doesn't it? Eeewww." And even though he couldn't really see her, he knew a shiver had gone through her.

There was a pall over the place. The air breathed different. Tasted different. Every three seconds, a goddamn cat yowled, sounding like something that lived in hell. Twice, one had yowled within a foot of them. The kind of thing that stopped your heart. Even Roy's, he was pretty sure.

They left the car behind two trees off the side of the driveway. Not much of a hiding place if Piggy came back early, but the farthest they were willing to walk with the two Marilyns. Mina had the old Marilyn because her dress was already a mess, and if she dropped her or had to drag her up the stairs, it didn't much matter.

The moon had started fighting the clouds about fifteen minutes before they got to Piggy's, emerging for longer and longer moments as the sky cleared. So, Roy had misjudged the length of the cold front. He glanced up as the moon brightened, then dimmed. The waxing and waning, the pulling and pushing gave him the feeling the night was alive, breathing.

"I'll go in first," he said, at the door.

Then things were running past them. Cats chasing each other. Or maybe a host of demons. And when the moon emerged, there were eyes everywhere.

"Okay," she said. "They're just cats."

He turned the knob and then had to give the door a shove with the heel of his hand to open it.

The smell was acidic. Vinegar. Cat piss. A lifetime of stogies. Ancient decomposing dybbuks. He tried not to breathe too deeply, stepped inside.

Behind him, Mina made a small unhappy noise as the moon waxed and a spidery light came through the windows like it was coming through waxed paper.

They stood there for the count and he had the feeling she didn't want to move any more than he did.

"We have the glass cleaner, right?"

"In my backpack," she said.

A crazy thought went through his head. What if they cleaned *all* the windows before they left? Maybe that's what you did in a place like this. Instead of smashing and dirtying, you fixed and cleaned.

He balanced Marilyn on one foot and pulled the penlight out of his pocket, turned it on and swung the beam across the room. There was stuff everywhere, piles of newspapers, cardboard boxes, furniture piled with more stuff. He decided he didn't really want to see anymore, just wanted to get it over with and get out.

"Ready?" he said to Mina.

"I guess."

He stuck the penlight between his teeth, wishing he hadn't smashed the headlamp when he fell on the road, and picked Marilyn up like he was carrying a five-foot long football. She wasn't heavy, just stiff and awkward. Like him, with his stiff-legged half hop.

"Think you'll be okay with her on the stairs," he said, around the penlight. "Maybe you should go first so I'm behind you."

"I'll be okay," she said. "Besides, I think I used up all my courage already tonight. I'll let you go first."

"Thanks," he said.

The stairs were straight ahead and he started up one step at a time, his stiff leg drawing the lower half of an ellipse to keep up. Slow as hell.

"Okay?" Mina said, sounding labored by the weight of Marilyn 2.

"Yeah," he said. Though he wasn't really. He was just trying not to think. About the fact there was another stairway to climb, another floor above this one. An attic. Like the attic when he was a kid that fed into his dreams. The door closing and locking behind him, screaming and yelling for someone to let him out, but like his dream about his rolling head and his inability to move, no sound coming out. Waking up with a sore throat.

Just do it, he kept telling himself. Just do it.

Near the top of the stairs, an explosion of cats came out of nowhere and rushed past them down the stairs. He yelled in spite of himself, the penlight fell out of his mouth, he reeled backwards. He imagined the four of them in a mess of broken fiberglass, wax, and bones at the bottom of the stairs. But something shoved him in the back, righted him.

"Jeez," Mina said.

"Cats," he muttered, "goddamn cats."

Two more steps and he was at the top. He moved onto the landing, set Marilyn onto her feet, waited for Mina to step up beside him. "Dropped my stupid light."

"I'll get it," Mina said, as moonlight dimly flooded the window at the top of the stairs. "But I've got to get rid of her first." She leaned her Marilyn against a wall, fished in her pocket, turned on her penlight and shone it down the stairs. A big orange cat stared up at them from the bottom. "Got it," Mina said, going down a step and bending over. She wiped it off on her jacket before she handed it to him.

She shone her light around. There was an open doorway to their right, piles of clothes on the floor, the smell of stogies strong enough to take your breath away.

"Piggy's room," she said.

To their left was a u-turn and a hallway, and Mina moved ahead of him. He picked up his Marilyn and followed. The hallway ended, and at a ninety degree angle to the left was one closed door. At a hundred and eighty degrees was a second.

Mina hesitated, then grabbed the first door's knob and turned it. She stuck her light in, then her head. "Another bedroom," she said. "We can stick my Marilyn in here."

Nate set his Marilyn on one foot and opened the second door. The attic stairs. Narrower, steeper than the ones they'd just climbed. "Give me the cleaner," he said, "I can do this myself." He hoisted Marilyn over one shoulder.

She stuck the plastic spray bottle and a rag into his hand. "Do a good job," she said, and he started up.

At the top, the window was two feet away from the stairs and he felt a terrific sense of relief that he wasn't going to have to walk across a length of space to get there. The glass was matted with webs, so opaque with dust that the light bounced off. He didn't look around, didn't want to know what was up there, didn't want to see weird shadows and false movements. He leaned Marilyn beside the window and swiped at the cobwebs. Then he sprayed and swiped at the glass. It took three times before the glass gained any shine. He picked Marilyn up and turned her so she was looking out the window, made sure she was sturdy. Then he whispered, "Sorry," and started back down.

"Mina?" he called, with a momentary flash of panic that he'd get no answer. But she was coming out of the room at the bottom of the stairs. She closed the door.

"You know," she said, "it might actually have been a decent house once. Maybe when his mother was alive. I think that was her bedroom." She cocked her head back toward the door. "There's three inches of dust all over everything, but whoever lived in it left it neat."

"Let's just go," he said.

As they came back around the u-turn to the top of the first floor stairs, their lights flashed into and across Piggy's bedroom. Mina clutched his arm and gasped, and a flood of disbelief hit him. At first, he wasn't sure what the hell he was seeing, and then, when he was sure, all he could do was say, "Holy shit. Holy fucking shit."

CHAPTER TWENTY-EIGHT

"Wait a minute," she said. "Let me move closer." She got up and pushed the wooden lawn chair nearer to his until the arms met.

The back yard smelled of sun and earth. A slight breeze was pushing at the bird feeder. Summer in the air for the first time this spring made her feel like slipping off her shoes and wiggling her toes in the grass. Not to mention this glow they were still sharing. A few steps down from the exhilaration of the last couple of days, but still very good.

She sat down and jiggled the arms of the chair until the legs felt solid, then she tipped her head back and looked up into a perfectly blue sky. The kind of day Scotty would have been shirtless and shoeless. The kind of day Lydia would have spread her dolls across a blanket for a backyard picnic. A day for Ben to pull the old iron grill out of the shed and scrub it with the wire brush because he never bothered to clean it in the fall.

She closed her eyes, told herself to stop. Because this was the way it always came. Unexpected. Slipping her out of a day that was real into one that wasn't. But not anymore. She had to make sure she knew the difference. Had to make sure every time.

A line of a poem slipped through her mind ... *If recollecting were forgetting, then I remember not...*

She concentrated on Nate's voice, on the newspaper in his hands, on the black and white photo in the middle of the front page, and on the headline: *THREE MARILYLNS FOUND!*

He reached the end of the column, muttered, "Page four," and opened the paper then folded it backwards neatly with a little inverted shake, a trick she'd never been able to master, but in Nate's hands the paper obliged.

Gradually she relaxed against the back of the chair.

He yawned a huge yawn. "Jeeze," he said, rubbing his head with his knuckles. "I can't get myself awake this morning."

She yawned, too. Not really morning, though. One o'clock Saturday afternoon and they'd only been up an hour. Three days of night-time adventure, followed by two nights of listening to the radio, a local talk show that hadn't stopped convulsing for forty-eight hours over the series of events — the third missing Marilyn, the fire, the found Marilyns, the arrest of one Peter Piggy Arpel.

Nothing about the yellow tires, the pumper truck, the river. Not yet. But the color photos of the truck and the yellow tire marks on River Road probably wouldn't arrive at the editor's desk until Monday.

Nate held the paper up so she could see the pictures, six of them. "Look how you can see her," she said, putting her finger on Marilyn's face in the attic window.

"Thanks to Roy," Nate said.

The pumper truck was there, too, in the foreground of the smoking tire pile, but its yellow tires were gray in the black and white photo.

He started to read again. "'Called by a report of a fire at the address, firefighters arrived to find a large pile of tires smoldering. This is the fourth time the fire department has responded to this address in the last twenty-two months. Mr. Arpel had been ordered to remove the tires from his property over a year ago.'"

"That was brilliant," Nate said, "setting fire to those tires. Which happened to be sitting smack in the middle of the field with a perfect view of a particular attic window." He chuckled. "Firefighters ... I mean, how much more reliable can you get than that?"

He cleared his throat.

"'It was while the fire was being doused that several members of the department noticed the wax figure of Monroe in an upstairs window of the house. Jim Woodley, a twelve-year member of the fire department said, 'At first we thought it was a real person, and then somebody said she looked just like Marilyn Monroe. That's when we put two and two together with the museum being broken into the night before and the wax figure disappearing again.' When asked if someone had gone into the house to substantiate what they were seeing, Mr. Woodhouse said, 'At that point it became a police matter. We called and reported it.'

"'The police report states that a call was logged at eight a.m. Thursday morning from the Niagara Falls Wax Museum to report a break-in. Entrance had apparently been gained through a window at the rear of the building. At that time, the museum also reported the theft of the Marilyn Monroe wax mannequin. In the last several years, the figure in that display has been stolen three times. No recoveries had been made until Friday morning, when the police entered the house belonging to Peter Arpel and discovered all three mannequins. Mr. Arpel is free on a one hundred thousand dollar bond.'"

"It goes on," Nate said, "but I guess we pretty much know the rest." He looked at her and smiled. "*Three* Marilyns. Can you believe that, Mina? All *three*?"

"Nope," she said. "I saw it with my own eyes and still don't believe it."

He set the paper down on his lap. "I keep trying to figure it out — did Piggy actually take her or get her from someone who did?" He chewed on his lip. "Or was it Roy, deciding to bang in every nail on the coffin just for good measure."

"Who knows," she said. "But whatever, it's a very satisfying ending."

"Will we see him again, so we can find out?"

"Roy?" She shrugged. "He comes and goes. Maybe."

Nate crossed his arms, settled lower in his chair. "We should get matching capes and fly around the world doing good deeds. They could turn us into a comic book. Maybe even a movie."

She leaned over and gently touched his knee. "Could you bear a new injury for every feat of derring-do? How is it by the way?"

"Much improved," he said. "And I assume my style would smooth out with practice." He looked at her. "You're laughing?"

"I keep seeing you standing there sniffing at the air while your pocket was on fire."

"Hmph." He shook his head. "You probably wish you were there when I fell off the garbage can, too."

"And still, you never faltered," she said.

"I talked to Pricilla yesterday."

"Friday," she said. "You always do."

"I told her to tell Kim I'd be there Monday night."

For a second, she couldn't think of a thing to say. "*This* Monday? The day after tomorrow?"

He nodded. "Her graduation's next Friday."

"So soon," she said, feeling her stomach cave a little. "With everything going on I lost track."

"And...?" he said.

She looked at him. "And what?"

"You said you'd think about coming."

Just then, Mrs. Dalloway stepped out from the bushes along the back edge of the yard and stood there eyeing Logan, who lifted his head and eyed her back. Then she came, trotting lightly across the grass, passing Logan's nose by less than a foot, looking straight ahead as though he was invisible. She stopped beside Mina's chair, began rubbing against the wooden legs.

"I have thought about it, Nate," she said, resting her hand lightly on the cat's back. "I have. And really, it's too soon. I'm going to stay here."

Three starlings landed on the shed roof, then whirled away.

"I'm not ready, Nate." She turned to him. "These five weeks have helped. *You've* helped. But I can still feel how close it is." She held two fingers an inch apart. "Besides, this needs to be time for the two of you. Just the two of you."

Mrs. D began to hum and Mina let her fingers trail across the cat's arched back, the warm fur a comfort.

He rubbed his knee. "Did you know that into the '70s and '80s they were still finding Japanese soldiers from World War II on islands in the Philippines? They'd been hiding, what … thirty, forty years? And the thing is they didn't want to come out. They couldn't believe the war was over."

She looked at him. "You're comparing me to an old Japanese soldier?"

He smiled. "Not quite. It just means I get the fact that you can't be hiding out one day and joining the world the next."

Beside him, Logan sat up and scratched at his ear, glanced sideways under Mina's chair, where Mrs. D had curled up, lay back down again, sighed.

"I'll leave early tomorrw morning," Nate said. "That way I'll get there Sunday night. I'll stay with Pris. She sounds like she could use some company. Though for the most part she'll treat me the way your cat treats my dog." He straightened his knee, did it gingerly. "Maybe this trip, all those hours alone in the car, will give me a better idea where to go from here."

She repeated the words to herself … *where to go from here.* Which meant what — that he wasn't coming back? Or if he did, he wasn't going to stay long? Not that she blamed him. Because what was there to come back to here when everything he loved, everything that was familiar, was somewhere else.

Nate leaned down and patted Logan. "I'm going to miss you, buddy," he said. "I think I'm even going to miss that crazy cat."

For a second, everything went still — the birds, the breeze.

"You're not taking him?"

He swiveled toward her. "Not if you're not coming. I figured he'd be better off here." Then she saw doubt register in his eyes. "I should have asked. I *can* take him."

"No," she said. "You can't. I mean ... I was thinking you'd take him, but of course you can't. I want him to stay. He's staying."

"You're sure?"

"Yes," she said. "It's fine and he's staying." And then, because she couldn't look at him, she asked the question to the trees and the sky. "And when do you think you'll be coming back?"

"A week. I'll be back late on Monday." He said it without hesitation. Something he'd already thought about, considered. "I'll try to get Pris out of the house, for whatever good it'll do. And I need to see Esther. Try to do it like a man instead of a seven-year-old for once. There's some questions she may still be able to answer. Before it's too late. And, then I'm going to check in with unemployment and dig up some leads on learning the back ends of computers."

She nodded.

He cleared his throat. "I mean..." Now it was his turn to not look at her. To ask his question to the backyard. "It's, uh ... I should come back, shouldn't I?"

She twisted in her seat, saw the set of his jaw. As though he was ready for whatever was coming. And it hit her that he was as uncertain as she. As vulnerable. As scared of whatever did or did not lay ahead.

She put her hand on his arm. "Of course you have to come back. The idea that you might not scares me to death."

He turned to face her. Doubt, relief, concern all there in his eyes. She almost laughed out loud. "Did you actually think I wouldn't want you to come back?"

He shrugged, his look settling, finally, to sheepish. "It crossed my mind." Then he frowned. "Why would you think I wouldn't want to?"

She shook her head. "Oh, you know — little things. This place. Me. Dangerous feats of thievery and entrapment. Insignificant things like that. It could have been nothing more than a kind of lark. An oasis before you moved on to the rest of your life. And I would understand."

"An oasis," he said. "Makes me sound like Lawrence of Arabia on sabbatical. But in case you need to hear it, I always intended to come back."

"And I always wanted you to," she said.

They both eased down into their chairs again, turned back to the yard. She left her hand on his arm.

"I'll take pictures," he said, "so you can see Kim. Watch her graduate."

"I'd like that." She looked around the yard, taking it all in, making a memory of the light, the warmth, the feel of Nate's arm beneath her fingers. All of it real.

And then, out of the corner of her eye, she saw Mrs. D's tail flick out from under the chair, hit Logan in the nose, and disappear. It made Logan start, and he fixed his eyes on the cat for a few seconds, until his lids slowly began to lower and the cat's tail shot out again and hit him in the nose a second time. Logan sat up and shook himself.

"It's okay, Logan," Mina said. "Mrs. Dalloway..." she tapped the bottom of her chair, "...you cut that out right now." And then to Nate's questioning look, "She's taunting him."

"Yeah," he said, "she's really good..."

But before he could finish, there was a yowl and a yelp, their chairs rocked and hers almost went over backwards. Nate jumped up. "Logan!"

Both animals were already half-way across the yard, Logan's nose inches from Mrs. Dalloway's tail, the cat flashing into the bushes, gone, and Logan stopping dead at the place she disappeared. He leaned forward, sniffed, then turned and trotted back, tail high, chest out.

"Finally," Nate said, "a little chutzpah."

Mina jiggled her chair back into balance and for a long time they sat there next to each other not talking.

She was thinking about spaghetti and meatballs for dinner when Logan's head came up, ears perked, his whole body on alert. They watched Mrs. Dalloway's head peek out from a bush.

"Uh-oh," Nate said.

The cat stayed still for a good two minutes, then slowly emerged, sat down, licked one paw, then the other.

Mina glanced at Logan, who hadn't moved a muscle.

After a while, Mrs. D stood up and started slowly toward them until she was about ten feet away, when she made a great circle of a detour around the dog and stopped beside Mina's chair. She stood there, unmoving, until Logan finally lowered his head back onto his paws. Then she carefully curled up on the grass.

"How about that," Nate said.

Gradually, sitting there in the sunshine, with the glow of their success still a satisfaction and with Nate's declaration, it came to her that right now, in this moment, she was feeling something she hadn't felt in a very long time. And almost as soon as she recognized it, she found she could barely breathe.

She concentrated on a bee flying a circle near the pear tree. Was it because she had no right to it anymore? To anything that felt remotely like happiness?

Nate squeezed her hand, which made her wonder if she'd spoken out loud.

"Nate," she said, when she could finally form the words, "I don't know if I can do this."

"This?"

"Us."

He was silent for a second. Then he said, "Why?"

"Because it scares me to death," she said. "Not being who I've been. Being … okay."

"So if 'okay' frightens you, then what does 'not okay' do?"

She glanced at him, then away. "Maybe it's the only thing I know anymore. I know it's ridiculous. *I'm* ridiculous."

"No," he said. "You're the least ridiculous person I've ever met."

"Then what am I supposed to do?," she said. "How do I go on? If living, really *living*, isn't something I can allow myself, how can I expect you to cope with that? With me?" Her hand lifted off his arm, fell back. "It's something you need to consider, Nate. Very carefully. That this peculiar person you're sitting next to may be as good as she ever gets."

Logan lifted his head off his paws, listened, then settled back and sighed.

"First of all," he said, "you may have noticed that my eyes are wide open. And have been for a while now. And second, I think what our situation requires is a short-range approach. For both of us. To everything. For instance, right now, all I need to know is that the odds are you'll be here with my dog in a week and won't change the locks before I get back."

She laughed. "Locks?"

"You know what I'm saying."

Yes, she knew. She nodded.

"And after that," he said, "we'll move through another week, and then, if it feels right, another."

She thought about taking life in small chunks. Never having to expect more from herself than she was capable of at any particular moment. She might be able to do that. Let herself be content for the next four or five hours, four or five days. After all, it was the way you learned anything new ... the way she'd learned to play the piano, dance the tango. One chord at a time, one figure at a time. Maybe it was the way she could learn to live again. In small chunks.

She saw Liddy standing for the first time in the middle of the living room, surrounded by a dozen stuffed animals, arms out, little bare feet gripping the floor, a look of wonder on her face. One step, then another, while Mina held her breath. Until a downy yellow chicken with a bright orange beak tripped her up, and down she went smack on her bottom. There'd been a moment of sharp surprise, then a look of indecision. Should she cry? She looked up at Mina for the answer, and Mina had put a look of wonder on her own face. "What did you do?" she'd said, smiling, "did you walk? Did you walk like a big girl?"

Instantly, Liddy's indecision had disappeared. She beamed; got herself up and did it again. And again. And again. So that by the time Ben came home from work, she was practically running.

Liddy was gone. Which made it all so impossible. Still, she had to try, even though she couldn't quite say why.

She concentrated on the feel of Nate's arm, firm and warm.

"Spaghetti and meatballs," she said.

"Spaghetti and meatballs."

"For dinner."

"Excellent." He squeezed her hand. "I'll make my famous garlic bread. And a salad."

"Your salad isn't famous, too?"

He shook his head. "No. Just my garlic bread. My salads..." he looked at her, "my salads are infamous."

BOOKS BY THIS AUTHOR

SHORT STORY COLLECTIONS

AFTERNOON DELIGHT BOOK ONE

AFTERNOON DELIGHT BOOK TWO

AFTERNOON DELIGHT BOOK THREE

AFTERNOON DELIGHT BOOK FOUR

AFTERNOON DELIGHT BOOK FIVE

COW HORMONES

NOVELS

CLICK

DON'T LOOK DOWN

A DANCE WITH THE DEVIL

PAYBACK

LOVE CANAL

RIDDLE

STINKBUG

50 ACRES MORE OR LESS

MOON OF THE DARK RED CALVES

www.ingramcontent.com/pod-product-compliance
Lightning Source LLC
Chambersburg PA
CBHW030918120626
46554CB00001B/201